Other novels by David Darling

The Noah Hunter Series

The Tipping Point

Grave Choices

Course of Action

Hunter's Gambit (forthcoming)

~

Standalone

Serve in the Shadows: Recruitment

Grim Measures (novella)

"Down these mean streets, a man must go who is not himself mean, and who is neither tarnished nor afraid."
- Raymond Chandler

Arrow Point Police Sergeant, Noah Hunter, isn't afraid to bend the rules to get results. But now he's faced with a decision —he must choose between justice or retribution.

While investigating two brutal murders, Noah finds a note warning him to back off or face severe consequences. When he doesn't heed the warning, someone close to him pays for that decision.

The investigation leads him to a Chicago crime family, so Noah brings the fight to them as he's left with no other options.

As Sergeant Hunter struggles to protect his friends, colleagues, and everyone else in Arrow Point, revenge is foremost in his mind. However, his actions create a ripple effect, and Noah's future is uncertain, especially when everything isn't as it seems.

Chapter 1

Mario Canetti had received a call to take care of a situation in the middle of the night, which came as no surprise. Those types of decisions usually were made under cover of darkness—where such deeds thrived.

What shocked him was the target, but he knew better than to argue. However, this was the first time a problem fought back with such skill and determination. Little Mario knew the risk, but what happened at the Greyhound Station was close. Too close.

He pressed against the side of his head where his earlobe used to be.

Blood seeped down his wrist, made a path along his forearm, and steadily dropped off his elbow.

Mario stood six-foot-six, and with his work boots, he had to duck so he wouldn't bang his head on door frames. At three hundred pounds, he filled that same opening. He had been the same size since he was old enough to drive, and at thirty years old, he had gained nothing but muscle.

Mario raised the shotgun with his right hand, edged forward around the corner of the building, and scanned the loading docks. The steel factory in South Deering, Chicago, looked abandoned. In the distance, a plane came in for a landing at O'Hare and blood dripped off his elbow to land at his feet. The steady drip reminded him of leaking faucet, and Mario would have to deal with it shortly.

Despite the adrenaline and his injury, Mario's breathing remained slow and steady. He had been in similar situations for most of his life, and in his mind, it was simple. Either he would be successful, or he wouldn't. If he failed, someone else would have to deal with the problem.

A glance at the eastern sky told him he had an hour before sunrise. The dark khaki pants and work shirt helped him blend into the shadows, but that advantage would soon be gone.

Since Wisconsin Steel closed, the receiving docks hadn't seen a truck in over twenty years. It allowed the local gangs and kids to decorate almost every square inch in graffiti and litter the docks with garbage. Not an ideal place, but there had been worse.

Time to wrap this up.

Little Mario pulled his palm away from the side of his head and allowed the blood to flow freely. He would need both hands available for what he had in mind. Mario wiped his hands on the back of his pants and gripped the shotgun tight.

He was ready.

He crossed the open area in several quick strides, and with a light jump, he landed on the loading dock. The heavy metal receiving doors were nine feet long, dented, and covered in gang tags. The doors were cracked an inch, the gap beckoning him inside.

He used the shotgun muzzle to swing the door open as he stepped to the side, his back to the wall. Mario expected further resistance, his finger twitching outside the trigger guard. He was surprised the hinges were well oiled and opened in complete silence. When no attack materialized, he grinned. It would happen inside. It was just a matter of when.

The moonlight didn't penetrate far past the door, and he quietly waited for his eyes to adjust. Mario could barely make out vague shapes and objects that littered the area. Oil and the sharp smell of urine wafted to him. Kids had used the inside of the door as a bathroom for many years. He forced himself to breathe slowly through his mouth until he grew used to it.

The distant sound of steel scraping on concrete briefly echoed off the walls, and he strained to identify the location, his head tilted to the side. Mario's index finger gently caressed the trigger, and he made a decision.

He tilted the shotgun back on his right shoulder while his left hand blindly swung side to side ahead of him. He stepped forward and made his way deeper into the building as he felt for a wall or an obstacle in his path.

He froze when his boot kicked what sounded like an empty beer bottle, but it was too late.

It rattled off a wall and skipped across the cement floor before it shattered. The noise echoed throughout the building and announced his arrival.

I may as well have brought in a marching band.

The large man pulled out his cell phone and turned on the flashlight application. The shadows leaped back, and a small form darted along the base of the wall.

Rats.

Only a few things bothered Mario; being shot at and dying were strangely absent from the list, but rats and spiders were near the top. His knuckles cracked on the walnut stock of the shotgun as his grip tightened.

"I have a pocket of shells," he whispered to the rodents. "Stay back, or I'll start firing."

An old mattress leaned against the long wall, and garbage filled the area. There wasn't a chance he could have made it through silently unless he had night-vision goggles. Straight ahead, a hallway led farther into the building, and an old metal sign hung sideways on the wall.

Driver's check-in with the shipping office.

Mario carefully stepped over the trash and passed the sign moving farther into the building. He leveled the twelve gauge across his forearm with the cell phone in his left hand. The cool barrel grew sticky with his blood.

After a dozen steps, he called out. "Just hand over the money, and this will go a lot easier."

Mario's deep voice echoed inside the building, and was lost to the shadows. He'd inadvertently announced his arrival and had nothing to lose, nor did he expect an answer, but when a low chuckle echoed throughout the derelict building, it made the hair on his arms stand on end. There was no way to pinpoint the location, but it sounded distant.

As he moved forward, deeper into the building, glass crunched under the soles of his work boots. He kept an eye out for more vermin, his imagination playing tricks on him as the shadows moved. The cell phone didn't illuminate the far walls, but it showed the hazards at his feet well. He was in a vast room, possibly a warehouse floor.

Out in the open, he was a sitting duck. He quickly tried to turn off the flashlight but lost his grip on the slick blood covering his hand. The cell phone dropped to the concrete floor, where it bounced a few times, settling at his feet. The screen was cracked and lay face up with the LED flashlight aimed at the bottom.

As if that were the signal, the assault began.

A muzzle flash lit up the darkness twenty yards away—at the same time, the sound from small arms fire reached him. The round passed harmlessly overhead, and he ducked in reflex. He raised the shotgun and fired the twelve-gauge toward the flash.

He couldn't tell if he hit anything or not, but he didn't want to wait around to find out. If he could see the weapons fire, his would be visible.

Mario ran forward, angling to the side when the second round caught him on the upper right arm. His hand spasmed, and the shotgun clattered to the floor. The force of the impact drove him back several steps, and he spun around in a half-circle. It didn't hurt right away, the feeling of numbness radiating outward. He dropped to his knees and tried to make himself less of a target while gripping his biceps to stop the bleeding.

The dim light from the cell phone only showed the immediate area, where a dark liquid stained the ground.

I'm bleeding too much.

Mario tried to remove his belt to use as a tourniquet, but the arm wouldn't respond properly. Lightning flashes of pain exploded behind his eyes as the feeling in his arm returned.

Another round struck the concrete floor to his left before it ricocheted off a distant wall.

He had a good visual of where the shots were coming from, but he needed a distraction. From his pants pocket, he pulled out a handful of shotgun shells. Blood slicked his left hand, and it wasn't easy, but he threw them out into the darkness. They bounced and rattled across the floor, but nothing happened.

Mario's choices were limited, and retreating wasn't an option.

He struggled to crawl forward and swept his left arm out in a circle on the cold floor, hoping to find the Remington. The pain in his arm and ear didn't help, and with clenched teeth, he did his best to ignore it. When his fingertips brushed against an object, Mario was momentarily confused.

It was a rounded piece of rubber.

A shoe someone was currently wearing.

"I ain't going back. Ever."

Mario heard the pistol being cocked above his head.

"I'm just doing my job." He was out of options. "Please, give me a moment to pray first."

Silence.

Mario mumbled his way through the Lord's prayer. Despite the crosses around the house and all the days he was dragged to church by his grandmother, he still didn't know the full prayer.

His work for the family came first. He had sold his soul at a young age for wealth, not faith.

With that in mind, Mario lunged forward and tried to hook the ankle in front of him. The sudden movement saved him, at least for the moment. The bullet hit him in the back of his shoulder instead of the top of his head.

The impact slammed his chest to the floor, and the air shot out of his lungs. As he struggled, it felt like a car had pinned him to the ground. He absently noted that he couldn't tell if the concrete was cold on his cheek or not.

"Sorry, Little Mario, I'm looking out for number one now."

"It's not too—"

Two rounds fired from three feet away, both entering his back.

As he lay there dying, the figure picked up his cell phone and quickly disappeared into the darkness.

This isn't my problem anymore.

It did not take long before he stopped breathing altogether.

Despite it not being his problem, Mario had known others would take the job.

They were family.

Chapter 2

Two shadows peeked around the maple tree with dark intent. The prospect of an easy score won the battle against their poor judgment and brought a smile to their faces. Across one-hundred feet of open asphalt, Sam studied the lone four-door-sedan in the parking lot, and his empty stomach decided for him.

"Worth checking out, Ben."

He patted his worn coat and produced a small flashlight, courtesy of the last minivan around the corner. Sam was dressed for stealth in black jeans and a dark blue jacket. Various addictions gave him a haunted look with prominent cheekbones and dark circles under his eyes. He wasn't sure the last time he had showered or eaten properly—other purchases took priority. While in his early sixties, he looked decades older.

Shortly, Sam's flashlight shone into the parked car and illuminated the dark leather interior. A yellow handbag sat on the passenger seat, and a few shopping bags filled with clothing and groceries were in the back seat.

Sam nodded to his partner. "Let's do it."

With their dark clothing and matching backpacks at one o'clock in the morning, they blended into the shadows. Despite the warm September weather, they wore dark winter caps, too. Ben looked like a teenager, despite recently turning twenty-one years old. Life on the streets caused him to resemble Sam, with a haunted look to his eyes, and the lack of nutrition started to show. A general odor about him announced his presence long before he arrived. They both looked like they could use a good meal and a fix to help calm their nerves.

With the car being the only vehicle left in the parking lot, it had caught their eye from across the street.

Another easy score.

The young man tried the passenger door of the Audi. With a click, it swung open an inch, and the interior light turned on.

"Fuck ya! Grab the bag, kid. I'll get the stuff in the back seat."

Ben picked up the purse, but it wouldn't move, "It's stuck or something."

"Just open it up and look inside."

"Huh? Okay."

As Ben struggled, Sam joined his partner to help. With the sound of a muffled gunshot, an explosion of red powder hit them both in the face and upper body. The vehicle's interior was suddenly filled with a red-mist cloud, the dye coating them completely. Struggling to breathe, Sam panicked and tried to wipe the red stain from his face. He failed to see the vehicle parked in the shadows, its occupants observing them.

Someone blinded them with a spotlight, and a voice yelled over a loudspeaker, "Arrow Point Police Department, get on the ground. Now!"

Ben had no desire or energy to run. He dropped to his knees and dry retched. Sam looked at his partner and took a step away.

"Get down on the ground!"

The police commands and the bright lights were too much for Sam. After a moment of hesitation, he bolted out of the outlet mall's parking lot.

Fear lent him energy, and with his head down, he ran for the east end toward the residential homes across the road.

After twenty feet, he heard the cop pounding the pavement behind him.

"Arrow Point P.D. Stop running and get on the ground."

Sam glanced over his shoulder as the officer closed the distance, with arms spread wide. They both clipped the curb at the edge of the parking lot and fell hard on the grass. The air exploded from his lungs, and he hit his head hard enough that he was temporarily stunned.

By the time he regained his senses, a set of handcuffs had secured his wrists behind his back. The big cop leaned over him, hands on his knees as he caught his breath.

Sam didn't have the energy to struggle. The officer began to read him his rights.

"You have the right to remain silent. Anything you say can and will be used against you in a court—"

Unable to hold out any longer, he passed out. A clump of dirt fell off his dyed face while the police officer swore.

* * * * *

"Dispatch, ten-fifteen. Two in custody. Request an ambulance to my location, over."

"Roger, ten-fifty-two to your location. En route."

Once he stood straight, Sergeant Noah Hunter took a few more deep breaths before rolling the suspect into the recovery position. Then he waited.

The cruiser's flasher lights came to life across the parking lot and lit the area with the red and blue strobe. The driver's side spotlight showed the other suspect was being dragged to his feet by his partner and placed in the back of the vehicle.

I hope he doesn't puke.

The other night they were called to a bar fight at The Tavern. The instigator threw up all over himself and the back seat of the cruiser. Noah shook his head as he remembered the smell. It's happened before and likely to happen again.

The ambulance lights were soon visible as they drove east across Main Street before they turned into the mall parking lot. His partner drove across the lot and joined him as the EMTs arrived on the scene. Noah removed the handcuffs and secured him to the bed rail on the gurney. He picked up the backpack, and something like coins shifted inside.

Noah briefed the paramedics as they loaded the suspect into the ambulance. While they secured the stretcher, Noah took a quick look in the pack. As suspected, he found several handfuls of loose change, a few pairs of sunglasses, and CDs inside. "Looks like they hit a few other cars in the area before we got them tonight."

Constable Bennett nodded. "The same thing in this guy's pack, Sarge."

After they watched the ambulance drive away, Noah turned back. "I'll have the bait car picked up. It needs cleaning again. We're done here for tonight. Drop us off at the station, and I'll start processing and paperwork, and you can go to the hospital. I didn't tackle him that hard. He'll be released soon."

At five foot eleven inches and weighing one-hundred and ninety pounds, Noah was relatively substantial. When you added the vest and utility belt's weight, the thirty-eight-year-old sergeant had packed a good punch when he collided. He intimidated many upon the first impression with that size. His short dark brown hair and goatee made him appear stern for those that didn't know him.

Bennett chuckled briefly. "No problem, Sarge."

Once he sat in the front passenger seat, Noah glanced over his shoulder, through the Plexiglas divider, at the young man in the backseat. "We're headed to the station to book you. Just hold tight."

As Bennett drove, Noah pulled out his notebook from his vest pocket and wrote down some information while the events were fresh in his mind.

Arrow Point Police Department (APPD), located off Main Street and Oak Avenue, was an older rust-brick building in the heart of the city. The department was founded thirty-five years ago when the town's population reached fifty-six thousand, and the Wyoming Highway Patrol had requested a separate police force for the city. The station had expanded to over one-hundred and sixty officers within the last decade, and with the continued population growth, they hoped for twelve new hires next year.

Over the past week, several cars were broken into in the west end of Arrow Point. Noah hoped that this was the responsible pair. He was sure the older man matched the description from a home security system that the owner had captured. The footage would also be submitted as evidence.

The young man groaned in the back seat, and Noah immediately spun around and held his palm out. "You will not throw up in my cruiser. If you're going to be sick, let me know, and we will pull over."

Stewart had a quick look in the rearview mirror, then he put the flashers on and increased their speed. Noah didn't know what was worse, the smell of vomit or the scent of the disinfectant they used to clean the cruiser.

The young man in the back started to cry. "My mom's going to kill me."

Noah and Steward shared a quick look. There was little they could do, and the kid seemed young enough that this episode may help straighten him out, especially with a vengeful parent watching over.

Noah turned and looked him straight in the eye. "Right now, I have one word of advice. Treat this as a life lesson. Do what others fail to do. Learn from this. Get clean and change your life, or you will spend more time in the back of cruisers once we catch you."

Noah offered advice, but not many listened. However, over the years, some had, so he would keep trying. The young man looked scared, and tears streamed down his red face to fall on his jacket, but he nodded.

Maybe he would be one of the few.

After they pulled into the station's rear parking lot, the young man was brought inside and processed for a night's stay. He would see the county judge in the morning after being transferred to Casper. If booked on a Friday night or the weekend, they were detained until transferred Monday morning, but there shouldn't be an issue mid-week. Arrow Point didn't have a court system in place, with Casper only seventy miles along highway twenty-six east. There were no problems having anyone transferred unless you counted the danger of an elk or deer collision along the route.

Once he handed the young kid to the staff sergeant, Noah went to the second floor of the precinct to the "cube." Originally, there were partition walls around thirty five desks for the officers to use. The low walls resembled a massive maze with small little cubicles for offices. Three years ago, the new chief had all the partitions removed and returned the floor to an open-concept office. However, the name had stuck by then, and the officers still referred to it as the cube.

Noah sat at one of the desks and logged in. Each desk was set up the same way, with a monitor and keyboard. The right upper drawer held any stationery required, and the lower right drawers contained several dozen blank forms and reports. Three years ago, APPD switched over to a paper-free system. That meant only twenty percent of the documents were a hard copy. Noah began the paperwork and booking reports. He also sent the request to have the bait car towed back to the station.

He heard Richardson raise his voice, and then a phone slammed. Noah looked at the captain's office at the end of the building. A few seconds later, Captain John Richardson opened the door and glanced around the cube to see who was there. Richardson appeared tired with dark circles under his eyes, and he wore his usual dark blue suit and tie. The captain had been a stable force at the department for over thirty years, and the older man had many more years left in him.

"Sergeant Hunter, homicide, west off highway twenty-six, just outside town. The state trooper called it in. It's within our city limits. Barely, but enough that it's our problem."

Their department didn't have enough officers for a separate homicide division. The senior officers usually filled in for those cases. Hunter, most likely, would have been assigned to it anyway. He was the senior sergeant on the force.

Noah nodded and logged off the system. "Sir, could you have Bennett finish the reports and booking?"

"No problem, and you're going to need some Vicks. It doesn't sound good."

"Yes, sir."

The station's main floor had an area set aside for lockers, and it took a little while to locate the small bottle of Vicks as he hadn't used it in many years. The small plastic container fit into his vest pocket, and new officers were encouraged to carry it. Vicks rubbed under the nose would take away the stench of a dead body. To help preserve a crime scene, it was better if officers weren't sick.

When the captain suggested he use the rub, Noah took it seriously.

The situation must be horrible.

In this case, it was worse than he could have predicted.

Chapter 3

Two miles west of Arrow Point, Sergeant Hunter saw the state
trooper's vehicle lights as they flashed two-hundred yards off a
nature trail. Noah had explored this area with his older brother
a few years ago and knew the country rather well. Iain had sent
him a few pictures of the two of them together when they hiked
and fished the mountain creek. They were pleasant memories
worthy of framing, and he hung them in the living room at
home.

After he slowed and pulled off the highway, he stopped
beside the black state police cruiser. Noah reached above his
head and turned on his flashers from the center console and the
driver's side spotlight. Before him, a path led north into the
woods. Tall grass and scrub brush grew on the sides. There
wasn't much in this area from what he could recall, except a
few old trapper's sheds another fifty yards farther off the trail.

"Dispatch, this is 4417, code eleven."

Sergeant Hunter has arrived on the scene.

"Roger, 4417. Code eleven."

For the most part, Arrow Point officers spoke plainly on the radio and not in codes. However, after two years of being in the infantry, proper voice procedures were deeply ingrained.

His flashlight illuminated the area as he followed the trail. Noah's right hand remained on the pistol grip of the holstered Glock 19, ready to flick the keeper and draw if required. The newer models had a friction-fit keeper, but he had the black leather holster for decades, and he wasn't about to fix what wasn't broken.

A gentle breeze came in from the east, making the trees sway and creak, and he heard night birds off in the distance. The trees had yet to change colors with the fall weather, but it wouldn't take long.

It was less than a minute before he saw the light and heard a muted conversation just off the pathway.

Once he stepped through the long grass, Noah saw three figures huddled outside the small trapper's cabin. He recognized the tall man as Trooper John Gaston from the Wyoming Highway Patrol. The young woman beside him wore the same uniform, but Noah hadn't met her yet. John held his flashlight between his shoulder and chin so he could write in his notebook.

The older man they interviewed wore a black and red checkered jacket and a camouflage baseball hat with the Remington logo embroidered on the front. He looked a little rough around the edges.

"Nice to see you again, John."

One look at the taller man's face, Noah knew this would be a tough one. There was wet vomit on the front of the trooper's uniform and on the sleeve where he wiped his face clean. A quick look at John's partner showed that she barely held it together. Her name tag read Trooper Eastman.

"Sorry, you were called here. Sergeant Hunter, this is Ryan Edwards. He arrived earlier and went home to call it in. We drove him out here forty minutes ago."

"Ryan, could you tell me what happened?" The man had probably already told everything to the troopers, but Noah needed to hear it firsthand.

The older man looked at the three police officers, then shrugged. "I crash out here when I get into fights with my old lady."

Noah heard a tremor in his voice. The man was still shaken up.

"What time did you arrive?"

Noah could tell that Ryan had smoked something recently as he looked strung out with pupil dilation, and the odor still clung to him.

"Ummm …" He shrugged again. "Little after eleven o'clock. Once I looked inside, I left and drove straight home to call it in."

Trooper Eastman spoke up. "He wasn't in any condition to drive back out here, so we picked him up."

"I'll send you my notes. And Noah," John looked straight in his eyes. "It's bad. Very bad inside."

As a general rule, police avoid describing things as 'bad.' When you see car accidents, sexual assaults, and bodies daily, labeling something bad falls too short. For Gaston to use that word, this was possibly the worst thing he had ever seen. If the vomit were any indication, Noah's suspicions were correct.

Noah reached into his shirt pocket and placed a small dab of Vicks under his nose before opening a utility pouch and removed a pair of blue latex gloves.

"You're going to need the boots as well and a mask if you have one." Eastman held out a pair of pale green slip-on foot covers. He nodded and accepted the protective gear.

Sergeant Hunter couldn't put it off any longer. It was time to investigate.

The shack looked fifty years old, and it was a simple twelve-foot square with a sloped roof. The night breeze shifted, and he caught the odor that drifted out from the building.

The two-state troopers escorted Ryan back to the cruiser while Noah tried to breathe through his mouth, just enough so that he wouldn't be overwhelmed.

Flashlight in hand, he used his right to open the door and look inside. The creak of the door and what lay inside was a moment he would never forget. No doubt it would be one of the reasons he would wake up in a cold sweat in the middle of a night's sleep.

He had been here many years ago, and he recalled an old wood stove and a long bench against the wall. There was a wall of pegs to hang various traps and coats as well. Once in a while, kids would come out here for a few beers or make out. That wouldn't be happening any longer.

Instead of a sleeping bag, a body lay on the extended bench. It was hard to tell with all the blood, but a black wire had cut deep into the flesh as it spiraled up and down the corpse. Noah was reasonably sure that the body was a male. He had been tortured, and a few pieces were missing, missing from the body at least. Large parts of skin hung from the pegs in the wall, along with the victim's left arm. It was separated at the elbow and also suspended from the peg. The hand was still partially clenched in a fist as if grasping for help.

Flies buzzed and crawled around the corpse. With the warm weather, it would be unavoidable. In the corner, the old wood stove looked like it had been used recently with fresh ashes that spilled out on the blood-covered plank floor.

Two rocks the size of a baseball rested on top of the stove. Two more stones of the same size sat on the abdomen of the body. It looked as if they had been heated and then placed on the stomach.

The flesh was blackened and seared.

Despite the odor of the rub under his nose, Noah caught the full smell of burnt flesh mixed in with the decomposition, which made his stomach churn. Arcs of blood were visible on the ceiling and walls. It looked like someone had dipped a broad brush into a bucket of red paint and flicked it around the interior. There was blood on almost every surface.

Jesus Christ.

A fly had landed on his face, and it almost sent him over the edge. It took enormous effort to continue with the flashlight and explore the small room further. He noticed that his left hand had a slight tremor while shining the light around. The beam wasn't steady by any means.

There were footprints on the floor, and it looked like the killer had stopped lifting their feet and had just slid back and forth through the slick blood.

A few cracks between the boards allowed the blood to drain below the cabin. There were even a set of small rodent tracks through the sticky liquid. Noah absently noted they appeared to be from a mouse. Once he shone the light under the bench, he spotted a little white object resting against the far wall. It glistened in the beam. At first, he didn't understand what it was. As he gasped, it came to him.

The lone eyeball stared back at him.

Noah had seen enough. He stepped outside and let the old wooden door slam behind him. He took a few deep breaths of the clear night air before walking back to the path. John was waiting for him. Trooper Eastman must have taken the man back to the cruiser while Noah was inside.

The two men stared at each other, the horror of the scene replayed in their minds.

Noah pulled off his ball cap and was about to run his hand through his hair but then stopped. He still wore the gloves.

"Did you check his shoes?"

John nodded. "Yes, he's clear. Whoever did this would be covered in blood. Drenched. There would be no way around it. Are you okay, Noah?"

He shone the light at the shack while he collected his thoughts. He didn't answer for a minute. "Yeah, I'm okay. Barely. Going to call it in more to secure the area, and we'll need forensics."

"I'll send you my reports."

Noah continued to stare at the trapper's shack.

John's hand dropped onto his shoulder, giving him a brief squeeze before heading back to his cruiser.

After a deep breath, Noah called dispatch to get reinforcements and inform the captain. As bad as it was to view the scene, he was glad he didn't have to process it like the forensic technicians. Those guys didn't get paid enough.

A glance at his watch showed it was three o'clock in the morning. There wasn't any chance of him being done his shift and getting home before seven. He peeled off the gloves and boots and left them beside the door. The state troopers piled their gloves there as well. The protective gear had touched the scene, and now they were part of the evidence chain.

Noah sent a quick text off to his girlfriend, Megan.

>> I'm working late. Have a good day at work.

He headed back to his cruiser and opened the trunk. He pulled out a roll of yellow barrier tape from the scene kit when he got a reply text.

>> Be safe. Love you. Xo

He smiled at her message, and despite the situation, it made him feel better. Noah put the phone away and went back to work.

It was going to be a long brutal night.

Chapter 4

Captain Richardson assigned Sergeant Hunter as lead to investigate the John Doe murder. As of yet, they had not been able to find an identity of the body. The first order of business was to check missing persons in the county. When that failed to turn up any results, Noah expanded the search to cover the state.

It was just after noon, and Noah sat at a desk in the cube as he finished off the requisition paperwork. Once forensics had finished with the scene, Noah would head back out and process the area. He would be in the way at this stage and wasn't needed to be a security guard. That was a junior officer's job.

He had done such duties for many years. It was someone else's turn.

After he logged off the system, he went down to the lockers to change before heading home for a few hours of rest. If he were lucky, he would still have three hours of light when he headed back out to the crime scene.

So much for having the weekend off.

Once he sat in his truck, Noah's mind couldn't help but recall the horror scene in the shack. He could still feel the fly crawling across his face. Quickly, he rubbed his hand over his goatee when the skin itched. Noah tried not to think of where that fly had landed previously.

When he started as a rookie, he had trouble turning off the "cop" switch when he left work and headed home. The new police officer syndrome hit him hard. He had gone through a few relationships early in his career because of that fact.

After eighteen years on the APPD, he could flip the switch quickly as he jumped in his pickup truck and headed home. However, today was different, and he had to open the window for some fresh air on his face to help take his mind off things.

Noah had a small one-bedroom bungalow in the north residential section of Arrow Point, only ten minutes from the station. For one person, it was fine. However, last Valentine's day, he had proposed to his girlfriend, Megan, and they both realized that they would need a slightly larger home.

They spent little time at her apartment downtown and more at his house. Neither place was suitable for two people.

They had met three years ago when Noah had volunteered for the safety talks at Red Creek Public School for the younger children. Miss Brooks had brought her grade-one class into the library.

Her long blond hair was pulled back in a ponytail, and she wore a simple slim white dress with yellow flowers. From across the library, Megan's green eyes had followed him, and he couldn't get the silly grin off his face every time she caught him staring.

Two days later, they ran into each other at the grocery store, and they ended up having a quick lunch, followed by dinner the next day.

For the first time that he could remember, Noah had been happy and looked forward to coming home each day. He tried to focus on those thoughts as he pulled into his driveway to lift the mood.

After three years, he had proposed, and it was the easiest decision he had ever made.

Megan would still be at school, and he could get a short four hours of sleep before she came home.

Despite wearing civilian clothing, Noah always carried his service weapon with him when he traveled to and from work. Depending on the case, he would be armed at all times. He also kept the matching Glock 19 loaded in his nightstand. Arrow Point was considered a small city, but he erred on the side of caution.

* * * * *

Twenty miles east of Arrow Point were the Powder River National Park and campgrounds. During the summer months, it was busy with families who liked to camp or tourists as they passed through Wyoming. Most stopped for an overnight stay on their way to Yellowstone. Sixteen dollars a night to camp versus one hundred dollars for a hotel room changed many people's minds, mostly when they were on a budget.

By the third week of September, most families were home and their kids back at school, and the tourist season had been over since Labor Day weekend.

With the slower season, the park rangers had cut back on staff. One ranger patrolled two or three national parks as a cost-cutting measure. Douglas Reynolds drove the white Chevy Tahoe slowly through the empty campsites at Powder River. Doug loved the job as a park ranger as he worked outside almost year-round. The thought of having to work in an office behind a desk made him shiver with dread. It wasn't for him.

He wore the brown and tan ranger uniform, and with his build, it was a good fit. It had been over six years since he started this career, and he still enjoyed it.

There were only two campers on the southern campgrounds at Powder River, and they looked like they would pack up and head out soon. It was ten-thirty in the morning, and the sites had to be cleared by eleven.

While he patrolled in the northern camp area, he found a site with quite a few empty beer cans around the campfire pit. When things were slow, teenagers were known to drive here and have a few beers. After he cleaned up the site and the cans were in a trash bag, Doug was about to place them in the back of the Tahoe when he paused. He could smell smoke from a fire, and a chemical odor filled the air along with it—possibly rubber.

He grabbed a long stick and checked the firepit where the beer cans were, but there wasn't so much as an ember that burned. After he jumped back in his vehicle, Doug lowered all the windows and drove up and down the laneways as he tried to find the source of the smell.

It didn't take long.

The third row down beside the service station. Tucked away at the end in a cul-de-sac, campsite #114 looked recently used. A stream of black smoke rose from the ashes into the morning sky.

The firepits were standard with all the national parks, a large circle of cast iron with a rack that can be flipped down for cooking.

When he pulled into the campsite, Doug turned off the Tahoe before walking over to check out the firepit. He put on his wide-brimmed hat to keep the sun out of his eyes. Intense heat still radiated off the coals and the metal grate. He turned around for a quick look at the campsite. It was clear that no one had camped here last night. Tents or RVs usually left a mark on the grass that took a few days to grow out.

Inside the pit was a pile of glowing embers. Doug spotted pieces of rubber with thin tendrils of smoke that drifted in the light breeze. It looked like the heel of a running shoe. The tread pattern had melted, but it was recognizable.

He had seen many campfires left to burn or flare up once the campers had left the area. However, he could tell kids or a careless camper didn't set this one.

Pieces of cloth had scattered on the grass from the intense heat. After looking at the material, Doug got a funny feeling in his stomach. It felt like the bottom had dropped out as his adrenaline spiked.

After peering closer into the firepit, he ran back to the vehicle seconds later. Doug grabbed his water bottle and emptied it over a few lumps. Billows of smoke rose, and he quickly reached inside and pulled out a severely burned wallet that still smoldered.

He placed it on the ground next to the piece of cloth, which may have been a T-shirt at one point. There were char marks around the edges, and a few holes burned through from the embers.

As he pulled out his phone to call the state police, he noticed that the strange marks across the cloth had formed a pattern. It was a design he recognized at once.

Blood splatter.

Chapter 5

The phone woke him up from a dead sleep. He opened one eye and saw it was four o'clock in the afternoon. Four hours of sleep was not enough, but it would have to do.

"Hello?"

"Rise and shine, we have the preliminary report. The scene is held for you."

"Thanks, Hutch. I'm on my way."

Steve Hutchings had trained Noah on the job when he finished the Law Enforcement Academy in Douglas. He had problems with his hips within the last few years, so he had taken himself off the road. Steve would finish his career working inside the station. With less than a year left to go for a full pension, he looked forward to retirement.

Noah rubbed his hand across his face and stumbled to the bathroom for a hot shower and shave. Ten minutes later, he grabbed a protein bar and headed out the door. As a general rule, he didn't drive to and from work in his police uniform. It could make officers' families potential targets, despite most neighbors knowing where he worked. He wore his usual jeans and T-shirt and hiking boots.

He wasn't in the station five minutes before the staff sergeant handed him the file from forensics. "It isn't much."

"Thanks, Steve. Does anything jump out at you?"

"Nothing. I would start with missing persons, state-wide, then across the country."

Noah agreed. "My thoughts, too. Take care."

After changing into his uniform, he headed up to the cube and logged in. There wasn't too much information in the preliminary reports. The bulk of the tests was still underway.

The victim was male, approximately forty-five years of age. One-hundred and eighty pounds. Fingerprints were burned off, and he was missing enough teeth that dental identification would be challenging, if not impossible.

The time of death was estimated at ten o'clock yesterday evening. The actual cause of death was blood loss, and after looking at the scene, Noah wasn't surprised.

After he flipped back through his notes, he saw that Ryan Edwards had arrived just after eleven p.m. He could have passed the suspect on his way to the trapper's shack. Noah wrote a note down to follow up with Mr. Edwards.

He headed down to supply and signed out a scene case. If he found new evidence, it had to be correctly documented and recorded. The chain of evidence had to be maintained and kept intact to be of any use, especially in court, where it mattered.

Fifteen minutes later, he headed west on Main Street before merging on the highway in an undercover Crown Vic.

The traffic was reasonably light, but that would change soon once everyone finished work.

Without cutting across the country, there was only one access point to the crime scene. Restricting access was a cruiser parked across the start of the trail. As Noah approached, vehicles ahead of him hit their brakes when they spotted the parked cruiser. If they thought it was a speed trap, all the better.

He flashed his high beams and then waited as the other vehicles pulled forward. He recognized constable Angie Dickinson, and when he drove past, he waved for her to follow. Two eyes are better than one when looking for more evidence at a scene.

Dickinson had joined APPD just over two years ago, and while Noah had never worked directly with her, he had heard nothing but good things around the station. Diligent and focused were the two words that described her most often.

There was a small clearing twenty yards from the road where they turned their cruisers around and backed in. As they got out of the vehicles, Noah had forgotten how tall Angie was. He was five foot eleven, and she was easily two inches taller, maybe more with her boots on.

"Are you up for a little fieldwork?"

"I still have two hours and nothing to do, Sarge. That sounds good."

She grinned, put on her ball cap, and then pulled her dark hair out the back in a ponytail. Despite her height, Angie still looked eighteen with her dimples and a few freckles across her nose. He knew it would be tough for her, especially when dealing with the public for her apparent youth.

He pulled out the scene case and an extra flashlight from the cruiser's trunk. For now, he would just wear his tactical gloves. The blue latex gloves made him sweat too much.

"Let's start in a wide perimeter and circle inward. If you see anything, call me over."

"No problem, Sarge."

Once they found the trail, Noah moved left, and Angie circled right around the trapper's shack. They started almost twenty yards out, the distance a healthy person could throw an object. Most men tried to toss away evidence at a scene in this method. It was reactionary.

The immediate area around the shack mainly consisted of pine trees and tall grass. Some juniper bushes had grown unchecked and were the size of a small car.

Noah had a telescoping walking stick that would lock into a position he would use to search a field. He used it to move the long grass aside as he walked. The only items he could find were a few old glass bottles and some garbage. Nothing appeared new, and they had a weathered appearance to them. Not what he hoped to find. Once he completed his arc, he took a few steps toward the shack and started working his way back. Slow and methodical got the job done.

He heard Angie as she searched through the long grass on the far side. Neither of them had any luck, or someone would have called out. After twenty minutes of bush-whacking, they met at the barrier tape strung up in a perimeter around the shack.

Noah knelt at the edge of the path and pulled out two sets of gloves, boot covers, and masks from the scene case beside the barricade.

"Try not to breathe through your nose. It's pretty bad in there."

They each grabbed a flashlight and ducked under the yellow tape. Noah paused to see if she was ready, then opened the door. Angie had heard about the scene, but she still wasn't prepared for the reality. The floor had mostly dried, and it had dozens of footprints visible in the blood. The warm September night with the light breeze had dried the blood into a rusty-brown color.

Noah entered, and he felt the blood cause a tacky grip on the bottom of his shoes. While the smell had lessened with the body's removal, it still reeked like week-old garbage dredged from a swamp—fetid and rotten.

All the body parts were taken away, and the wire that held the body down was still present, but they were all cut and hung loose.

"Umm ... Sarge?"

When he turned around, Dickinson's eyes were watering, and she dry heaved.

"Get outside," he said. "Quick."

Angie darted outside, ripped off her mask, and took a few deep breaths of fresh air. Although her mouth still watered, she got it under control within a minute.

"That was close. I'm good, Sarge."

The flashlight had caught an area in the grass, and Noah saw the place where trooper Gaston had been sick beside a large bush.

He mentioned only being sick once.

Noah's eyes widened as the information settled in. "Just step back and don't go any farther."

He strode back up the trail toward the vehicles and ducked under the yellow barrier tape. Two steps off the path, he looked through the tall grass where he had started his perimeter search until he found the spot again seconds later. Someone had thrown up just off the trail. Noah had thought it was the state trooper that had vomited or another officer. However, it may have been the murderer or someone else that hadn't been accounted for yet.

Excited, Noah marked the area with an orange flag from the kit and called dispatch to get forensics back out to the scene. He had to look through some reports, reach the state trooper, and confirm, but he may have found a solid lead. DNA can be extracted, and it could lead to a match and suspect.

Noah wondered what else the killer could have left behind. Caught in the moment, people grew careless.

If there were something out there, he would find it. Slow and methodical did get the job done.

Chapter 6

The laptop lid closed with a muffled click, and Ernie sat back and looked around the hotel room. They had arrived in Cheyenne, Wyoming, two days ago, and the place already looked like someone had lived here for a month. Clothes were scattered, and several pizza boxes were stacked on the floor next to a pile of empty beer cans.

Nick had pulled a blanket over his head, and he snored like a grizzly, which made the double bed shake.

For a solid eight hours, the hotel room echoed with the deep rumble of Nick as he breathed through his open mouth. Ernie had enough. He found an empty coffee cup and threw it at the covers.

"Get up. We have work to do."

Ernie paced back and forth in the small room while Nick struggled to sit and squinted at the light streaming through the windows.

Ernie was already dressed for the day and wore jeans and a short-sleeved dress shirt, his usual outfit. He stood just under five-foot-eight and was bald except for some short dark hair above his ears that circled his head like a ring.

"Did you hear from Donny or Frank?"

Nick pulled on his pants and brushed his long hair out of his eyes. Both men were the same age, thirty-five, yet Ernie looked fifteen years older. Where Ernie was slim and on the short side, Nick was considered a giant by comparison. He stood six-foot-two-inches and over two-hundred and fifty pounds. His long dark hair was shoulder-length, and he kept it brushed to the side.

"Nothing. They should have been here a few days ago."

Nick scrolled through the various screens on his cell phone. "No texts or missed calls."

Ernie nodded. "Same here. We can't wait for him any longer. Pack up, and we'll head out."

Nick pulled out a hundred-dollar bill and left it on the pillow before throwing his things in a gym bag. His mother had drilled in him at a young age to tip well, and with the mess they left, it would be well earned. He certainly did not want to clean it up.

A few minutes later, both men left the hotel room, and Ernie checked them out of the main office while Nick brought the rental car around the front. After the fourteen-hour drive west across I-80 over two days, neither man felt motivated to get back in the car.

Once he was in the passenger seat, Ernie pulled out his phone and looked at the map. "Donny should be at the next meet-up location. I'll try to get a hold of either of them. We'll be there in three hours."

Nick brought out his sunglasses and started up the rental. Within a few minutes, they were on the I-25 northbound. They would be in Casper, Wyoming, by noon.

* * * * *

After forensics arrived at the scene, Noah left to let them do their job while he went and knocked on doors. There were a few homes in the area, and they had to be canvassed. The small subdivision was less than a mile away on the west end of Arrow Point.

Edwards lived in that neighborhood, and Noah checked in to see if he recalled anything new. However, he had nothing further to add. Ed hadn't seen or passed any vehicles the other night that he could remember. The distraught man had smoked a large quantity of weed to try to deal with what he discovered. After the state trooper dropped him off, his memory wasn't as clear.

Noah couldn't blame him.

Constable Bennett joined him later in the morning. They sat at the station and went over the forensics reports and the crime scene photographs. Bennett has been with APPD for over six years, but this was his first major case and the first murder.

One step would be to visit the garbage dump outside of town. It had been a popular place for people to hide things they didn't wish to be found in the past. Eight and a half years ago, Noah had found a hammer at the dump that a housewife had used on her husband. Going through tons of garbage had been an incredibly messy task and not one he wanted to do again if he could help it. Before Noah began working at the station, someone had found the body of a homeless man at the dump. He may have died in a garbage bin downtown, or someone dumped the body and got collected by a truck. In the end, they couldn't prove if there was foul play or not. The dump holds many secrets and may help with this case.

They had almost finished their brainstorming session when Noah's cell phone rang. He didn't recognize the number.

"Hello?"

"Sergeant Hunter?" The voice was that of an older woman.

"How can I help you?"

"This is Nina Rodriguez, park ranger control office in Casper."

Noah grabbed a pen and paper, ready for the bomb to drop. "Go ahead."

"One of our rangers found something that someone tried to burn at one of our parks. It looks like it could be evidence. The highway patrol mentioned you have a John Doe, and possibly your case may tie in with this."

Nina promptly told Noah the details, and he thanked her before he hung up.

"Bennett, grab a car. We may have a lead on our John Doe."

After he pulled on his jacket, Noah went and knocked on Captain Richardson's office door, but there was no answer. When APPD operated outside the city limits, they needed an exception authorized—should they have a due cause. In this case, Sergeant Hunter believed he did.

In some states, police officers had jurisdictional authority throughout the whole state or county. Arrow Point Police Department was limited to their city limits for now.

He headed down to the main floor, where he ran into the duty staff sergeant. "Hutch, I need the authorization to work outside the city limits at the national park. They may have evidence for my John Doe."

Steve frowned. "Captain Richardson has headed home. He wasn't feeling good. The LT won't be in until tonight's shift."

Noah filled him in on what he needed and the reason. Steve shrugged. "I'm the ranking officer. Permission granted, but just to gather evidence."

They all knew the problems with arresting anyone outside their jurisdiction. The courts would dismiss the case nine times out of ten.

"Thanks."

He headed outside to the rear parking where Bennett sat in the cruiser, the same unmarked interceptor that he had used last night, ready to go.

Twenty minutes later, they pulled into Powder River National Park and stopped at the information booth beside the front gate. At this time of year, people paid on the honor system as the employee shack was empty. Anyone that wished to camp did the paperwork themselves and displayed their pass on the dash of their car. The second copy went on the post at the end of their campsite.

Noah stepped out of the vehicle and grabbed a map for the park. The main campsites were north or south of the main road and the large day park area was next to the river. While they drove through the campground, each site they passed was empty. The late summer weather seemed to be over. Gray clouds and a cold wind blew in from the north.

"Next right, then end of the road." Noah twisted the map around as he tried to make sense of it. It was more a drawing of the campground rather than an actual plan.

After five minutes of navigating the small laneways, they could see the ranger's Chevy Tahoe parked next to a comfort station. He had erected a ten-by-ten white portable shelter over the firepit area, and he sat on the picnic table while he waited.

He was dressed in the brown and tan ranger uniform and wore his wide-brimmed hat that looked like a state trooper's headdress. He appeared to be in his mid-thirties and looked physically fit. All the work outside had given him a deep tan. When he stood, he was slightly taller than Noah, at six feet. Ash from the fire had flecked his short brown curly beard.

He stepped down and walked over to meet them. "Doug Reynolds."

They shook hands briefly and introduced themselves before he continued. "I came across this site yesterday at ten-forty-five in the morning, and the fire was still hot. It may have burnt all night."

Noah went under the tent and had a quick look at the firepit. It was mainly ashes, with a few lumps underneath.

"I was out here early this morning once the highway patrol called back and said you would be coming out. It looked like rain, so I put up the shelter."

"Good job." Noah was impressed. The ranger had preserved the scene nicely. "Where are the items you found?"

Bennett knelt and used his finger to stir through the ashes, examining the pit for other items. Reynolds led Noah over to the back of the Tahoe and dropped the gate. There was a cardboard box in the back with several sealed evidence bags.

"I didn't know you guys used the same bags." Noah couldn't believe the park ranger's performance. He had seen seasoned officers that were not this prepared.

Doug shrugged. "They're in the system, but most rangers don't carry them."

Noah picked up the evidence bags and turned each one over. The first contained a charred black leather wallet, and the other bags had charred pieces of cloth with a few holes burned through them. The dried blood stains were noticeable.

"Wow, almost as good as a smoking gun." Stewart Bennett joined them.

The last bag contained what was left of a running shoe's heel. It had been distorted from the heat retained in the rubber. "Sorry about that one. I didn't know the piece of the shoe was that hot."

Noah turned to Bennett. "Anything else in the firepit?"

"Nothing, just some burnt wood, and ash."

Noah slid on a pair of latex gloves and opened the bag to examine the wallet. The right side of the driver's license was heavily charred, but they could see the photo of a large man, middle-aged, with dark, slicked-back hair. The state of Florida issued it.

He was a long way from the Sunshine State.

As he stared at the picture, Noah couldn't be sure if it was the man from the trapper's cabin or not, but he found something mixed in with the money that he didn't expect.

He pulled the card out of the wallet and showed it to Bennett. "We better go."

Chapter 7

At the police station, Noah and Stewart logged the evidence. The park ranger would submit a full statement when he was off work the next day. Noah removed the thick white card from the wallet and photographed it. Once it was in a smaller evidence bag, he was ready. Their destination was the Sunset Hotel, which was less than a block north of the station on Oak Street. The hotel was the tallest building in the area at eight stories. There were a few low-rise apartment buildings nearby, but they were only three stories.

Above the hotel's main entrance was the Sunset logo, a half sun rising above two mountain peaks. The same symbol that appeared on the white room key that they found in the wallet.

As they pulled into the lot, Steward asked, "Do we need a warrant?"

Noah nodded. "Yes, the fourth amendment protects privacy rights, and they are extended to a hotel room, but there are circumstances around it. Let's see where we're at."

The parking lot was relatively empty, and they pulled into the visitor spot right at the main doors. Noah called the station, and they confirmed that the driver's license recovered was registered to a false address in Florida.

"Now, we have reasonable suspicion that a crime may have been committed."

The lobby was decorated in rich dark wood and highly polished light multi-colored stone. Across the foyer, couches and chairs faced a television and fireplace, with free coffee and newspapers on a buffet table.

Arrow Point had one hotel in the downtown area, but there were a few motels on highway twenty-six. Without the tourist trade and those passing through, Arrow Point wouldn't survive.

The young lady behind the counter had bright purple shoulder-length hair, and she smiled when she saw Constable Bennett walk up to the counter.

"Hi, Stewy!"

Noah turned to his partner and grinned. "Stewy? I'll have to remember that."

"Hi Donna, this is Sergeant Hunter. We need your help."

Donna frowned. "What can I do?"

Noah pulled out his phone and showed her the picture of the driver's license. "Do you have a Donald Jones registered here?"

The young lady winced. "I'm not supposed to give out customer information."

Noah nodded. "I know, but we believe he turned up dead the other night." He pulled out the room security key they found in the wallet and showed it to her. "He was using fake identification, and we found his room key."

Donna turned to her computer system and typed away for a moment. "Room 412 is due to check out in ten minutes. At that point, our privacy policy lists that room as vacant."

"Thank you. Is it okay to have a coffee and wait?"

"Of course."

Noah helped himself to a black coffee and sat on the couch while looking over his notes. Bennett stayed at the counter and continued to talk with Donna. Noah found out later, she had dated Bennett's younger cousin a few years ago, and it hadn't worked out. Despite Arrow Point having almost one-hundred-thousand people living in the city, it still felt like a small town, and you always ran into people you knew regularly.

Moments later, Bennett came over. "Donna said that they didn't pay for an extra day and that they have to check out but haven't. We're allowed to go in."

"Sounds good."

Noah finished his coffee and threw the paper cup into the garbage. They took the elevator to the fourth floor, followed the signs, and then turned right. Room 412 was at the end of the hall. A white DO NOT DISTURB sign hung on the doorknob.

Noah stood to the side and knocked on the door. "Arrow Point police. We are coming in."

Once he held the pass key against the sensor, the LED display changed to green, and with a muffled click, the door unlocked. Inside was the standard hotel room with two double beds opposite a long low dresser with a TV on top. The back corner had a desk right next to the window and an air conditioner unit. The bathroom was immediately on their left. All the lights were off, and the thick curtains were drawn.

While they stood in the hall, Noah called out into the room, "Arrow Point PD. Is there anyone here?"

After a slight pause, he reached inside the door and turned on the lights. They couldn't see or hear any movement, and Bennett made to step inside. Hunter put his arm up across the doorway to block him.

"Let me go in first," he whispered.

With one hand on his Glock, Noah repeated himself, louder in the room. "This is Arrow Point Police Department. I'm coming inside."

Bennett also kept one hand on his pistol, ready to draw if needed, while he watched their back and covered the washroom. Noah went into the room, and it only took a few steps to confirm that the place was empty. There just wasn't anywhere to hide.

"Clear."

Two red gym bags lay open on each bed with clothing scattered all around. The dresser drawers were pulled open, and they appeared to be empty. On the desk chair, a gray sports coat hung off the back. It looked like the room had been torn apart and searched. Neither officer could tell if the search was successful or not.

Noah walked over to the windows and pulled back the curtains, which allowed a small amount of light into the room. The skies over Arrow Point had turned dark, and it started to rain.

"Sarge, over here."

Noah turned to see Bennett slide on his tactical gloves, and then he picked up two pieces of paper that lay across the one pillow on the bed closest to the bathroom. After a quick look, he passed them over to his partner.

"This isn't good." Bennett held them out.

Both sheets of paper were a printout of two faces. The first page had a black and white picture of Donald Jones, and it had a large X drawn through it with a red pen. The next page had a similar image of an unknown man. Printed in black ink below, it read, "You're next."

"Jesus Christ." Noah looked back and forth between the two sheets of paper.

The second picture showed an older man around his mid-sixties, wearing thick dark glasses over a rather large nose. The pages didn't have any names or other writing, but they were folded at one point, the crease marks still sharp.

"Go downstairs and follow up with Donna, see if she has seen the second man. I'll look through here quickly and see if we can find anything. We may have to get a team in here."

Stewart pulled out his phone and took a quick picture of the second man before heading back to the elevators. Noah studied the room and wondered where to start.

In the bathroom, he found two small brown leather ablution cases. Noah had a similar travel case—they were fairly generic. They held a few disposable razors, soap, toothbrushes, deodorants, and so on. The bag on the left was dumped in the sink, and a large bottle of Aspirin lay on top.

Noah had a look through the second bag. It didn't have anything exciting. Just the same contents as the other. He double-checked the dressers, but they were empty, and the clothing had nothing in it. The beds were on a fixed frame, and there was no access to underneath. Near the window, Noah paused when he looked at the air-conditioning vent. There were no signs of tampering.

At the desk, he found a few menus from a local restaurant and pizza take-out coupons. When he moved the chair, he heard a metallic noise from the suit jacket. The inner pockets were empty except for a pen. In the front pocket, he found a set of car keys with a Toyota remote fob.

Noah headed downstairs, where he found Bennett outside the elevator. "Donna has never seen him. He wasn't registered to the room."

Noah held up the car keys. "Found these. Hopefully, there's something more in the car."

The rain had turned into a heavy drizzle, and the wind had picked up. The eastern sky showed darker clouds that moved in with the brisk breeze.

Noah pushed the alarm button on the key fob. Neither officer saw any lights that flashed nor heard a horn. Noah pulled his ball cap lower against the rain as both men walked around the building to the rear parking lot. Two Toyota sedans were parked against the back fence next to a minivan and a small blue Honda. All within fifty feet of the hotel rear door and smoking area.

The lights on the dark blue, four-door Toyota Avalon flickered, and the doors unlocked when Noah once again pressed the remote. With the steady rain and the tinted windows, it was hard to see in the backseat. Noah pulled his flashlight from his utility belt and opened the front passenger door, and a quick look inside showed it was empty.

He then pressed the trunk icon on the key fob, and the lid popped an inch. Once they lifted it and looked inside, Noah swore under his breath as they took in the scene. A large white bath towel from the hotel was bunched up in the corner against the right rear taillight.

It was soaked in blood.

"I think we found how Donald was moved around." Bennett shone his flashlight over the rest of the trunk and found dried blood smeared all over the interior, soaked into the fabric.

"If it wasn't him, it could have been the other man. Hopefully, this isn't from a third person."

Noah couldn't believe the series of events. One body may have turned into two. Things like this don't happen in Arrow Point, but the blood-soaked towel proved him wrong.

Hopefully, this would be over soon, but the feeling in his stomach proved otherwise.

Things were just getting started.

Chapter 8

Megan finished cleaning the classroom, ensuring that the chairs were up on the tables and the boards were cleaned. Every Friday, the janitor would come through and mop the floors, but if the chairs were not on the desks, your classroom might be skipped. A lesson she had learned the hard way when she first started teaching at Red Creek public school over five years ago.

At four o'clock, she had finished for the day and headed home to her apartment. The rain fell hard enough to bounce an inch off the road, and she wouldn't have been surprised to see it turn into a thunderstorm. The weather wasn't an issue as she lived six minutes from school. A seven-minute commute if she hit the red light. There was something to be said for small towns.

Noah was going to come over for dinner. It was their 'date-aversary.' He teased her about her memory for dates, but Megan knew he liked it. Soon as she pulled into the underground parking at her apartment, she heard the chime for an incoming text from Noah:

>> I have to work, won't be done until later. Sorry xo

She knew it was silly to be celebrating the three-year mark from their first date now that they were engaged, but she had looked forward to a night together. Megan sent a quick reply back, then took the stairs to the top floor. Track pants and a T-shirt with a glass of red wine or two would have to work.

Once she stepped inside the apartment, Megan hung her coat in the closet, kicked off her shoes, and then headed into the small kitchen. She froze for a second and took a deep breath, then held it before tears fell down her cheeks. On her kitchen table was a massive bouquet of fresh flowers, and a card leaned against the vase.

With one hand, she wiped her face clean and grinned. After a deep breath to calm down, Megan took a moment to enjoy the fragrance and then picked up the card.

Happy Date-aversary, Love Noah.

Megan grabbed her phone and sent him a text:

>> Thank you so much! I will wait up for you ;)

Despite the weather and the dinner plans that had changed, a warm glow filled Megan's heart. After she opened a bottle of red wine and poured herself a glass, she turned on the radio.

Megan looked down at the engagement ring on her third finger and smiled. She couldn't help but bring it to her lips for a kiss. It used to be Noah's grandmother's, and Megan loved how it sparkled in the light. After a week of being around six-year-olds, she looked forward to some adult time. She hoped he wouldn't be too tired.

* * * * *

Sergeant Hunter sat at his desk with the LT as they went over the information accumulated on the case thus far. He just finished another report and printed it off with the actions taken at the hotel. The forensics team had tarped the vehicle and loaded it on a flatbed to be analyzed. It seemed that most of his time was spent doing paperwork and reports, which was part of the job.

The hotel only had one security camera, and it didn't cover the rear parking lot, which didn't leave him with any substantial clues. With one finger, he tapped the picture of the unknown man and slid it across to Lieutenant Piekenbrock.

"This is the person we believe is next, according to the warning. A definite person of interest."

The LT picked up the photocopy. "Because it was coupled with the first picture, you're right. I will put out an ATL." *Attempt to locate.*

Zane Piekenbrock stood two inches over six feet and had a military bearing about him. At fifty-eight years of age, he kept his white hair short in a crewcut fashion. The LT usually dressed in a suit for work, and he never seemed to wear the same tie twice. Today it was a black tie with a gold diagonal stripe. The guys had long since given up on counting the various ties he owned. They figured there must be a whole closet dedicated to them.

"Would I be able to get more help on this?"

The LT thought about it, then nodded. "Definitely. What do you have in mind?"

Noah sat back and rubbed his hand over his face. He was tired from the long day, and switching from the night shift to the day had caught up with him. "Would I be able to get a full team?"

Large cases automatically had six members that worked full time, plus support. The overtime was usually the sticking point. It always came down to the budget.

Zane offered a wry smile before he shook his head. "Not now. Bennett and one other." He tapped his finger on the report from the original body that was found. "This was horrible, but so far, there aren't many options. Let's find who did this and the next target. When you have more information or something solid, help will be there."

When the LT stood, he kept the photocopy of the second man. "I'll get this to comms and have it sent out statewide."

Piekenbrock turned and walked into the captain's office with a glance at his watch, leaving the door open.

Looking around the cube, Noah saw six other officers typing away on the computers, logging in, filing reports, and checking email. He crossed the cube to stand beside the corner desk and waited until she finished on the computer.

"Ready for a change of pace?"

Constable Dickinson looked up and gave him a half-grin. "What do you have in mind, Sarge? I thought you were engaged."

Noah chuckled and held up a folder of paperwork. He gestured to the conference room just off the cube. "Ready for your first homicide?"

"I was going to set up a speed trap just off the highway, but I will gladly pass and join you."

"I can get that reassigned easily enough, but if you are not interested, let me know."

Angie logged off and stood. "Sounds good. I'm interested."

It took an hour to go over the findings and various reports. Angie sat back in the chair and looked worried. Her fingers tapped on the table absently.

"Where would you like me to start?" she asked.

"Right now, find the rental company for the Toyota and follow up with any information they have. The first ID was false, but maybe we can identify this second man the killers after. Security video would be good."

Dickinson nodded and quickly went to work. There was a time to delegate and disappear. This was one of those times, so he left her alone. As he turned to walk away, his phone vibrated with a text. When reading Megan's reaction, he smiled and looked at the time. Since he had to wait on reports from the coroner's office on the John Doe and the forensics report, he decided to head out early.

"Sergeant Hunter?"

Lieutenant Piekenbrock waved him into the captain's office, pointing to the chair inside. He was on the phone. He held up one finger to indicate he was almost done.

Noah took a seat and scanned the small office. There were a few awards to Captain Richardson and photos on the outside wall. Behind the desk were three shelves packed with regulation and procedure manuals. The large wooden desk took up half the space, and it was covered in paperwork with two computer monitors.

Piekenbrock sat down behind the desk and, within a minute, finished the call. "The forensics unit called. They finished processing the data from the first crime scene, and they made the comparison to the car. The blood matched with the trapper's shack and the towel you found. There's nothing else from the cabin they could identify. No prints, hair, nothing that wasn't from the victim."

Noah raised his eyebrows in disbelief. "The killer didn't leave any trace? That's amazing and hard to believe."

"Same with the car. It was wiped clean, and any prints they found were too smeared to be usable. I have authorized them to process the hotel room for prints and hopefully identify both men."

"I have Constable Dickinson working with me now, and I'll have the staff sergeant reassign her."

The LT drummed his fingers on the desktop. After a moment, he nodded. "Good. Find this other man. I hope that we will have more answers in the morning. Rest up."

After working fourteen hours straight on little sleep, he was ready to call it a night.

"Dickinson, any new information, give me a call. I'll see you in the morning. You can start the day shift tomorrow, so don't stay up all night."

She smiled and gave him the thumbs-up sign before turning back to work. The constable had the phone to her ear, held in place with her shoulder, while she typed away on the computer.

Noah changed out of his uniform before he headed to Megan's apartment.

He couldn't help but grin. He was tired but not that tired.

Chapter 9

Ernie rubbed his hand over his head and wiped the water. The rain hadn't let up all night. The meet-up in Casper was a dud, and they headed farther west to Arrow Point. After they checked into another hotel, they headed out for a few drinks. The place nearby was The Tavern. It may be the only bar in the small town, as far as they could tell.

The Tavern was the local watering hole for Arrow Point and relatively popular on the weekends. The bar and dining room had tables, chairs, and booths that lined the exterior wall. Each Wednesday night, an area was cleared for the local dart teams to use the space for their tournaments.

The room adjoining the lounge resembled a traditional bar, more than a restaurant. Large wooden beams crossed the ceiling and walls, and a large gas fireplace was on the north wall between two huge windows. The dozen small booths and tables were seldom used. Most sat at the long wooden bar or gathered around the lagoon tables to watch sports. Each corner of the bar had a television, and there were two behind the bar, mounted on the wall. A game was broadcast at all times on the various screens, from darts to baseball. The third room in the building was toward the back, and it had a small dance floor and stage where local bands would play on the weekends.

Ernie and Nick sat down on the bar stools and ordered two large pints. After a few minutes, both men lit up a smoke and immediately were asked to step outside. The bartender, Sarah, was quite firm. They weren't even allowed to bring their beers with them. Ernie shook his head at the new rules.

"Fucking hick town," he whispered.

Nick stood inside the doorway, his long hair wet and hanging down in his eyes. "They should have a separate room so you can smoke while you drink. Brutal. Not like it used to be. So, what's our next step?"

"I'll contact the boss and see if Donny or Frank checked in with them. I've worked with Donny for almost twenty years. He wouldn't jackrabbit. I don't know Frank that well, but something happened. We just have to find out what."

Once they flicked their smokes out into the parking lot, they headed back inside. Once they finished their beers, they ordered another round. Despite the label of a hick town, both men were impressed with the chicken wings.

They had just ordered their third round when Ernie's phone chimed and vibrated on the bar top. Nick continued to drink while Ernie took a deep breath and picked up his phone to read the email.

After a minute, Nick couldn't take it any longer. "What's up?"

Shaking his head, Ernie handed his phone over for him to read while he stood. Opening his wallet, he threw some cash on the bar.

"Jesus Christ. Do you think that was Donny?"

The phone showed a news article of a John Doe found in the woods at the Arrow Point city limits. There were no pictures, but the story was rather graphic.

"Let's go. We have work to do."

Ernie opened the door hard enough to slam it into the wall as he stormed out. A few turned to stare. Nick sighed and threw another twenty on the bar as he turned to follow.

* * * * *

By midnight the rain had stopped, and a warm breeze came in from the west. The streets were dry when Noah made his way home. As much as he loved being with Megan, her bed was a smaller double, and he never got a good night's sleep when perched on the edge of the mattress. On more than one occasion, he had fallen out—not something he wanted to do again if he could help it.

He held a piece of paper in his right hand and tapped it against the steering wheel while his brain continued to process the information. It was a copy of the listings for two-bedroom homes within their price range for Arrow Point that Megan had given him earlier.

His house was too small for them both, with only eleven hundred square feet, so they had to get a new place. It just seemed to make it more real for Noah. He had lived in the same home for over eleven years. However, the thought of a large two-car garage with a workshop perked him up.

He pulled into his steep driveway and parked the Chevy truck under the carport. The water from the rain slowly dripped off the roof into a large puddle where a flower bed had been several years ago.

Once inside, he turned off the security system and headed straight for bed. Noah didn't last long, falling into a dreamless sleep.

* * * * *

Noah woke up a few minutes before the alarm to start his day. Eight hours of sleep had fully recharged him, and there was a little bounce to his step. The sun was already up, and with the breeze that blew in the bedroom window, he could tell the day would be humid.

Fifteen minutes later, he had showered and was dressed in jeans and a green T-shirt. On the way out the door, he grabbed a protein bar and stepped out the side door. When he stood beside his truck, he dropped the bar on the ground, and his right hand slid down to grasp the grip of the Glock while he gazed through lowered eyes at the area.

He could see the fence that divided the neighbor's property from his, with large bushes on the far side through the backyard. Across the street were a few more homes. However, there wasn't anyone awake and outside this early on the weekend.

Noah took a few steps over to his truck and pulled a white piece of paper out stuck in the crack of the front door. The page was folded in half and dry. It had been placed there recently, after the rain. It read: Stay off this case—first and only warning.

It was printed on regular white paper and creased where it was folded. There wasn't a signature or any other marks. Noah performed a perimeter check of his property with one hand on his weapon, but he came up empty.

He examined the note a few more times before he went back inside, closed his bedroom window, and then made sure the security alarm was on. There wasn't much else he could do before he had to leave and head to work.

He pulled out a spare set of tactical gloves from the glove box to avoid contaminating the note further, should it be processed.

Strong but confident hands gripped the wheel of the truck as he wove in and around the light traffic. Soon he was parked in the back of the station after six minutes of leaving home. As he got out of his truck, he met with Lieutenant Piekenbrock as he finished the night shift.

"LT, is the captain in?" Noah held the note in his hand along the edges.

"He seems to have the flu. What can I do to help? Lieutenant Hodges is already upstairs."

With the gloves still on, Noah held the note open for the LT to read. "This was in my truck window this morning when I woke up at home."

"Son of a bitch. Follow me."

The LT headed into the station at a brisk walk. Once they were on the elevator, Noah noticed a redness creeping up LT's neck—the man looked angry. The police station's third floor dealt with call services, dispatch, administration offices, and the deputy and police chief offices.

As they approached the offices at the north end of the building, Noah could tell the chief or deputy chief wasn't at work. The doors were closed, and the lights were off. The receptionist for both men was absent.

"The deputy chief should be in." Piekenbrock turned to Noah. "Get that in an evidence bag, then submit it under your case file number."

The LT's phone rang, and after glancing at the number, he gestured for Noah to follow him to the administration area. The main switchboard operator for the station had their own corner office. The LT knocked on the door, then entered.

"That was quick." Erin had worked at the station part-time long before Noah had even finished high school. She resembled everyone's grandmother, right down to the sweaters and a pair of glasses on a chain around her neck. A second pair perched in her hair. She liked to work weekends and one shift per week, and without her, the whole station would not run quite the same.

"Lieutenant, I had a call for you from the state police in Casper. The coroner's county office was broken into last night, and they said you are now missing your latest John Doe."

Noah stepped back once, not knowing how to react to the news. However, the LT certainly did. He slammed a fist into the doorframe in frustration. "Thank you, Erin."

As they turned to leave, she added, "Once the fire in the offices was out, they found him missing."

Noah raised his eyes at this. "Fire?"

Erin nodded. "They are still investigating, but it may not be related."

Lieutenant Piekenbrock closed his eyes for a moment and took a deep breath. He seemed to think something over and came to a conclusion. His eyes opened, and he turned to Noah. "You now have your team, and I'm on it."

Chapter 10

Arnold Sharpe woke every morning with the sun to make his coffee and breakfast. He was eighty-three years old and still fairly active. He contributed his long health to daily walks, eating right, and a few sips of whisky every night.

Once dressed in his gray pants and matching hoodie, he ate breakfast and fed the dog. Sonny was a four-year-old golden retriever that his granddaughter had left with him while she was on vacation. After he grabbed the leash and a few plastic bags, they headed out for their daily walk.

The rain had stopped the night before, but most things were still wet. The dog seemed to take great pleasure walking through each puddle. Arrow Point Rotary Park was less than a mile from Arnold's house, on the east end of town. Once they arrived, he reached down and took Sonny off the leash. There was no one else about at this time, and the dog loved to run.

"Go on, boy. Keep me in sight."

Now that Sonny was free, he only ran three feet and started to sniff around a park bench before he walked over to the trees and kept an eye out for squirrels.

Arnold kept his routine and walked the full trail through the park and past the baseball diamond. Sonny barked and ran by at top speed, headed for the woods just north of the path.

"Do your business in there so I don't have to pick it up."

Arnold loved the dog but bending down with his sore back to clean up after him was getting a little much. The sun burned off the moisture, which made his shirt stick. It would be a warm day.

Once he reached the bridge that spanned the creek, Arnold turned around and didn't see the dog. He gave a short whistle, and after a moment, Sonny came bounding out of the woods.

"Let's go back home. I could use another coffee."

As he reached down to clip the leash on, Arnold paused. The front of Sonny's muzzle and along the side of his head was a dark red smear.

"Are you okay, boy?"

He rubbed the dog's side for a wound but didn't find anything. When he looked at his hand, it was covered in sticky blood mixed with dog hair.

"Jesus Christ. What did you find, pup?"

Sonny tilted his head sideways and opened his mouth when he panted. He was a good boy at times—Arnold swore he could almost talk. He wished this was one of those times.

"Okay, let's go see."

He kept the retriever on the leash while Arnold made his way through the short grass as he followed the dog's track. The trees were mostly maple, with a few fir and birch clumps spread out along the park's northern side. They didn't have to go far.

A dozen feet into the trees, a man was leaning back against a lone birch tree. His chin slumped down on his chest, and he appeared to be asleep. He was an older man with short curly hair, deep lines on his face, and a large nose.

"Are you okay?" Arnold moved closer, but the man didn't respond. "Sir?"

Once he got within a few feet, Arnold realized the man wouldn't be answering him. Not from this side of the grave, at least.

The man wore a dress shirt and khaki pants with a dark blue sweater. There appeared to be several gunshot wounds to his chest and one to his right leg that soaked his clothing in blood.

Arnold wasn't much for religion or God, but the first thing he did was say a prayer for the poor man.

"Come on, Sonny, good boy. Let's go home and call the police. It might not be too early for a quick drink, either."

* * * * *

Noah sat in the conference room and looked over his notes before writing down suggestions the rest of the team had proposed. Lieutenant Piekenbrock sat on his right and constable Bennett on his left. At the head of the table, Angie Dickinson went over the findings on the vehicle found at the hotel.

For the first time in years, the lieutenant wasn't in his usual suit, but he had changed into his class "A" blue uniform, wearing the same gear as everyone else. Except for his sidearm. He preferred the Browning HP 9mm.

At the other end of the table, Constable Ken Horne sat with Sergeant Stan Bydal. Noah asked the two men to join the team for this case, to which they readily agreed.

Both were seasoned officers, with Stan having the most experience with homicides from his years with the Denver Police Department. Stan stood five foot eleven and had a slim waist but broad shoulders and chest. At fifty-five years of age, he appeared to be easily twenty years younger. He had the tapered look of a quarterback and carried it rather well.

Constable Ken Horne was one of the larger men on APPD, standing six feet four inches and almost three-hundred pounds. His biceps were the size of most men's thighs, and Noah was reasonably sure that Ken could lift the back end of a cruiser if needed.

One look at him, and most people complied right away with his orders. Ken was also one of the smartest people he knew, and he was lucky to have him on this team. As long as there weren't snakes involved in any way, Ken would be there for them. His fear of reptiles was legendary, which led to a series of pranks around the station. Jokers beware—he would get you back and usually twice as bad.

Angie took out another set of papers. "Vehicle registered to Apple Rentals, out of Des Moines, Iowa. It was rented by Mr. Donald Jones on Tuesday morning this week."

Noah checked his notes. "Do we have credit card information on him? Video feed?"

Angie shook her head. "There wasn't any video, and the rental company is getting back to me on the payments."

Noah pulled up the forensics report from the Toyota. "Initial report, blood matched the victim from the towel and trunk. Zero prints on the vehicle. The techs believed it was a full wipe-down, and they smelled bleach as well."

Stan cleared his throat before he spoke. "Anyone else thinking this is too organized? It seems they are watching too much television about covering their tracks, but they are doing the right moves."

The meeting was interrupted when LT's phone vibrated and danced on the tabletop. He was about to mute the call when he caught a glimpse of the display, then Piekenbrock answered.

He paused to listen for a moment, then, "Okay, send me the information. We'll be there in a few minutes."

After he disconnected, he took a deep breath and shook his head. "It seems we've found the other man from the hotel too late. Grab scene kits, and I'll call the coroner's office. They have another body to collect."

Chapter 11

By noon Rotary Park was one of the busier places within Arrow Point. Parked along the edge of the wood line, police cruisers and an ambulance, along with the coroner's van, were in a single line. They closed the park, and the pathways had turned into vehicle lanes.

Yellow barricade tape decorated the tree line as it encircled the area in a sixty-yard perimeter around the body. A few people tried to see what had happened, and soon after, two reporters arrived. The lieutenant brought them off to the side to give them a statement and keep the photographers away from the area.

Noah knelt and listened to the county medical examiner as he pointed out the various gunshot wounds on the body. He had met Doctor George Hall a few times previously, but he hadn't worked directly with him. A heavy-set man in his late fifties that usually wore blue scrubs and a Dodgers ball cap. He wore a leather coat and rain boots, and when he crouched beside the body, his knees sounded like dry branches when they cracked.

"Not much blood. The victim had five gunshot wounds to the chest and one to the left leg. I can see the residue from here. All fired close enough to cause stippling."

Noah nodded. "He was killed somewhere else and dumped here."

After they stood, George scanned the area. "Someone had to carry him in here. No room for a car."

Stewart and Noah were the first on the scene, and they had driven through the park. He hadn't noticed any other tracks.

"Could he have been in the area and walked here to die? Or forced to walk here." Noah called a few other police officers to join him as the medical examiner headed back to the van.

"He wasn't killed where the dog walker found him, but it could have been nearby. Let's start at the far end of the woods, closer to the park, then work our way to the creek."

After the reporters moved to the far end of the impromptu parking lot, the LT joined them, and they walked to the far edge of the wood line.

One of the basic search patterns the police used was an extended line. They could comb a large area with that method. For larger areas and fields, Noah had seen fifty officers together as they searched. However, he only had half a dozen available now, so he had to make do.

Once they were in position, he called out, "Stay on the center. Slow walk."

The six officers strode through the woods at a slow pace. They moved branches and looked under bushes, but they found nothing other than the usual trash. Eventually, they passed the tree where the body was found and continued downhill toward the creek.

Constable Angie Dickinson was on the far right. They had just walked into a small clearing when she called out, "Halt! On me."

They were twenty yards away from the creek, and the area was filled with short grass and large dirt patches, the ground sloped toward the water.

As everyone converged to her location, Angie pointed at the grass. "Over here. Another over here."

Two brass nine-millimeter shell casings lay at her feet, and Piekenbrock pointed at another large stain in the dirt.

Blood.

"Stop moving! Look for prints in the dirt."

Although Noah was in charge, Zane had been at the game for longer, and his lieutenant rank came out full force.

Everyone froze and studied the ground at their feet. Stan was closest to the bloodstain, and he pointed out a few scuff marks, but they didn't lead anywhere.

Noah held a hand in the air, and he turned in place as he tried to pinpoint the location. His head tilted to the side as he strained to listen. "What's that noise?"

Angie pointed to a sapling next to the creek. "Garbage."

There was a piece of paper stuck to a tree, five feet above the ground. "Horne, go and check that out. Bennett, head back and walk forensics over. We will need to rope off this area, as well as a direct line from here to where the body was found."

"No problem, Sarge." Both constables turned and walked in different directions while the remainder continued to examine the scene.

Noah knelt and searched the grass for more casings and tried to figure out where the shooter had stood.

Horne swore a few times before he called out, "LT, can you come here?"

Piekenbrock dusted the dirt off his suit pants when he stood. "Coming."

Curious, Noah watched as Zane walked over to stand by the creek, and they talked in low, hushed tones.

When the LT pulled out his phone and took several pictures of the paper, Noah strode over. Horne tapped the LT on the shoulder and gestured behind him as he got close.

Lieutenant Piekenbrock stepped to the side and blocked Noah's view of the paper. "Sergeant Hunter, I will be removing you from the case. Effective immediately."

At this, Noah's eyes opened wide in disbelief. "What's going on, LT?"

Stepping around the officer, Noah had a good look at what they tried to hide. A long-blackened survival knife had pierced the paper, and it stuck deep into the tree trunk. The wind had flipped it over, and he reached out to correct it.

"No! Don't touch it."

When Horne blocked Noah, the wind died down and allowed the paper to hang flat.

"Oh, my God."

You were warned. Now pay the price.

Underneath the bold writing was a picture of Megan Brooks, printed in black and white.

It was the same style as the note found on his truck and the papers found at the hotel. Noah whispered, "She should be at my place. We're looking at houses tonight."

He didn't wait for a response. Noah turned and bolted through the trees toward his cruiser. Fear lent him strength, and he focused on nothing but his efforts. The sudden adrenaline surge made his heart pound in his chest. He heard the LT broadcast over the radio, "Code eight. Officer needs assistance. One three niner Beach Street West."

It was just six weeks ago that Noah had a large backyard barbecue. Quite a few of the station had swung by for a beer and to meet his new fiancée. Piekenbrock remembered the address.

The LT yelled for Dickinson to secure the scene. "Horne, you're with me."

Both men ran for their vehicles, hoping they would be in time.

Chapter 12

Megan opened the trunk of her old four-door Honda and lifted her duffel bag of clothes and purse out before closing it with a free elbow. The sun felt good on her face, and she took a moment to close her eyes and enjoy the warmth. There were a few clouds in the blue sky, and the light breeze felt good as it blew a few loose hairs across her face. She wore her favorite cut-off jean shorts and a white T-shirt. It was laundry day, and this was one of her last outfits.

Once she unlocked the side door, she placed her things down to enter the code to disarm the system. Usually, Noah didn't have the alarm on and just kept his doors locked.

On their first anniversary, Noah had given her a key to his house, and every Saturday, Megan usually came over to do her laundry. She loved the apartment, but going to the basement to use the coin laundry machines wasn't ideal. It was one thing she wouldn't miss.

Over the years, she kept some clothes here and a few items that she would need regularly. Noah had emptied a drawer in his dresser, and she kept her things there. He had the same cache at her apartment, even though he didn't sleep over as much.

Once she settled in, Megan turned on the radio and started her routine. She watered the plants and put a few things away. Noah never spent much time at home, and the place never seemed to need any serious cleaning.

Off the kitchen, a steep set of stairs led into the basement. Megan could stand straight when she was downstairs, but Noah had to bend slightly with the lower beams.

Most of the basement was storage for Noah's camping equipment and a few fishing rods, tackle boxes, and tools. Two large windows at the north end of the basement filled the area with natural light, and there wasn't any need to flick a switch. Megan's favorite appliances were under the large windows, a massive new front-loading washing machine and a dryer. No coins were needed.

After separating the clothing into a few piles and starting the machine, she sat at the kitchen table and opened Noah's laptop.

There were a few new listings for homes in the area, and Megan wrote them down.

As she sang along to an Eagles song and scrolled through the real-estate listings, she didn't hear the cell phone as it rang several times. It sat in her purse, next to the washing machine. The noise from the cycle covered up the multiple incoming calls.

When people panic, their thought process gets jumbled, and they have problems functioning. Logical thought goes out the window. Confusion sets in, and poor choices end up being made.

Noah wasn't sure if it was his two years with the infantry or the eighteen years of being on the police force, but when he found himself in moments of high stress, he was able to shut down that part of his brain that caused panic—and lock it away in the back of his mind.

That left him a highly functional, emotionless computer for a brain that had an elevated reaction time, and he became focused on the task at hand. Emotions and second-guessing were processes that he didn't have time for, and they got in the way.

As he approached the police cruiser, he slammed the trunk lid closed and jumped behind the wheel. Once the vehicle was in drive, he slowly accelerated across the grass. Had he floored it, the rear tires would have spun, and it would have slowed him down.

Noah absently noted he was detached from the situation mentally. He would do his best to move with all possible haste. Once the flashers were on, Noah buckled in. He automatically shifted his holster forward an inch—it had always caught on the seatbelt release.

Rotary Park was in the east end of Arrow Point and the fastest route to his house—west along Main Street before short-cuts along a few back roads. That way, he avoided high residential areas.

He smoothly accelerated through town with his head on a swivel, cars pulling over quickly. Those that didn't, Noah swerved around and continued on his way. Almost routine.

As he turned left on his street, Noah turned the flashers off and unbuckled his seatbelt while he slowed. He parked in front of his neighbor's house, turned off the cruiser, and drew his pistol in one smooth movement.

Once he stood on the street, he glanced around and saw nothing unusual. A few vehicles parked on the road several homes away, but there didn't appear to be anyone watching his house.

He kept the Glock pointed along his right leg as he slowly walked along the grass between the two homes and stopped at Megan's car. He flattened his hand on the hood of the Honda.

The metal was cold.

Once under the carport, he moved past the side door and did a quick turkey-peek around the corner. The backyard was empty. As calm as he appeared, Noah absently noted his breathing had picked up.

He duck-walked below the kitchen window as he moved through the backyard. Absently, he noted sirens in the distance and the smell of clean clothes from the dryer vent. He checked the far side of the house.

Clear.

Back at the side door, he tried the handle. It was unlocked. He brought the Glock into the ready position as he slowly opened the door with his left hand. With a deep breath, he quietly stepped inside his own home.

Music emanated from the living room.

Slowing his breathing, he brought his left hand under his right to support his wrist and pistol while he stepped into the kitchen. The living room was empty, and nothing in the short hallway to his left. It led to the bathroom and bedroom. He could smell Megan had cooked something for lunch, and the laptop was left open on the kitchen table.

He went down the small hallway and cleared the back room—no sign of Megan.

He turned off the music in the living room and retraced his steps through the kitchen. With the music off, he heard the dryer going and started down the steps. The Glock led the way.

A sudden ear-piercing scream caused him to jump, and he rushed the last three steps. Megan dropped her folded clothes, leaned back against the washing machine, and brought her hands to her face. Wide-eyed and scared to her core.

But alive.

Noah quickly holstered his pistol. "Are you okay?"

As she tried to get her breath, Megan nodded. Once she settled down, her temper flared. "What the fuck was that all about?"

Noah glimpsed two figures run past his laundry room window. The dark blue uniform pants with yellow stripes were visible. Simultaneously, the front and side doors were slammed open, and multiple people rushed into his house as they called out for him.

"Downstairs. Code four!" *Code four—no further assistance is needed.*

He turned to Megan and finally began to let the tension ease in his shoulders. "I'm sorry. I can explain."

Noah stepped forward and gave her a big hug and a quick kiss. The message was passed along to his brothers upstairs as they stood down.

The note was a bluff.

Thank God.

"Let's go upstairs. We need to talk."

Noah sat at his kitchen table and held Megan's hand. His small house was filled with people, and a few cars lingered out front. He skipped a few details, but he told her what he could.

"I still can't believe it. How will you catch them? Are we safe?"

Lieutenant Piekenbrock reassured Megan. "I'm going to have a protective detail on the house, twenty-four seven."

Noah smiled and added, "I'll be here as well. There's nothing to worry about."

"Sergeant Hunter, what I said earlier still stands. I'm removing you temporarily from duty."

Noah looked like he was about to say something, but Megan squeezed his hand and nodded. "Okay. I'm due for a few days off. Keep me informed if you can?"

Piekenbrock shook his hand and turned to Megan. "If I can, I will. Glad you are safe, watch over him."

Stan held out his hand. "Give me your truck keys. I'll drop it off."

Behind a cupboard door, Noah pulled down his spare set of keys and handed them over. "Thanks." He would get the other set from his locker when he returned to work.

The LT turned and brought the rest of the men outside with him. After a quick word, one man pulled his car around out front and watched the house from the road.

The first protective detail shift had started.

Soon as everyone had left, they sat back down in the kitchen. "Sorry, we scared you. I was worried."

Megan had calmed down, and she didn't seem too concerned. "I'm fine. Nothing going on here except some laundry."

"I guess we can postpone looking at homes until this is over."

"That sounds good." Megan turned to her notes and passed them over. "There were only a few within our price range, but there will be others."

Once he stood, Noah looked down at his uniform. "Okay, I'll go change. Be right back."

Megan stood as well and grinned. "You don't have to change right away, do you, Sergeant Hunter?"

Chapter 13

When all the cop cars drove past with lights and sirens screaming, Ernie had a moment of panic, and he pulled the rental car over in front of the National Bank downtown Arrow Point.

Nick laughed nervously. "For a second ..."

Ernie swallowed, his throat suddenly dry. "Same here. All good."

They waited a few minutes before they pulled back out on Main Street and headed west. Traffic started to flow behind the parade of police cars once again.

"I'm not getting a good feeling from this." Ernie slowed down and started taking a few side streets with endless rows of family homes.

Nick just hummed in agreement. Despite the fact they headed in a different direction, they seemed to have found where all the cruisers went. The same destination that the GPS map on their phone had led them to.

"Don't make eye contact. Keep driving past."

Instead of turning on Beach Street, the rental car slowly drove by.

"Jesus. There are easily seven cop cars and two undercover cruisers out front."

A quick look at the bags in the backseat reassured Ernie. "All will be fine. Let's go get some lunch."

* * * * *

Around midnight, Noah was still restless. Megan did her best to wear him out, but in the end, she was the one snoring in his bed. Dressed in jeans and a T-shirt, he slid the Glock onto his hip. For the third time, he went around the house and checked that the windows and doors were secure.

Noah could see a police car parked out front from the living room window. He headed to the kitchen and grabbed a couple of water bottles and protein bars. Noah turned off the alarm system, stepped outside, and headed down to the road.

Once the cruiser's windows lowered. Bennett and Dickinson sat together in the front.

"Why didn't you guys tell me you were out here?"

Stewart winked. "None of your business, Sarge."

Noah chuckled and handed over the bars and water. "Here you go."

"Thanks."

"Any new information come in?"

Bennett looked at Angie quickly, then back. "Nothing yet. I can tell you we are not supposed to brief you on anything new."

Noah shrugged. "I know. I had to give that same order myself. That doesn't mean I won't ask, though."

After they spoke for a few minutes, Noah headed inside the house. He locked the door, activated the alarm system once again, and then checked the windows a fourth time.

He tried going back to sleep but just tossed and turned all night. At five o'clock in the morning, he'd been lying awake for hours. He gave up, crept out of the bedroom, and gently closed the door behind him. Megan still slept soundly.

After he made a pot of coffee, Noah went online to see what information, if any, he could gather from the reporters at Rotary Park, but there was nothing new.

There was a follow-up story on the first murder, but there wasn't any latest information, nor any word on the break-in at the coroner's office.

Noah had planned to go over there today to see how the highway patrol and sheriff's department were doing with that investigation, but that would be someone else's job now.

A couple of hours later, Megan woke and stumbled into the kitchen wearing one of Noah's T-shirts.

"Did you sleep at all?"

He shrugged. "Here and there. I'm still wound up."

"I tried to wear you out." Megan poured herself a cup of coffee and sat beside him.

"You did a good job." He kissed her on the cheek and opened the fridge. "What do you want for breakfast?"

"What are our options?"

They were interrupted when Noah's phone rang. After he checked the display, he held a finger in the air. "Morning LT, everything's going good here."

"The chief is in, and I've briefed him. You need to come in and make a formal statement."

He looked at Megan in his T-shirt and how much leg she showed. "Now?"

"If you can, the car will stay at your place. You should be back in half an hour."

"Okay, sir. I'm on my way in."

Noah looked at Megan. "How about I pick up breakfast on the way home?"

She hugged him and kissed his nose. "I'll be here. Don't worry."

He slipped into his running shoes, brought something out of the bedroom with him, and laid it on the kitchen table. The Glock 19 was the same as the model he carried. "It's loaded. Just point and shoot if you need to use it."

Megan nodded and made a face at the pistol. "You know I hate guns."

"I'll be back soon. Love you."

"Love you, too."

Another kiss goodbye and this one lasted a bit longer.

"I think I'll hurry home." Noah caught his breath and turned off the alarm. "Turn this on behind me, and don't open the door to anyone."

Megan made a shooing gesture. "I'll be fine. Go."

Noah caved and locked the door behind him. Once inside the truck, he took a minute to rearrange his holster but gave up and placed it on the seat next to him. They always caught in the seatbelt release no matter what vehicle he was in. Left-handed officers had it made. He backed down the driveway, then lowered the driver's window as he pulled alongside the cruiser.

Constable Glen Luttrell lowered his window as well. "Hey, Sarge."

"I'm just heading down to the station. Back in thirty minutes or so."

Glen grinned and pointed over to his house. "I think someone is saying goodbye."

Noah turned and looked at his front living room window. Megan stood there as she sipped her coffee, and when she saw Noah look over, she waved, then leaned forward and breathed heavily on the glass. Quickly Megan drew a large heart in the condensation, then blew him a kiss through the center. As she turned and walked away, she flicked the back of her shirt and mooned him.

"I will make sure that that isn't in the report. I don't think I even saw anything." Glen laughed and pretended to look away.

"I'll check the logs. You better not. I'm guessing you haven't seen anything in the area?"

"Nothing. A few residents are going to and from their homes, but that's it."

They talked for a few minutes when Glen asked him about his current case. Noah was about to answer, but he never got the chance, nor would he ever remember what he was about to say.

The first explosion blew out all the windows of his house in a brilliant yellow flash. Glass flew and sprayed his truck like a hail of stones at seventy-feet. A crack radiated along the length of the passenger window. A long shard of aluminum, which used to be part of a window frame, buried itself into the truck's rear quarter panel. Noah brought his arm up in reflex while he turned away. He barely saw the second explosion as it lifted the roof of his house slightly while the front wall blew out.

The noise hit him all at once as his truck was rocked back by the force of the blast. The police cruiser was partially sheltered, but Constable Luttrell could see the full pyrotechnic effects.

Bright flames shot out the windows while a small mushroom cloud of black smoke rose in the morning sky. Flaming debris rained down over the lawn and both vehicles, as well as the neighbor's homes. The right side of the house fell over as the carport was crushed along with Megan's car. It wasn't long before that caught fire as well.

Noah had no recollection of how he got to the front of the house or how long he knelt on the lawn. He could only hear a high-pitched ringing in his ears as he struggled to breathe. It felt like only seconds had passed before he noticed flashing lights behind him. Strong hands gently picked him up and walked him to the back of an ambulance.

No one noticed the red Toyota drive by the end of the street.

The two men inside grinned at the anarchy and continued on their way.

Chapter 14

Noah was in shock and disoriented. He had trouble concentrating or thinking of anything but Megan.

Eventually, an emotion swept away the muddled thoughts.

Anger.

It burned through the confusion, and Noah grasped at it like a lifesaver. It clarified his thoughts and shook off the fog.

The police chief, Jason Birch, came by the medical center to check on him and easily a dozen other officers. The Arrow Point Medical Center didn't have the full resources as the hospital in Casper, but they had a couple of private rooms, a doctor, and a few nurses. Once Noah started to regain his senses, he insisted that he was fine and wanted to leave.

As he was getting ready, Piekenbrock and Bennett arrived.

"Please tell me you have something."

The LT shook his head. "Sorry, nothing yet. The chief asked the feds to step in for the explosion. We don't have the resources to analyze that properly."

"How are you doing, Sarge?" Bennett seemed worried and upset. His eyes were red and puffy. Megan had liked to tease him, and it seemed to strike him hard.

"I'm not hurt, but I know finding the people that did this will make me feel a lot better."

Noah pulled the plastic hospital bracelet off and threw it on the bed, then picked up the white paper bag the doctor had given him. He was to take two Ambien thirty minutes before he went to bed tonight. It would help him sleep, and after seeing the events today replay over and over in his mind, he would need some help.

The LT put his hand on Noah's shoulder. "We'll find them, don't worry about that. Do you have a place to stay?"

Noah thought for a second. "If you can take me back to my truck, I'll swing by the station and grab my keys. I can stay at Megan's apartment. I already have a few things there."

"Anything you need, you let us know."

The nurse wouldn't let him leave until they checked his blood pressure again and a few other items before they signed him out. They seemed to care, and Noah appreciated the concern.

Minutes later, Noah walked out of Arrow Point Medical Center. They drove across town and parked at the end of Beach Street.

It had been three hours since the explosion, and the fire trucks remained out front of his home. There wasn't much left of it. The roof had mostly collapsed in a charred heap, and the walls had caved in. Everything was a blackened mess with smoke that rose from a few spots. However, the fire was out.

Debris had scattered over eighty yards, some pieces landing on his neighbors' homes and lawn.

Someone had moved Noah's truck to the end of the street, and the keys were still in it. With all the police presence and the activity, it was about as safe as it could be.

A few of the neighbors were out on the sidewalk as they watched the fire crews check the debris for hot spots.

A white cube van parked next to a dark blue Crown Vic at the other end of the street. Two FBI agents leaned against the truck while they talked to one of the technicians. Once the fire marshal finished his investigation, the feds would start their own.

It seemed too much to take in. Noah closed his eyes and took a deep breath. The burnt smell of wood covered the area, and despite the few tears that trickled down his cheeks, he knew he would be okay for the moment at least.

He turned to the LT and Bennett. "Thank you *very* much. I promise I'm fine for now. I need to make some phone calls and relax."

He shook the paper bag that held the sleeping pills.

"If you need anything, Sarge, let me know. Even if to just sit and have a beer or twelve." Bennett seemed to tear up, and he almost seemed like he was going to fall apart. Noah stepped forward and hugged him and slapped his back in comfort.

"It's okay, buddy. We'll get them."

Bennett nodded. "I'm supposed to be comforting you."

He wiped his eyes and got back in the cruiser. The LT added, "You need anything, you just let me know."

"Will do, thanks."

Inside his truck, Noah looked for his Glock and found it in the glove box. Someone had placed it there to keep it out of sight. He pulled it out of the holster and racked the action to confirm a round was still in the chamber. He didn't trust the round-chambered indicator on the Gen 4 model's extractor and liked to check visually. It did him no good if it wasn't ready to go when needed.

He adjusted the position once it was holstered and back on his side. It would stay with him, and if he were lucky, it would be used shortly on the people who did this. That was a cure he could live with.

Barely.

* * * * *

Sitting on the bed's edge, Ernie leaned forward and shrugged, his hands raised in the air.

"Not sure exactly, but what I do know is we still have a job to do."

Nick paced back and forth in their hotel room and eventually gave up. Brushing back his dark hair from his eyes, he nodded. "Okay. What's our next step?"

They had received a copy of Donny's autopsy report, and they knew he would have talked. With what was done to him, there wasn't anyone that wouldn't have spilled everything they knew. No one could hold up to that.

Ernie also couldn't believe Frank was dead as well. Someone was targeting them, and he would find out who.

"I think we need to set a trap. I know what kind of bait to use as well."

Chapter 15

Unlocking the door and stepping into Megan's apartment was a surreal moment that Noah relived over and over. Everything seemed normal, yet he could still feel her presence. If he pretended hard enough, he could feel her waiting for him inside.

Locking the door behind him, he left his keys on the kitchen counter and looked around. The flowers he bought still sat on the table, and the light was on above the stove. Everything looked as if she had just stepped out and would be right back. Half a bottle of red wine sat on the counter. Noah pulled the cork and grabbed a glass from the dishrack.

Megan didn't have any family left, but he thought there were a few people he should be calling. Her school principal, for starters. He would also call his mother. She had been in a nursing home in Casper for the last two years in assisted living. She liked to do most of the things herself but still needed supervision. They had met several times, and Megan had grown to love her. It had been almost a month, and he would have to go out and visit, but with work, he was having trouble coordinating the time.

His brother Iain was still deployed and should be coming home from Afghanistan in two months, just before Thanksgiving. He would send him an email soon, filling him in.

Sitting on the couch, he sipped the wine and opened Megan's laptop.

My laptop now?

He wasn't ready to start thinking that way yet.

Despite Arrow Point being over one-hundred and thirty thousand people, rumors and word of mouth worked faster than the internet at times, and Noah received a steady stream of calls.

Unable to deal with it any longer, he turned off his ringer, popped two pills, and washed it down with the last of the wine. Getting ready for bed, Noah found the loneliness almost more than he could bear. When he lay down, he could still smell Megan on the pillow.

The drugs, coupled with a glass of wine, soon had him drifting off into a deep sleep without dreams. For that, he was thankful.

~

For the first time since he was a teenager, Noah had slept just over twelve hours. He needed the rest, for when he woke up, he was still groggy and had a slight headache.

He was sure that his mental process was back, and he was able to function once again. His training took over. He pushed his emotions—and to a certain extent—his memory into a corner of his mind and locked the door.

He took stock of the clothing he now owned, which sat in half of the top drawer of Megan's dresser. He would need more, but it would do for now.

He fell back into his morning routine quickly and had a few cups of coffee and a shower. He kept his pistol with him at all times and even rested it on the back of the toilet while he cleaned up.

Wiping off the bathroom mirror from the shower, he looked at himself, and he couldn't believe the man that stared back. Dark circles under his eyes made him look like he hadn't slept in a week. His goatee and stubble made him look older, and in a spontaneous moment, he pulled out some shaving cream and his razor.

A few minutes later, he ran his hand over his smooth face.

Much better.

Getting dressed, he finished the third cup of coffee while he checked the messages on his phone. Eighteen missed calls and twelve voice messages.

He listened to the messages, deleting most. The last one was from Chris Curry, the fire marshal for Arrow Point. They had recovered the body from the house. It was so severely burned and damaged from the explosion that there was no way to identify it. The cause for the blast was still underway. The source seemed to come from the basement. Megan was the only one inside. A few minutes later, one more lingering kiss, and he would have gone up with her.

Noah and Megan had talked about funeral arrangements, and he made a mental note to contact Mankiewicz Funeral home to arrange a cremation with no service.

A sudden need for fresh air came over him, and Noah grabbed his light jacket from the closet and locked up the apartment. He darted down the stairs to his truck. At eleven o'clock on a Monday morning, Arrow Point's traffic was almost non-existent, and Noah drove aimlessly around town. He stopped at a drug store to pick up a few things. While he was in line to pay, his phone rang.

Bennett whispered, "Sarge, there was another murder last night. In the new construction, north end. Gotta go."

Looking down at his cell phone, Noah realized his partner had hung up rather quickly. It didn't take long to come to a decision. After he paid for his things, he jumped behind the wheel of his truck and headed north. A few years ago, the area used to be a farmer's field. Several streets were recently completed, and just east of that was a whole new area under construction. Slowly but surely, Arrow Point was growing.

A cruiser parked sideways and blocked one of the new, partially completed streets. The officers held back almost a dozen people on the other side of the yellow barricade tape.

Pulling over fifty yards away, Noah walked in and stood in the group of people that were waiting. He recognized two of them as reporters, and the man with them was a photographer, a large camera hanging around his neck.

Noah didn't remember the rookie assigned to keep everyone out, which was okay with him. He wasn't up for talking with anyone. He was here to observe.

The police were concentrated around a partially built home with a main floor and three walls. A pile of lumber lay off to the side. He couldn't tell what was happening from this angle, but he could hear the reporters talking around him. A man was nailed to the wall and gutted sometime last night.

A few more people joined the crowd and watched, and a few tried to take pictures with their phones, but they were too far away. A murder counted as 'new and exciting' in Arrow Point. Turning to the young woman with the camera, Noah asked, "Do they know who was killed?"

She shook her head, her long brown hair moving slightly. "They aren't saying."

"Okay, thanks."

"I did manage to get a picture before we were forced back here."

She held her camera up and showed Noah the display. She zoomed in on the figure right in front of an unfinished wall. The man's head leaned forward slightly. It looked like he was sleeping. His long unkempt hair almost covered his eyes, and Noah could see his long gray beard hanging down on his chest.

His eyes opened wide in recognition and shock. "Umm … thanks."

Quickly, Noah turned and walked back to his truck. The woman with the camera shrugged and turned around to the reporter and kept talking.

Why would someone kill Pete?

It didn't make any sense, but he was determined to find out, and he knew where to find some answers.

Chapter 16

Despite growing up in Arrow Point, Noah never truly saw most of the city from an adult's perspective. He went to the Gerald Ford public school in the west end, but he never knew they had a mouse problem. Noah would often go shopping downtown with his family, but he never noticed the people that sat on the corners or slept in the alley.

The first year on the police force opened his eyes to what people mostly see when they went about their everyday business in Arrow Point.

A group of kids that would magically disappear when a cruiser showed up on their street. A few ladies who hung out at The Tavern were not there for drinking but to sell their bodies for cash or drugs. There was also a growing population of street people with nowhere else to go. They just shuffled from one place to another, depending on handouts.

Pete was one of those men who rarely asked for help, but he would stay in the church on occasion when it was too cold to sleep outside. He would find pieces of wood that people had thrown away and carve them into animals to sell. Pete would spread out his little display blanket downtown with all his small carvings on it. He would never ask for a price, but he would gladly accept anything anyone would be willing to give, either food or money.

For over twelve years that Noah had known, whenever a cruiser drove by and saw Pete, they would always wave, and he would wave back with a smile.

He knew one man that may know about Pete, and that was Gerry. They were usually seen together, spending time out at the park or down at the men's shelter behind the church. Noah never asked Pete nor Gerry what their circumstances were and why they were living on the streets, but he treated them with respect and always asked how they were doing.

Both men were always cheerful, with no problems that they shared. When he asked how things were, they simply shrugged and gave him a big smile.

Noah parked behind the church, then walked over to the shelter and asked around for Gerry. A few social workers directed him to the next block over, and Noah gave a few waves to a few of the men he had seen about town. They all knew the sergeant checked in on them, especially during the cold months.

On the corner of York and Main, Gerry sat on the street bench and sipped from a coffee mug. Noah wasn't sure how old he was, but he could guess easily over seventy or close to eighty. A long white beard tickled his chest, and thick, black-rimmed glasses perched on the end of his nose. Gerry wore an old Red Sox baseball cap in the summer months that he traded in for a winter hat from the same team. He wore a mix of clothing, which seemed to be in various layers, despite the warm day. The few large bags that sat at his feet contained all his worldly possessions.

"How are you doing, Gerry? Mind if I join you?"

At seeing Noah, he smiled ear to ear. "I'm doing good. Just enjoying the nice weather. Sit down, please."

Leaning back on the bench, Noah closed his eyes for a moment, enjoying the warmth of the sun.

"I wish this were just a visit, but unfortunately, it's not."

The smile washed away from Gerry's face. "I figured someone would be coming soon."

Noah turned to face him. "I need to know. I can't tell you details, but if you know something about Pete …"

Gerry leaned forward, deflating like a balloon. "I told him not to go with those men, but they knew his name. Pete thought they were taking him home, but he wouldn't listen to me."

"Can you describe them, Gerry? It's important."

He rocked back and forth slightly with his eyes closed. "Two white guys, one was big and the other small. The little guy did all the talking. He was smooth to have convinced Pete. We were out behind the Tavern, and sometimes the cook feeds us."

Noah knew all about Charlie at the Tavern. Many meals have 'accidentally' slipped out the back door. "Do you know what they were driving?"

"It was a little, four-door red car. It was dark, and I have trouble seeing at night."

"That's okay. Do you remember anything else?"

Gerry opened his eyes and faced Noah. His eyes were cloudy in the sun's bright light, but they still had a spark to them. "There was a sticker of a green apple on the back. I saw it when they drove away."

Noah's brows furrowed as he tried to remember something, then it clicked.

He pulled out his wallet and gave Gerry a couple of ten-dollar bills. He also handed over his business card from APPD with his cell phone number written on the back. "If you need anything, you give me a call."

Gerry stuffed it all into a pocket and then closed his eyes and faced the sun once again.

Noah's thoughts already spun with the new information as another piece of the puzzle clicked together. He had to hurry to keep ahead of his colleagues. They would not be far behind.

Chapter 17

Noah drove to the station, picked up a few things from his locker, and threw them into a small gym bag. He left his uniforms hanging, but he did pack a few clothes changes before going upstairs to the cube. Instantly, the guys came over to see how he was doing, and all work stopped. It took fifteen minutes before he assured everyone that he would ask for help if needed, and he appreciated their condolences. Their heartfelt concern almost brought him to tears. They were indeed a brotherhood and family.

Noah did notice that the door to the captain's office had remained closed.

At a far desk, he logged in and checked his email. He also wrote a short letter to his brother to tell him what had happened. Opening the case file, Noah quickly found what he was looking for. The blue Toyota was rented to the man from the trapper's cabin, Donald Jones.

The vehicle had been checked for prints with no success. However, forensics took pictures from all angles. The last picture showed what he was looking for—Apple Car Rentals, written inside a large green apple sticker.

While looking through the other pictures, Noah couldn't tell if the red car parked beside it was another rental as well, but his gut was telling him it was. Same model with the same year, just a different color.

Two rental cars from Des Moines, Iowa, would be too coincidental. One of the rules he had learned while on the force was that coincidence rarely happens. A mantra he lived by and had proven over and again.

Sitting up straight, Noah looked around the room, taking it all in. What he was about to do could get him fired or, at least, suspended.

When someone died, they were usually told to wait at least a year before making any significant decisions. That way, your grief had a chance to play out and not influence your choices.

Everyone would know that it was Pete they found up north on the construction site, and they would be talking with Gerry shortly, maybe even now. Gerry did like to talk, so they would know that Noah came to visit.

Sighing, Noah concluded that a thirty-minute head start wasn't worth blowing his career over.

The lesson he learned while in the infantry, CYA, echoed in his mind.

Cover your ass.

If the LT were as busy as he thought, he wouldn't be checking emails until later.

Noah quickly sent Piekenbrock an update on a possible tie-in for the case, then logged off. A quick look at the time confirmed that he had missed lunch. After saying goodbye, he quietly made his way back to his truck. Eating was foremost on his mind, but first, he had a few stops to make before heading back to Megan's apartment.

Before pulling into a parking spot at the Sunset Hotel, Noah drove around the building a few times, but the red Avalon wasn't there.

Donna stood behind the counter, and she smiled when she recognized Noah as he walked through the door.

"Sergeant Hunter, how are you?"

"Good. I'm looking for two men that may have been staying here." Noah quickly described them and added, "They also may have been driving a red Toyota Avalon."

Donna turned to her computer and pecked away at the keyboard. "I have only been here since noon and didn't see anyone, but there was an Avalon registered to a room. They checked out this morning."

Grabbing a pen and paper, Donna wrote down some information and passed it over to Noah. "You didn't get this from me. Okay?"

Smiling in appreciation, Noah nodded. "What information?"

Laughing, Donna gave him a wink before he turned away and headed back to his truck and looked at the note.

GE55 P93, Ernie Jones, FL.

The second Florida driver's license was most likely false, and a second rental car from Iowa.

There were no such things as coincidences.

* * * * *

"Are you sure they work?" Nick looked down at the computer screen and zoomed into the area.

"Best thirty dollars I have ever spent." Ernie took the tablet back and took another sip of coffee.

They sat in a donut shop twelve miles west of Casper. The gas station and rest area were next door and shared the same parking lot.

When everyone stared at the crime scene this morning, Ernie had quickly walked up behind Noah's black truck and dropped the small plastic device into the bed before he joined the crowd at the barrier. He stood right next to the cop when he talked to that girl. Pigs are all the same, no matter where you go.

"I bought a bunch of them online. Just pull the tab, and the GPS is paired up with the program. Too easy."

The locator connected to the local cell phone towers, and it broadcasted its location to an online tracking program. The locator moved as a blue dot on the map.

They watched the dot drive around town. Hunter stopped at various locations but never in one place for too long. Nick patted his shirt pocket. "Going outside for a smoke."

Ernie put away the tablet and stood as well. "How about we head into the city for dinner? We have to pick up a few things for tonight."

"Sounds good." Nick already lit a cigarette before heading outside.

"We should be on our way home tomorrow. It'll be just like shooting pigs in a barrel."

Chuckling to himself, Ernie knew he would enjoy what was coming up. It always gave him a thrill when a plan came together.

Chapter 18

Noah finished talking with the superintendent of Megan's apartment building and tried to make arrangements to continue paying the rent. However, to his surprise, she had paid fifteen months in advance. Maurice had Noah add his name to the form, and just like that, he had a place to live. He didn't realize how much that weighed on his shoulders. Now he only had ninety-nine other things to worry about, but it was a start.

After an afternoon driving around Arrow Point, at times aimlessly, he tried not to grow anxious. He was on the lookout for a small red car but had no success. Frustrated, he called it a night and looked in the cupboards at the apartment, finding more than enough food. When he was busy, Noah was fine and could concentrate on the task at hand. However, back in the apartment, he had trouble getting Megan and the case off his mind.

When his phone rang, it was a welcome distraction. The display showed it to be from the station.

"Hello."

"How are you doing, Hunter?" Lieutenant Piekenbrock sounded tired.

"I'm coping."

"The feds are done with your house. A mixture of C4 and dynamite caused the explosions. It wasn't an accident."

Noah collapsed on the couch. "Jesus ..."

"They are willing to step in and help us with the murder investigations. The chief's making up his mind as we speak. Also, we've identified the second man as Frank Morello."

"What do you know about him?"

The LT punched away on the keyboard and pulled the information. "Heavily involved in organized crime as an enforcer. CID is sending us more information, long as we keep them in the loop."

The Criminal Investigative Division was the FBI's task force that oversees drug, violent crimes, and organized crime. They have thousands of special agents tasked with holding back the tide of corruption. At times it was a fruitless effort.

Noah came up with a decision. "LT, I've heard from a source."

He passed along the information of the driver and plate number. If organized crime families were involved, it would be well above the sergeant's paygrade from the Arrow Point Police Department.

"For someone not on the case, you're doing remarkably well at gathering more information."

There was no appropriate answer to this. Noah stayed silent.

Zane sighed. "Rest up, and I'll continue to keep you informed if I can."

"Yes, sir."

After saying their goodbyes, Noah leaned back on the couch and closed his eyes. There was one thing that nagged at him.

How would a homeless man be involved in organized crime?

After a quick meal, Noah tried to watch television, but he gave up within five minutes. Sitting still wasn't possible, so he grabbed his coat and keys and left the apartment.

Even if he weren't productive, driving around town would at least keep him busy. Besides, he wanted to check out some of the motel parking lots north of Arrow Point. They were right off Highway 26, and many tourists kept them busy on their way to or from the national park.

At ten o'clock on a Monday night, there wasn't much traffic. There were a few cars still outside the Tavern, but Noah recognized two of them belonging to the staff.

Since he was heading west, he continued until he came to the trail that led to the trapper's cabin. He backed in, turned off the truck, and pulled out his flashlight, then went for a walk.

Despite being only two miles from the city center, Noah couldn't hear any other sounds except that of the county. The night had cooled, and he could feel the temperature change. It wouldn't be long until the fall weather took over, and nights like this would be typical. Shining the light on the trail, Noah noticed deep tracks. A large vehicle had driven up here fairly recently, possibly even earlier today.

Noah soon found the reason.

The entire trapper's shack was gone, leaving a large patch of bare earth. Once all the evidence had been collected, the town couldn't leave it standing. It would never be adequately cleaned. Right now, it was probably burnt to ashes.

Glancing around, Noah wasn't sure what he hoped to find out here, and after a quick look at his watch, he decided to head back to town and bed. The goal was a few hours of sleep. The last few days have taken their toll, and he was starting to feel it.

The apartment building's underground parking was too difficult to maneuver his truck around in, so Noah parked in the visitors' area. As he got off the elevator, he stifled a yawn. However, when he was about to put his key in the door, he froze.

A new scratch circled the deadbolt—brown paint flecks littered the hall carpet at his feet. Drawing his pistol, Noah crouched and put his ear to the door and listened.

The fatigue was washed away, replaced by adrenaline in the blink of an eye.

Silence.

Trying the handle, he wasn't surprised to find the door unlocked, and he opened it a crack. All the lights were on, so he opened the door wide and rushed inside with one smooth movement. With both hands on the Glock, he turned left into the kitchen and checked the corners. His prior room-clearing training with the infantry was never forgotten.

Two steps back, he then turned and hurried to the living room while he continued to scan the small apartment. Still nothing. He absently noted that the place was trashed.

The bedroom and bathroom were empty as well.

Starting his secondary search, Noah checked the closets and under the bed, even the kitchen cupboards.

Nothing.

Once he calmed down, he locked the door and took stock of the apartment.

Whoever ransacked the place must have been quiet about it, or the neighbors would have heard. The couch was turned over, and the cushions leaned against the window. The fabric underneath was pulled away from the frame. Everything on the small bookshelf was taken down and restacked on the floor in neat piles.

All the coats and jackets were removed from the front closet and strewn on the floor. The pots and pans were taken from the kitchen cupboard and stacked on the counter.

In the bedroom, the mattress was moved, and the dresser was emptied of clothes and dumped on the bed.

Someone had been searching for something.

What were they after?

The fatigue was gone, and he holstered his pistol. He skinned the knuckles on his right hand when he punched the wall and let out a growl. Frustrated, he had some work to do and calls to make.

Chapter 19

Noah called the break-in to the station, but far as he could tell, nothing was missing. He told them to send someone over in the morning to file a report and let Lieutenant Piekenbrock know. Whether he was on the case or not, he seemed to be involved. There were no such things as coincidence. The break-in had to be related.

Noah then spent over an hour and placed everything back, but what intrigued him the most was the scratch marks on the apartment door. It was a perfect circle with the deadbolt in the center, barely deep enough to scratch the paint. The only thing it could be was a professional lockpicking device. The door-latch wasn't broken or forced.

Noah sat back on the couch and looked around. Everything was back to its position, and nothing was destroyed. Far as he knew, Megan didn't have anything of value that would warrant a targeted break and enter. He couldn't morally decide if Megan's possessions were now his or not. Everything he owned could now fit into a small gym bag.

When Noah trained for his sergeant's exam, one of the instructors said a coin always had two sides. When in doubt, try a different view. Find results and understand a person's perspective as only one side of the coin. With that in mind, Noah had a hard time grasping that anyone would have been after Megan. There was one way to find out, and that was to eliminate the obvious.

He started in the bathroom and began his own detailed search. In Douglas's Law Enforcement Academy, Noah was limited to afternoon training for Interior Evidence Gathering. It was divided up between vehicles and homes. They learned about false doors, hiding items in plain sight, and various methods of searching. At times tools were required, and flat-out destruction has its time and place. Noah wasn't ready for that level of the extreme, but he would give it a good look.

He started with the cupboard under the bathroom sink. He removed everything, placed it on the floor, and checked the walls and base for false panels. Each toilet paper roll was examined as he put it back, as well as the cleaning products. He lifted the tank lid for the toilet and had a good look inside. This was a common place to hide items but more for drugs.

Nothing.

The search was going to take all night, so Noah put on a pot of coffee. He wasn't going to be able to sleep anyway.

* * * * *

Neither man had spoken during the hour-long drive, but occasionally Ernie would open the tablet, watch the blue dot, and then shut it down. Nick checked them into Motel 8, north of Casper, at two in the morning and paid for two nights. The office had a blue neon light stating they were open, and you could drive straight to your room. The tall sign out front offered free Wi-Fi and air-conditioning with every night's stay.

The building was only one story tall. However, there were thirty rooms for rent. After opening the door to room four, each man threw their small bag on a bed, then looked at the other.

"I'm out of ideas."

Nick patted his pockets and pulled out a pack of cigarettes. "I know the next step. Going against a cop without backup isn't too smart, ya know?"

"I know, I know. I'll make the call."

Glad it was not him calling this in, Nick headed outside for a butt. He had never heard of so many places in one state that were non-smoking. A good reason never to move to Wyoming if he ever heard one.

Leaning against the car's hood, Nick lit up a smoke and glanced upward. The night sky only showed a few stars, and the low clouds moved in with the night breeze. Blowing a plume of smoke straight out, Nick followed it up with a few smoke rings.

"You happen to have an extra smoke?"

Startled, Nick looked over his left shoulder and saw a woman next to the driver's door. Bright red hair, wearing a gray sports bra with a short brown leather jacket and matching mini skirt and dirty white running shoes. A dozen bracelets matched her large hoop earrings. She was good-looking enough to get his attention and hold it.

Patting his shirt pocket, Nick handed over the pack while he continued to check her out. "No problem."

"Thanks, honey."

With a wink, she pulled a lighter out of her bra, lit one up, and passed the smokes back. Nick got quite an eyeful, and suddenly he was in a better mood.

"Kinda late for a stroll."

Taking a deep drag, the woman shrugged. "Yeah, but couldn't sleep, and I'm trying to quit. Ya know?"

Nick grinned. "Been there."

Exhaling through her nose, the woman rolled her head back and forth from shoulder to shoulder. "Much better. Thanks."

"No problem."

They stood there with an awkward silence for a few seconds, and the woman smiled. "Guess that's it. Thanks. Just going to head back to my room for a drink …"

She nodded toward the other end of the motel. The only other car was parked at the far end—room thirty.

Giving Nick a quick wink, she walked across the parking lot and headed back to her room. He couldn't look away. It was quite the sight.

One minute after her door closed, Nick made up his mind. He dropped the smoke on the ground and rubbed it out with the toe of his shoe. Back in the room, Ernie was still on the phone. "Will be back in a bit, don't wait up."

Ernie waved him away before he turned back to the call. Nick tucked in his shirt and fixed his hair in the mirror before going for a quick walk. In a good mood, he hummed a Green Day song as he crossed the parking lot.

He was about to have the time of his life.

Chapter 20

The sun beamed through the gap in the curtains when Ernie awoke and stretched. The clock on the nightstand showed it was almost nine in the morning. Six hours of sleep wasn't too bad, just enough to get him through the day. Coffee would undoubtedly help, as well.

He was on the way to the bathroom when he noticed Nick's bed was still made, and his bag sat on top of the dresser.

Fuck.

Ernie got ready and packed his bag, then checked his phone. There were no messages or texts from Nick. He said not to wait up for him, but this was ridiculous.

He sent him a quick text and then waited. There was a small coffeemaker in the room, and Ernie fired it up for a quick cup to help kill some time.

After a few minutes, he called Nick directly. It rang several times before he gave up.

Ernie stepped outside and scanned the parking lot. His car was the only one there.

He was pretty tired when they arrived late and couldn't remember.

When he moved closer, he saw Nick in the backseat of the rental vehicle, sitting sideways across the bench. He leaned against the rear passenger door, and it looked like he was sleeping. Ernie got a shiver, and the hair on his arms stood on end.

When he peered through the window, he realized Nick wouldn't be waking up from this nap.

His throat was cut ear to ear. The blood had drained straight down like a sheet and soaked his shoulders and chest.

"Fuck!"

Ernie kicked the car door several times before he noticed that each tire had been slashed. The Toyota sat on its rims.

Eyes wide, Ernie spun around, looking for anyone watching, but he was alone. The motel was a twenty-minute drive north of Casper, and there wasn't much in this area except vast tracts of forest and open fields. He pulled out his cell phone and snapped a quick picture of the scene.

He ran back into the room, quickly went through Nick's bag, and pulled out some extra clothing and a few snacks he had stashed. He took down the extra blanket from the closet shelf that no one ever used and placed everything in his gym bag.

He didn't have time to wipe down the room or car. He had to move quickly. The small window in the bathroom was barely big enough for a three-year-old. He didn't have a choice. The front door would have to do.

Outside, he darted past the office and stopped at the vending machine next to the ice maker. He quickly loaded up on chocolate bars and bottles of water.

When he heard the sirens in the distance, Ernie wasn't surprised. In fact, he would have been disappointed if the cops hadn't been called.

Once he turned the corner of the building, Ernie glanced over his shoulder and then disappeared into the woods. Help was on the way. He just had to survive and hold out.

* * * * *

Early in the morning, Noah gave up. He was reasonably sure there wasn't one square inch that he hadn't checked. With the sunlight warming the apartment, he went around and turned off the lights, and opened the curtains.

With his finger on the light switch in the kitchen, he paused.

There were a few places he hadn't checked.

He opened the third drawer in the kitchen and dug around until he found what he had seen earlier—a yellow-handled flathead screwdriver.

Starting back in the bathroom, Noah used the screwdriver to remove the switch plate for the light and had a good look inside before he placed it back. The electrical outlet by the sink had nothing behind it either. He methodically worked his way through the apartment.

Finally, in the bedroom, he had taken off the light switch plate and looked inside, and found something. In a small clear plastic sleeve, tucked into the small space with the wires, was a brass-colored key.

Noah stared at it for almost a full minute in shock before he pulled it out to examine it. He wasn't sure how long Megan had lived here, but it could have been from a previous tenant. However, with the series of events that led up to this, he doubted that train of thought. He pulled the key out of the plastic sleeve and looked at the engraving. Master Series 445.

From the heft, he could tell it was for a more solid security lock, and after a quick internet search on his phone, Noah confirmed the lock brand.

Putting the switch plate back on, he made yet another coffee and sat on the couch. The key felt new, with sharp ridges on the cut. A key tends to wear with use, but he doubted it had been used, if at all. By the time he finished his coffee, Noah had an idea. Turning off the coffeemaker, he rinsed his mug and left it in the dishrack. Inside the first cupboard door were a few hooks with keys on them. One set was for Megan's car, and the second was for the apartment building.

Noah remembered giving Megan a key to his place, and the next weekend they had gone out and made two copies for her apartment keys. One set for him and the second set in case of an emergency.

He grabbed his jacket and clipped the holster on his belt before heading out of the apartment.

Once inside the elevator, he pushed the button for the basement instead of the ground floor.

He hadn't been on the lower level before. Megan hated it and only came down here to do laundry when there were no other choices. For years she would come over once a week to wash her clothes at his place.

The laundry room floor was decorated in a light blue tile with white subway tiles halfway up the walls. Five washing machines sat against the right wall, and directly across were five matching dryers. There were a few folding tables set up in the middle. The machines had an attachment on top where coins could be inserted to use them.

Past the laundry room was a large metal door. On a brass plate next to the handle, *Storage Lockers* was engraved. When his mother moved into her senior's apartment building in Casper, the units also had a storage locker in the basement.

On the chain were four keys. One for the front door and one for the underground parking garage entrance. The third key was to open the mail compartment off the lobby. The last key fit perfectly into the locker storage door and turned. When Noah stepped inside, the light sensor activated, illuminating the interior. A series of cages stretched along the walls with two rows in the middle. Each unit was four-by-six feet and built with a thick hog wire over wooden frames. The lockers were secured by various padlocks the tenants used. Evidently, most people stored Christmas decorations and large coolers and lawn chairs, along with towers of packed boxes.

The numbers on each locker door didn't correspond with the building's unit numbers, but Noah just walked down the three aisles until he found the appropriate lock. In the second aisle, against the back wall, was a large black and silver Master Series lock, model number 445.

Inside were six boxes stacked against the back wall in two separate piles, otherwise, it was empty. Noah didn't expect the key to open the padlock, but with a sharp click, it turned. Taking a deep breath, he opened the door and entered to see what Megan went to such great lengths to keep hidden.

Chapter 21

Casper/Natrona International Airport barely qualified for the global status, with only two runways and one terminal. With the upgrades to the airport in the late eighties, the runways were expanded, and they could handle the larger aircraft. The terminal's interior had been recently remodeled, and the man's shoes made a slight clicking noise against the polished stone floor. He wore an older gray business suit, carried a briefcase, and pulled a worn travel suitcase behind him. One of the wheels was damaged. It veered randomly, letting out a small squeak every time the interior weight shifted.

The man was five-foot-nine-inches tall, and he appeared to be slightly hunched. It made him shorter by almost an inch. There wasn't anything memorable about him. In fact, people looked right at him and promptly forgot about him within the same thought. He kept his short hair mostly brushed to the side, but it seemed to have a life of its own, and tufts stuck up randomly. If any were to guess his age, they would estimate between twenty-five and fifty.

Just inside the doors for arrivals were two car rental agencies. He picked the closest one and lined up as a family in front of him dropped off a vehicle. The process for renting a car didn't take more than five minutes before the woman behind the counter handed his license back.

"Thank you, Mr. Anderson. Enjoy your stay in Casper."

"I will, thank you."

He picked up the key for his rental and walked outside to find it in the parking garage.

Fifteen minutes later, Anderson pulled into the parking lot of the FedEx shipping center on Circle Drive. The customer pickup offices were empty, but after he rang the bell, a man dressed in a blue uniform came out of the back office. He showed the young man his verification slip.

"I'll be right back."

He went through the double doors and into the warehouse area. He didn't have to wait too long before the doors swung open again. "Here are your car parts, Mr. Anderson."

The young man dropped the two reinforced boxes on the counter. Each box was twice the length of a standard shoebox, yet they weighed eighteen pounds each. After signing for the parcels, Anderson carried them out to the rental car and put them in the trunk.

By this time tomorrow, he figured he would be flying home.

He loved these quick jobs.

* * * * *

Noah knelt in the storage locker and took down one box from the top. There was a layer of dust he had to wipe off, but there were no markings. The boxes were all the same dark brown with a lid, the type you would see in an office from a paper shipment.

The first one contained old clothes, everything from jeans to sweaters and T-shirts. The next four boxes were Christmas decorations. At this point, Noah didn't think this was Megan's locker. Far as he knew, she never liked decorating for the holidays.

The last box on the bottom was heavy, and once he looked inside, Noah sighed in relief.

The paperwork on top was for a Rachel Parisotto. Income tax forms and an old rental agreement for the building were in a plastic bag, dated several years ago. A quick look confirmed it was the same apartment as Megan's.

In the bottom was a stainless-steel container, and after he lifted the lid, Noah whistled in surprise.

On top were two boxes of 9mm rounds and an old M1911 Colt handgun with a detailed fox head carved into the wooden handgrips. It was a lot heavier than his Glock, but he could feel the weapon's quality. A quick check revealed it wasn't loaded. He couldn't tell the pistol's age, but he did know that they didn't take 9mm rounds. Far as he knew, they used .45 ACP cartridges.

He placed the gun to the side, then opened the ammunition boxes and saw stacks of money inside. After looking through them, he figured there must be ten thousand dollars in various denominations.

The only other item in the metal box was a survival knife sealed in a large plastic bag.

It was the large type of bag used for freezing a roast. With the flashlight from his cell phone, Noah took a closer look at the blade. There were several scratch marks along its length, and where the hilt met the edge, a dark substance was built up and stuck to the metal.

Old, dried blood.

"What were you doing with this, Rachel?"

He considered all the possibilities, and each one wasn't promising. In the end, the police officer's side of his brain won out, and he placed the knife, money, and the gun back in the box and brought it with him.

Doubtful, this had anything to do with Megan. However, the CYA rule kicked in.

Instead of going back upstairs to the apartment, Noah jumped in his truck and headed to the station.

After a long night, Noah was looking forward to sleeping. He was running on coffee and adrenaline, and both were fading rapidly.

Hopefully, he would find out about the previous tenant and focus on more important matters.

Chapter 22

The 2020 Dodge Ram Caravan was a deep red and quite clean, inside and out, and still smelled new. It was one of the more excellent rentals that Jim ever had. Once he placed the two boxes from FedEx on the floor behind the driver's seat, he broke the seal on the smaller one, and a few seconds later, he got back behind the wheel and unlocked his briefcase.

Inside, a few pale blue folders dealt with stocks and investment trading, along with a calculator and a few pens. Tucked into the leather pocket was a new burner cell phone.

After the phone powered up, he sent a text message and waited for less than fifteen seconds before the reply returned. Jim sent another message before shutting down the phone and headed north.

Fifteen minutes later, he passed the Motel 8 on the east side of I-25 N and pulled over when he was at the Harford Field Airport sign. Once the hazard signals were on, Jim got out of the rental, walked through the grass ditch, and headed into the woods. His plain gray suit seemed out of place, but he was comfortable nonetheless. If anyone cared, they would assume he was taking a quick bathroom break in the trees—a common occurrence.

"Anderson!"

He paused when Ernie stepped out from behind a few trees and headed his way. He carried a gym bag loaded with blankets and clothing. His jeans were dirty, and he had a long scratch across his bald head.

Ernie grinned from ear to ear at the familiar face.

"What's going on?" Jim had a deep voice that cracked as if he wasn't used to talking.

"Donny and Frank are dead, and when I woke up this morning, this happened." He dropped the bag and pulled out his cell phone. The picture of Nick was in vivid detail. There was no mistaking what happened. He now had a second smile.

"Someone got Nick? Jesus." Jim looked worried. "Tell me what you know."

Ernie nodded and started at the beginning, leaving nothing out. Running his hand through his hair, Jim took a deep breath. "There will be a lot of things to fix. Do you still have the tablet?"

Nodding, Ernie dug around in his gym bag and pulled it out. He hit a few options, then started the program.

The street map filled the screen, and a large blinking blue dot moved north through Arrow Point.

"Perfect, let's go." With a grin, Anderson quickly turned and walked away, startling Ernie. As he bent down to pick up his bag, Jim turned back, brought up a silenced Glock 17 from inside his suit jacket, fired off one round, paused, and then two more. The first went through the middle of Ernie's back. He fell flat on his stomach, and the other two went into the back of his head.

Anderson picked up the three brass casings and slipped them into his jacket pocket before removing the silencer and tucking the Glock into his belt.

After searching the body, he found Ernie's wallet and cell phone. He found Nick's wallet and phone in the gym bag as well, along with his favorite chocolate bar. After filling his pocket with the items, Jim headed to the road. He held the tablet in his left hand and ate the chocolate bar with his right.

After a while, the blue dot stopped. Smiling to himself, Anderson thought he should be able to catch a flight home tonight and sleep in his bed. Happy, he made his way back to the minivan.

~

An hour later, Anderson sipped his coffee while leaning back in the chair on the patio. It was mid-afternoon, the sun was still warm, and a light breeze had picked up. The donut shop wasn't busy, and he had an excellent view.

Many were outside with the warm weather, and all the high school students were getting out of school. They seemed to walk in clusters, and they all looked the same with their backpacks over one shoulder.

The traffic increased steadily for the last twenty minutes, and Jim casually watched them drive by. His focus was on the police station across the street. Although more than a few officers crossed at the light and ran into the coffee shop, he remained focused.

The double chirping noise drew his attention. He flipped up the tablet and watched the blue dot start to move. He glanced up in time to see a black pickup truck turn right out of the police station and head west on Main Street. Casually he took another sip and looked at his watch. Smiling at the thought of wrapping this up, Jim finished his coffee, then got in his rental and quickly followed.

It was time to work and earn the big bucks.

Chapter 23

Noah spent most of the afternoon at the station, filling in report after report, despite not being back on the job. The LT interviewed him, going over a few questions about the break-in and finding the key.

The knife was treated as a piece of evidence, and it was properly logged. It would be going out with the afternoon shipment to forensics to be tested. After looking at it himself, Piekenbrock agreed—it was probably blood.

"Did you touch it at all?"

Noah shook his head. "Not a chance. I know better than that."

"Okay, had to ask. I'll be looking into the background of Rachal Parisotto. If she has a potential murder weapon or was involved in one, we'll find out."

Noah nodded, aware of the problems she would face. "I handled the colt pistol, though, just enough to make sure it wasn't loaded."

The gun and money were also turned in as evidence, with a total of nine and a half thousand dollars. Neither man had an answer as to why those items would have been together. It did not look good.

Zane tapped his pen on top of the desk. "Is the break-in related to the key you found? Or would the break-in be related to the current murders?"

Shrugging slightly, Noah didn't have the answers. "Odds are there are no such things as coincidences. Right?"

The LT laughed and stood. "Right. Go home and sleep. Let me know if you need anything. I checked into your accumulated leave. You have five weeks' holidays left for this year. I would suggest using up some and getting everything sorted out."

Noah wasn't sure if he could handle that much time off. "Keeping busy is helping me keep my mind off certain things."

"I understand. Think it over and get back to me tomorrow."

Lieutenant Piekenbrock was paged over the PA system and then left. As he wondered what the next step was, the funeral home called Noah and confirmed the arrangements were completed. He could pick up the cremated remains any time, as well as the death certificate.

Noah grabbed his extra civilian clothes out of his locker to bring back with him. Mankiewicz Funeral home was across town, and it was right next to a clothing store. Having only a few outfits, Noah would have to buy more essentials. The fact that he had to figure out how to use the coin laundry just hit him. Another thing he had to do was settle the insurance with the house.

The list of things that he had to do grew, making him consider that the LT was correct. Taking some time off would be best to sort out his life. Soon as he sent a text message to Piekenbrock, he felt better about that decision.

Time is what he needed.

As he jumped in his truck and drove off, Bennett pulled into the station and gave a little wave. It seemed like months ago when their job was to catch the guys doing the car break-ins. As he pulled into the funeral home, his phone rang again. The display showed it was Zorch and Associates Law Office.

"Hello?"

"I am looking for a Noah Hunter." It was a woman's voice, and she had a slight accent that he couldn't quite place.

"Speaking."

"Do you have a moment to come to our office? Megan Brooks made you the sole beneficiary of her estate, and we are acting as executor of her will, as per her wishes."

Noah was speechless. He had no idea that Megan had changed her will to include him or that she even had an estate that needed managing.

"Yes, I can come in. Where are you located?"

The woman gave an address in Casper, then added, "Make sure you bring a copy of the death certificate as well and your identification."

Looking up at the sign for the funeral home, Noah took a deep breath. "I'm getting that now, actually. I'll see you in an hour."

After saying their goodbyes, Noah went inside the building. After he filled out a few forms and shook hands with the director, he picked up the cedar box that held Megan's remains and walked back outside to his truck.

The urn was twelve inches square and eight inches tall, and it weighed more than he thought. He placed the box on the floor behind the driver's seat, and he put the folder with the death certificates on the dash. They had given him a few extra copies in case they were needed.

"Excuse me, Noah Hunter?"

Noah turned and saw a man in a gray suit beside a new red minivan. He was about five-foot-nine inches and approximately one-hundred and sixty pounds. Noah guessed the man was at least thirty years old. He couldn't help but appraise him, but he appeared not to be any threat. The vehicle was one parking space away, and the rear passenger door was open behind him, showing an empty interior.

"How can I help you?"

The man smiled and gestured to the seat. "If you could come with me, please? I have quite a few questions, and I would prefer it if we could do this elsewhere."

Noah closed the truck door and faced him. He let his right-hand drift closer to his holstered Glock. Despite the man's casual attitude, alarm bells were going off in Noah's head.

"Tempting as that offer sounds, I'm going to decline."

The small man gestured once again. "I have to insist."

At this point, Noah moved his right hand onto the pistol grip. "I need you to get in your vehicle and—"

The smaller man exploded from the minivan's side and covered the distance across the parking space in a blink of an eye. Noah had automatically started to draw his weapon when the man's left hand crushed his wrist and slammed the Glock firmly into the holster. His right hand came up under Noah's chin, snapping his head back into the truck window.

The move would have knocked him out, except he had turned his head slightly. The blow skipped off his jawbone and slid across his cheek.

Dazed, Noah brought his knee up to strike the man in the groin when the stranger grabbed the hair at the back of his head, turned, and dropped to one knee.

Airborne, Noah flew in a tight circle and landed on his back. The wind whooshed from his lungs, and he had trouble understanding the speed at which things had turned. As Noah rolled over to get to his feet, the last thing he saw was the blur of a polished black dress shoe arc toward his head.

Chapter 24

Noah slowly came to as if rising from a great depth. The darkness gradually gave way to the light, and when he opened his eyes, it was blinding. His right eye had trouble opening fully as the swelling interfered.

He was on the ground leaning against a tree, his arms tied behind him. He took in the area and saw he was on the edge of a tree line, with a view of the foothills several miles away.

This wasn't Arrow Point. They were somewhere in the western area of Wyoming. His jaw felt bruised, and he had a throbbing pain in front of his right ear.

He couldn't tell how long he'd been unconscious, but the temperature had dropped, and the shadows from the trees stretched out in front of him.

It was late afternoon or early evening.

"Ah, you're awake. I hope you had a good nap." The man stepped in front of Noah and smiled.

"What the fuck is going on?" Noah struggled against the ropes, but they were too tight.

"Relax, all will be well."

He still wore the same light gray suit with a dark blue tie. He seemed fairly average, except for a gleam in his eye. Noah could tell he was crazy, or he got off on this whole situation.

"You assaulted and abducted a police officer. Things will not go good for you."

The man chuckled and crouched just beyond the range of his feet. He stared straight into his eyes. "Little things like that don't worry me. Shall we get started?"

Noah tried to jerk his shoulder forward and slide one arm out but to no avail.

"I'll take that as a yes. This whole thing can all be over in a minute. Just answer the question. Where's the money?"

Noah couldn't suppress his chuckle. "What money?"

The man just shook his head. "Last chance."

"Hey, man. I have no fucking idea what you're talking about. What money?"

The man stood and brushed his suit straight. "I thought you were smarter than this, but apparently not."

He must be crazy.

Noah studied the area in search of a way out, but he was immobilized. There wasn't a quarter-inch of free play in the ropes. He could hear the man working behind him. There was a little clanking of metal. Noah had no idea what he was doing. He continued to struggle and would not give up. It wasn't in his nature.

"You're going to love this." Stepping in sight, Noah was slightly confused as to what he held. It was a long tube, twenty-four inches long. Two prongs were on one end, and a coil of wires connected to a small unit clipped onto his belt.

The tube was white, with stylized lightning bolts halfway down. There was a digital display on the controller with a switch and a red dial, illuminated with a white light.

"Before we begin, I will start at the lowest setting and work my way up. Feel free to scream all you like. There's absolutely no one around for several miles."

Noah noted the sticker read Zappo Cattle Prod on the underside as the man stepped forward.

The two connectors touched his chest. Noah's jaw slammed shut, and his teeth ground together when the low voltage coursed through his chest.

His muscles spasmed head to toe, and after several seconds, the pain increased. The smell of cooked flesh filled his nose.

"How was that?" The man in the suit stepped back and rested the cattle prod on his shoulder. "So, where is the money?"

Taking a deep breath, Noah tried to see the damage. The burning sensation spread out across his chest, and his muscles still twitched with the memory.

Noah only knew about one sum of money. "I turned it into the station as evidence."

The man raised his eyebrows, and his eyes opened wide in disbelief. "Really? I find that hard to believe."

"All true. I found it this morning and turned it in."

He spun the wheel on the control unit at his belt. "Let's confirm that, shall we?"

He jabbed it back into the same spot on Noah's chest. Unable to control himself, Noah screamed and thrashed, but the ropes held his hands behind his back too well. Smoke rose from his chest at the contact point.

The ten seconds the cattle prod touched him seemed like an eternity, and when the man pulled it back, Noah slumped forward in relief.

"That was level five. You did better than some others have. You should be pleased." He smiled at Noah, almost as if he were proud of him, before he spun the control wheel to the end.

"This setting is going to suck. No other way of phrasing that."

"Look, I turned the money in to the police station. All ninety-five hundred dollars. I didn't keep any of it." Noah had bit down on his tongue at one point. There was the taste of blood in his mouth.

"Ninety-five hundred dollars? Do you think I would be doing all this for that little amount?" The man waved the cattle prod in a gesture, encompassing the situation.

"That's all that was there." Noah tried to regain control of his breathing. He was having difficulty, and he gasped a lungful of air through his mouth.

"Trust me. Rachel had a lot more than that." The man tapped the long stick into his left hand.

Noah must have looked confused because the man laughed. "She didn't tell you?"

"Who?"

"Rachel, that's who."

Noah laughed. "Are you kidding me? I don't even know her. She lived in my fiancée's apartment before she moved in. We've never met."

For the first time, the man in the gray suit seemed unsure of what to do. He was processing this new information, and after a moment, the man seemed to come to a decision. His grin didn't reach his cold eyes when he leaned forward with the cattle prod.

"Look, mister, I think you have the wrong guy. I don't know this—"

Inches before the prongs neared his chest, it looked like an invisible hammer picked the man up. He flew backward three feet before he slammed hard on the ground. Half a second later, a rifle shot echoed from the trees behind him.

Noah saw where the round hit, just slightly off-center of the man's chest. Dead center of his breast pocket. A large plume of blood radiated outward and soaked into his shirt and jacket while a spray decorated the ground fifteen feet away.

The cattle prod rolled off his chest and fell on the ground beside him, his right hand still clutching the base.

Noah struggled to see who had fired the weapon, but he could not turn his head far enough. He could hear someone as they tramped through the woods. Branches cracked, a heavy weight stepping on the occasional twig as the person drew closer.

Soon the footsteps stopped just behind the tree. "Hold on. I'll get you out."

Once he heard the voice, Noah couldn't have been more surprised.

"You have some explaining to do."

Chapter 25

The ropes gave way as they were cut, and the sudden rush of blood back into his hands was quite painful. Not as bad as getting electrocuted, though. Strong arms helped him stand, and it took him a second to feel sturdy enough to stand on his own feet without help.

"You okay, Sarge?"

He stared at Bennett before he nodded. "I will be."

He pulled up his T-shirt and glanced down at his swollen and red chest. Two circles the size of dimes were burned into his skin. It was already starting to swell, and the pain could be felt in his jaw.

Bennett had a .300 Winchester Magnum slung over his right shoulder. Noah had seen that rifle many times. He usually kept it in his car and went to the range outside of town to shoot after work. Bennett still wore his uniform, and he looked like someone had just shot his dog.

"First, thank you. I'm not too sure where this was going to go. Odds are it wasn't going to end well. Second, it's time to explain."

Stewart walked over and kicked the man's feet a few times to see if he would move. The round would have left an exit hole the size of a softball in his back. He would not be getting up again.

Bennett met Noah's eyes. "I fucked up pretty bad. I posted a few pictures last month from your party, and ..." He choked up and had to take a minute to collect his thoughts.

Noah had the guys from the station over for a barbeque and a few beers to celebrate his engagement. Bennett was there for most of the afternoon.

"I have friends from Chicago that I haven't seen in over ten years. A few of them saw the picture of you and Megan."

Noah could tell he was having a hard time with this, but once he realized he might have been a part of the reason why Megan was dead, his heart grew cold.

Bennett pulled out his phone, and it took a second to find what he was looking for, then he showed it to Noah. It was a picture of an old house, and a man and woman were unloading some groceries from a vehicle. The next photo was of the same place but taken at night. The lights from the windows showed the shadow of someone walking by inside.

"That's my parents and their house."

Handing back the phone, Noah guessed what was coming next. "They threatened you for information?"

Unable to meet his eyes, Bennett nodded. "They wanted to know about Megan, not you. I think these were some bad people. I don't know what they wanted."

Noah couldn't figure out if he was furious and wanted to shoot Bennett or feel sorry for him. Both options were on the table.

"How did you know where I was?"

"As you were leaving the station, I saw someone watching you from the coffee shop." Bennett jerked a thumb toward the corpse. "I saw him take you down at the funeral home, grab my rifle, and follow. I just couldn't sit by anymore."

"Your 'friends,' what line of work are they in?"

"When I was a kid, I used to run with a gang. I think they moved up and are working for organized crime. I don't know details, I left all that behind me, or so I thought."

Noah looked around at the trees and the body. The sun would be going down within a few hours.

He searched the man's pockets and found his wallet. "The driver's license is from Chicago. His name is Jim Anderson. There's an address as well."

The other IDs they'd discovered were from Florida and ended up being fake, but this one looked real. There were other things in the wallet with the same name: a CAA membership, a credit card, and even a library card.

Noah pointed at the corpse. "Do you know him?"

Bennett shook his head. "No. I'm so sorry, Sarge. What do you want me to do?"

At this, Noah still hadn't made a final decision. "I don't know whether to shoot or arrest you or hug you."

Bennett nodded slowly. "I understand. I'm responsible for my actions."

"Damn right, you are!" Noah paced and tried to stop yelling but wasn't successful. Damn, it felt good, though. He needed an outlet, and his partner was right there. After two minutes of cursing, he eventually started to repeat himself, so Noah stopped and came to a decision. "First thing you should do is phone your parents and let them know they have to go into hiding. Get out of town and not tell anyone where they're going—even you. Don't wait. Right now."

Bennett stepped away to make the phone call while Noah searched the body. He only found a key to a rental minivan. Then he opened the small bag that Jim had brought.

Half a dozen knives, rope, pliers, and a few other things that Noah wasn't sure of their purpose. Anderson took his torture game seriously.

Taking a deep breath, he felt the skin tighten on his chest. Noah knew he would have to put some cream on it and cover it. Infection would be likely. No doubt he would have a new scar as well.

By the time Bennett finished talking to his father, Noah had come to a decision.

"Are your parents okay?"

"Yeah, they don't fully understand, but they are leaving now."

"Good." Jerking a thumb at the body, Noah decided. "He stays here for now. I'll call it in later, anonymously. Then you're going to take some personal time off work."

Bennett readily agreed. "Whatever I can do, I will."

"Good. We're going on a trip."

Chapter 26

Piekenbrock and Richardson sat in the conference room off the cube. They each had a pen and notepad of paper, and the LT had a tablet propped up on the stand that faced them both.

They were not waiting long before staff Sergeant Hutchings knocked on the door, and they stood. "Captain Richardson and Lieutenant Piekenbrock, this is Special Agent Brandon Gardiner, FBI."

Standing beside him was a tall man who wore a dark suit and tie. He held an accordion briefcase in his left hand, and he reached out with his right to shake their hands. "Pleasure to meet you."

The man had a firm handshake, and he smiled slightly at each of the men. Zane figured he was close to sixty years old and looked physically fit. Despite his age, the shirt was stretched tight across his chest and shoulders. He carried himself like a retired football player. No longer in his prime but still graceful and powerful.

"Please, sit down." Captain Richardson sat at the head of the table, and both men sat to either side. "Thank you for meeting us."

"I have the results of the prints and some of the DNA matches from some of your bodies."

The FBI agent pulled out a sheaf of papers and flipped through the first few pages before continuing. "The first man is Donald Scafidi." A large photograph spun on the table to face the police officers. It showed a large man posing for his mug shot. He seemed to be amused, and he smirked into the camera.

"He worked for the Luciano family. They are becoming more of a problem as they are expanding their syndicate. Donald was an enforcer, and we believed he handled some of the dirty work for them."

They had organized crime working in Arrow Point? Piekenbrock just shook his head.

The captain looked at Lieutenant Piekenbrock in surprise.

"The second man is his cousin, Frank."

The picture wasn't a mug shot, but the photograph was taken from a distance. Frank stood outside a restaurant with a pretty young woman in his arms. They appeared to be laughing, and he held the door for the girl.

"Frank Scafidi has never been arrested. However, we have intel that he was the reason they started to branch their dealings into synthetic drugs. The H-Bomb was the product which made them millions."

Even the Arrow Point police heard of the H-Bomb drug. Kids used them at raves and parties. It was as simple as ordering them online directly and untraceable.

Special Agent Gardiner pulled out the picture of the man found at the hotel yesterday, dead in the car's backseat, and tapped it with his finger.

"This is Nick Luciano, nephew of Anthony Luciano, the head of the family. Nick was stepping up and becoming more active, and we believe he was under orders from Anthony, or he wouldn't have left Chicago. Organized crime pays well, and we have been working for over ten years to bring them down before they get larger."

Lieutenant Piekenbrock looked over at the pictures and then back up at the FBI Agent. "Why are they here and dead in Arrow Point?"

Gardiner leaned back in the chair. "The FBI has no idea. This area of Wyoming isn't even remotely near a shipping route, and there's no big business here that would interest them."

Captain Richardson clicked his pen a few times before putting it down. "Is this some type of mafia gang turf war? Do you have anything on who killed them?"

"As far as we know, there isn't an organized crime family operating out here. As to who killed them? No idea, but you should get them a medal and a parade through town. These are some bad people for sure."

Zane turned the tablet around and showed the homeless man's picture found at a construction site. "Do you know anything about this man? We don't know how he's related to any of this."

Gardiner shook his head. "Sorry, we don't have any information on him. He isn't known to us."

A knock on the door startled them. Staff Sergeant Hutchings leaned inside the room. "Gentlemen, there has been another body found, quite possibly related."

Piekenbrock looked over at Captain Richardson, and his eyebrows rose. The captain looked down at the last picture before he nodded.

He turned to Gardiner, and the LT asked, "Do you want to go with me to find out who turned up next?"

Packing up the papers, he handed them over to the captain. "Sounds good. I've been in the office for too many years."

"Hopefully, you'll have more information to help us solve the increasing body count."

~

Captain Richardson stayed at the station, and Piekenbrock drove the FBI agent out to the crime scene west of Arrow Point. The APPD had a few new Chevy Tahoes painted in a gunmetal gray, and the vehicle quickly drove up on the grass and across the field.

The forest went for a few miles before opening up into vast fields. With the sun beginning to set, the police car's flashing lights and an ambulance were easy to spot.

Piekenbrock turned the vehicle off and opened up the glove box. Inside was a box of latex gloves. "Help yourself."

Both men tucked a pair into their suit jackets. There wasn't any barrier tape around the crime scene. Sergeant Horne came over when he saw the Tahoe pull up.

After brief introductions, Piekenbrock asked for an update.

He pulled out his notebook, and Horne checked the time. "Forty minutes ago, we received an anonymous lead. Upon arrival, we found one male dead from a gunshot wound to the upper chest. State police are on the way."

"Identification?"

Horne shook his head. "Nothing. We did find a few interesting items near the corpse."

The FBI agent followed the men over to the area, where a green tarp covered the body, and a few men looked at a small bag that lay behind a tree.

"LT, there are some weird items in there." Some cut rope lay on the ground, and sitting on top were various knives and pliers—even a small butane torch.

Lieutenant Piekenbrock slid his hands into latex gloves, then picked up a long-bladed survival knife. "Do you think these items were used in the first murder? He was definitely tortured."

"Not too sure." Agent Gardiner put his gloves on, then walked over to the tarp and lifted the end. "Jesus Christ."

At the tone of his voice, Piekenbrock placed the knife back and hurried over. "Do you know him?"

"Yes." The agent seemed excited. "I'm fairly sure this is James Anderson. He's known as a fixer for the Luciano family. We have never had enough to convict him. He's walked several times."

They stared at the body, and Piekenbrock shook his head. "Another member of the same mafia organization is dead."

"Lieutenant, I'm sorry to say this, but the FBI will be taking over these cases. Something big is going down."

The LT chuckled. "Good. All yours, we have nothing but bodies. You're welcome to the case."

"If Anderson is dead, things are bad and probably going to be getting a lot worse."

The FBI agent appeared to be shaken. Piekenbrock wasn't sure what was going on, but for the first time, he was glad the feds were taking over. If things were getting worse, they were welcome to take the brunt of it.

Chapter 27

The last flight from Casper to Chicago left at eleven-thirty at night and flew direct. Noah and Stewart were the last two people to board, and they quickly found their seats. They only had a small carry-on bag, which they stored overhead before they buckled in.

Noah had driven the minivan back to the funeral home to get his truck while making arrangements for the flights. He was glad to find his wallet, cell phone, and weapon in the back seat of the rental.

Bennett headed to the station and cited a family emergency as the reason he would need some time off. After each man had gone their separate ways, they met up at the airport's long-term parking in Casper, sixty minutes later.

Noah had grabbed a few clothes, cleaned up, and was on the highway in record time. His eye had stopped swelling, but he knew the next day might prove different when it would start to bruise.

The burn mark on his chest wasn't as bad as he first thought. He would need to take care of it once they landed. Right now, there just wasn't time.

Bennett seemed resigned to his fate and wanted to make amends, but Noah could tell he was still torn apart by the choices that lay before him. That made two of them.

The silence stretched on for the first hour before Noah had enough.

"I understand that you were in a rock and a hard place, but I wished you had come to me first."

Bennett looked down at his hands. "The fact that they were stalking my parents just …"

After a minute, Noah came to a decision. "No one else knows about this except me. When we get there, you will point me in the right direction and then disappear. I don't want you involved."

Bennett looked confused. "What are you saying?"

"I'm determined to get answers, and I don't want you messing up your career or wind up in jail."

"What choices I make are my own. As long as my family is safe, I'll help."

"We shall see. I'm going to try and rest a little. I don't think I will be getting much sleep once we arrive."

Noah turned off the overhead light for his seat, and after a second, Stewart did the same. The old saying he learned in the army leaped to mind. Sleep when you can, you may not know when your next rest will be.

With that thought, he was out within two minutes.

Three hours later, the chiming of the fasten seatbelt sign and the announcement that they were about to land woke Noah. Bennett still snored, and a soft elbow into his arm made him stir.

After listening to the pilot's announcement, Noah adjusted his watch forward an hour. It was now four o'clock in the morning, local time.

Forty minutes later, Bennett drove a new Hyundai SUV rental into the Little Village district of Chicago. The homes built after the war were well maintained. Most were a small bungalow-style with long driveways and a garage in the back. Many families had given up their front lawns for more parking, leaving only a long strip of grass along the side. Most of the area had seen better times, but you could tell that some made an effort to keep their homes and yards pleasant.

Slowing down, Bennett pointed at a large building out the passenger window. "That's FC Academy, where I went to high school. My parents' house is the next block over."

They turned south on Homan Avenue, and the vehicle slowed at the fifth home from the corner. It was directly across from a small playground park. The lights were off, but it appeared to be the same house from the picture. "That's where I grew up."

Noah insisted on driving by to give Stewart peace of mind and get a sense of the area.

"Have you heard from your parents at all?"

Bennett shook his head. "Nothing. They know what line of work I'm in, and they took the warning seriously."

"Good."

Pulling out a brown leather wallet, Noah showed him the address. "That's the next stop. I'm fairly sure it's safe."

Bennett knew the general area of Humboldt Park, and after a few false turns and roundabouts, they arrived on the street.

After searching the body and the car, Noah had found a wallet, cellphone, and tablet. The driver's license address—3344 Potomac Avenue—was only a twenty-minute drive from their current location.

Unfortunately, they had to leave their guns back in Arrow Point, but Noah wasn't worried about entering a dead man's house armed. It was the next step that worried him.

After eighteen years on APPD and two years in the military, coupled with the events of the past week, not many things could have surprised Noah. However, soon as they arrived at the location, both men were shocked. It was a small detached home beside a vacant lot. A little white picket fence surrounded the front lawn, and in the gardens underneath the front window were pink flamingos, windmills, trolls, and about twenty other types of lawn ornaments.

"You have to be kidding me."

After passing several other homes, they turned around and parked across the street to watch the house.

A quick look at the time showed it to be almost five-thirty in the morning. People were starting to wake and get ready for their day. The sun would be up within the hour, but right now, it was mostly dark, and the streetlights were still on.

The house was pitch black, with no vehicles in the driveway. The single car garage they could see at the back of the home was also dark, and despite the low light, they could tell it was painted a bright yellow. Odd.

"I want you to stay here. I'll be in and out within eight minutes. If I'm one minute longer, I want you to leave without me."

They knew that any alarm systems within most homes would give the owners two minutes to enter their code before the alarm activated. That left thirty seconds for the security company to contact the police, and the usual response time is five to six minutes. The timings could all change if the system were hardwired to the authority directly. But with the type of person that they were dealing with, Noah doubted that would happen.

Getting out of the Hyundai, Noah walked west along the street for a hundred yards, then crossed the road and back along the opposite side. He wanted to make sure no one was watching, even at this early hour.

He kept a lookout for security cameras and people at their windows when he got to the driveway.

The small backyard looked well maintained, with a small patch of grass next to the garage and a little lounge set off to the side. Next to the rear door were two large flowerpots, making Noah doubt that he had the right home.

What if the address was fake?

The next part was harder to do than he thought, actually breaking into someone's home. Opening the rear screen door, Noah looked for alarms or a security panel inside the window. Nothing.

He wasn't surprised to find the door was locked.

When he checked the rear windows, he could tell one led into a kitchen, and the smaller window was for the basement. Testing both, he found them locked, but an explosive backkick with the heel of his running shoe shattered the basement window, and three seconds later, he stood inside the home.

There was no doubt he was in the correct house. Noah started at the sight in front of him, and he couldn't help but pause for a moment before he sprang into action.

Chapter 28

As he had done for over seventy years, Anthony Luciano woke early, went down to the kitchen for a glass of water, and started his day. He wore a set of red and white checkered flannel pajamas with dark blue slippers. It wasn't exactly his style, but he loved his granddaughter, and it was a gift from her. That more than excused any sense of style or fashion faux pas.

Anthony stood six feet even and kept his broad shoulders back at all times, giving him proper posture and an intimidating look. He hated people that slouched. In his youth, Anthony was powerful, with layers of muscle rippling over his frame. Even at seventy years old, you could see the hidden strength he still possessed. However, time seemed to have won out in the long run.

His once thick dark hair was a source of pride for him, but it had thinned and had turned a dull gray over the last decade.

The kitchen light turned on, and Anthony walked over to the refrigerator. He grabbed a water bottle, opened the blinds, and stared out at his backyard.

The sun was about to rise, and he had a great view of the gardens and pathways, which stretched for half an acre. Tall hedges surrounded the property and gave him the illusion of being in the country, not twenty minutes from downtown Chicago.

He was pleased to note that his gardener worked away in the backyard, raking the leaves that had fallen from the fruit trees. He paid his employees well, and he expected results, or they could easily be replaced.

The glass table seating had a good view of the morning sun and his backyard when he opened the laptop and checked his email. For over eight years, he had stopped using email to send messages, but one of his grandsons just smiled and shook his head when it was mentioned. Sent emails can be tracked and monitored from the servers. However, *saved* can't. Instead of sending the message, you simply kept it in the draft folder. Then anyone else opened the email to read it. The letter was never sent, yet it reached the people you wished it to, as long as they knew how to log in.

The email address and the password changed every two weeks, making it one of the most secure methods of passing information that his family has had in a very long time. The world was full of free email clients and options.

"Porco cane." *For God's sake*. Patting the shirt pocket of his pajamas, he pulled out his reading glasses and continued with the computer to confirm.

Nothing. The folder was empty.

Anderson had never failed to update when an assignment was completed. He absently tapped his fingers on the kitchen table while staring at the rising sun.

All the possibilities spun through his mind as he smiled, closed the laptop, and stood.

He hasn't finished the job. There must have been complications.

Reassured, Anthony made his way upstairs to get dressed and start his day. There was no time to lounge around.

The family came first.

* * * * *

Noah looked at the workbench and the items lying across it and the long white cardboard box. Written along the box's length, Zappo Cattle Prod and the foam packaging were still inside.

The workbench's back wall was made of pegboard, and hanging on the wire hooks were various tools. The large gray metal cabinet beside the workbench had a shelf full of 9mm ammunition boxes, and on the cabinet's rear wall were two Glock 17 pistols and two Glock 19s. Sitting beside the ammunition were two silencers.

Selecting the Glock 19 and a full magazine, he loaded the pistol and slipped a silencer and an extra box of ammo into his pocket. The basement was otherwise empty.

Noah went up the stairs using the application from his cell phone to light his path. The little light that came in through the small window wasn't enough to see without stumbling.

He immediately felt better for having the weapon. The grips were different from his own. He may like this new one better.

The stairs opened into a short hallway. To the left was the kitchen, which overlooked the backyard, and to the right was a living room with stairs leading up to the bedrooms. Noah was cautious with anything he touched, aware that the house would be investigated thoroughly once the body was identified.

A glance at his watch confirmed he had only five minutes before he asked Bennett to leave without him.

The kitchen was simple and had a small table in the corner for eating, and the living room had a television that faced a comfortable chair and leather loveseat. Both rooms were clean, and nothing was out of order.

Moving up the stairs, Noah heard every step as it creaked under his weight when he went to check out the bedrooms.

If the house weren't dead silent, he never would have noticed, but the fourth step didn't squeak or make any noise at all. The others certainly sounded like gunshots throughout the old home.

He went back to stand on the first step, where he placed the pistol down. After running his hands over the fourth step, he looked for a trigger or locking mechanism with no luck. His fingers tight under the front lip, he lifted, and the step opened back on hidden hinges.

"Bingo."

Inside the small space was a black duffel bag and two blue binders. Lifting the load, Noah guessed it weighed slightly over ten pounds. With the Glock in his waistband, he picked up the books and headed to the front door. His time in the house was over, and he didn't want to get caught. There would be too many questions to which he didn't have an answer.

With his jacket sleeve, he wiped his prints off the step and headed out the back door.

He would get an answer and those responsible.

It was only a matter of time.

Chapter 29

"Are you sure? I don't want any problem or anything to come back on them."

"They would insist. It's just temporary."

They dropped their bags on the kitchen floor, and Bennett started to make a pot of coffee. Noah dropped the bag and folders on the floor while sitting at the table. The kitchen was small but recently remodeled with white stone countertops and stainless-steel appliances.

Bennett maintained that his parents wouldn't mind if they used their home for a day or two until they received the all-clear and returned.

"Here you go, Sarge." He slid a mug of hot black coffee in front of him.

"Thanks."

Noah had a sip and chose a binder at random. It contained lists of jobs Anderson had done.

- Businessman Carl Owlstead, Orlando FL, 2245 Winfield St. 02/99

"Jesus Christ."

Noah flipped through the pages in disbelief. There were hundreds of entries.

Handing it over to Stewart, Noah opened the second book. It dealt with payments received and various bank accounts and investments. The last page showed a total of over ten million dollars.

Bennett gave a short whistle. "Crime does pay, apparently."

Noah privately agreed and opened the small bag. Stacked inside were bundles of money, wrapped with the brown paper bands as if they were directly from the bank. He grabbed a random pile and flicked the ends. They were all one-hundred-dollar bills. "Two million? Wow."

Both men stared at the bag of money for a moment before realizing how it was obtained.

Noah looked across the table at Bennett. "I need to know who contacted you and where they are."

Bennett went into the living room, and after a few seconds, he came back with a pen and a small pad of paper. "My dad always keeps this near the phone."

He came up with a list of three people and passed it over to Noah. Joey and Adam Peddle and Carmelo Marrelli.

"Joey and Adam were in school with me before they dropped out, I'm not sure what they're doing now, but they used to be errand boys. Carmelo was the one who sent me the messages. I never really knew him. He mostly hung out with Adam."

"Where can I find them?"

Bennett shrugged. "I know they used to hang out at Blackies Poolhall on West 18th Street, in the Lower West Side. That was over ten years ago, though."

After looking at the clock on the stove, Noah stood. "It's seven in the morning. I doubt they're open or if anyone is hanging out there until later."

He paced the kitchen like a caged animal. He had the energy to burn but no outlet.

Bennett took a sip of his coffee before he grinned and held a finger in the air. "I have an idea. I'll need your phone, but this should work."

* * * * *

Anthony gave his wife and daughter a kiss goodbye before he got into the back seat of the Cadillac. Gently, the driver closed the door before walking around the vehicle and sat behind the wheel. He could barely hear the engine from the back seat as the driver smoothly accelerated.

Anthony opened the buttons on his suit jacket and waved goodbye to his granddaughter as she ran down the steps, a pink teddy bear clutched tight in her right hand. He had given it to her last week, and she hadn't put it down yet. He smiled when she blew him a kiss, and he sent one back.

The morning traffic was horrible, and the drive downtown to the offices took longer than expected. Thirty minutes later, they pulled up to a six-story modern building.

The stainless-steel sign above the glass doors read Luciano Property Development. Soon as the black Cadillac stopped, an older man in a dark suit opened the rear passenger door. "Good morning, Mr. Luciano."

"Good morning, Jack."

Anthony got out, strode into his building, and headed to the sixth-floor offices. His secretary, Andrea, already had a cup of coffee waiting for him on his desk.

Anthony smiled at her. "Thank you. How much longer do you have?"

Andrea was petite, barely over five feet tall, her hair back in a ponytail. She was also thirty-six weeks pregnant. "Any time now, my due date isn't until the middle of October. It can't come soon enough, sir."

Usually, Andrea wore a smart dress suit to work, but she had great difficulty fitting into anything lately. She seemed only to wear large dresses or a blouse that hung down over her like a drape the last few weeks.

"Let me know if you need time off. Family comes first."

"I will, sir. You have a call waiting for you."

He nodded, closed the door, and sat behind his desk. For all the apparent wealth, Anthony liked to keep his office simple. The small wooden desktop was almost empty except for a monitor and keyboard next to a telephone and one picture frame. The walls were filled with over two-dozen photos that hung about the room. Pictures of a young boy holding his mother's and father's hands were black and white, while more recent photos were stunning in brilliant colored detail.

The most recent picture was Anthony holding his latest grandson, taken three months ago when they arrived home from the hospital. It sat on the desk opposite the monitor.

He picked up the phone, hit the glowing red button, and accepted the call.

"Go ahead."

"Mr. Luciano, I have a lead on the previous deal we discussed." The man's voice was intense and seemed to rumble slightly.

Anthony tapped his finger in a nervous habit once he recognized the caller. "Can we close this deal shortly?"

The man on the phone paused. "I think we can. We need to apply a little leverage. The situation could be wrapped up by noon."

Anthony glanced at the Rolex on his wrist and noted the time. "Do what you feel is appropriate to close the deal."

He didn't wait for a reply and leaned back into the office chair after hanging up the phone. He closed his eyes, tilted his head back, and prayed for forgiveness. He didn't want to finish this off, but obligations forced his hand. Despite the rule that guided his beliefs and had been drilled into him since he was a toddler, he made the decision.

Some things were more important than family.

Chapter 30

Carmelo drove past his old high school with barely a glance, but he did unbuckle the seatbelt. He took a deep breath and began to calm down for the job ahead. He forced his strong hands to loosen their tight grip on the steering wheel.

The BMW X3, a new four-door gray sports utility vehicle, handled the corners smoothly, and it was the quietest car Carmelo ever drove. Even when he accelerated, the engine just thrummed with power, and the tires gripped the road as it took off.

Carmelo wore a freshly ironed blue dress shirt and black dress pants with polished black shoes. His new gold watch caught the morning sun, and a reflection danced across the SUV's interior.

As he slowed, he turned on a side street and pulled over. He pulled out an eight-inch fixed blade in a hard-shell plastic sheath from the storage space under the armrest.

It's time for some quiet work.

Before Carmelo got out of the car, he had glanced around the street to make sure no one watched from their windows.

All clear.

It was mid-morning, and everyone was either in school or working. However, the car in the driveway was reassuring.

He tucked the knife into the waistband at the small of his back and locked the BMW before he strolled up the driveway. He wanted to avoid the front door, so Carmelo headed around to the rear and passed the Hyundai. The lights were on inside the kitchen, and he could hear a radio playing rather loudly.

The tall maple tree in the backyard obscured any neighbors that may have tried to watch. He pushed the backdoor open and walked inside. The smell of coffee filled the small house, and he thought he might have a cup after he finished the task that awaited. He had a few things to do first.

Carmelo pulled the knife from the sheath and slowly moved up the three steps into the kitchen.

His dress shoes clicked on the tiled floor when he crossed the kitchen and had a quick look in the living room before he moved down the hall to the back bedrooms.

The shower was running, and the bathroom door was closed. As his hand was about close on the handle, he felt cold metal press into the side of his head.

"Move, and you're dead."

He almost wet his pants when he saw the gun and figure that suddenly appeared beside him.

Fuck.

As they sat at the kitchen table, Stewart Bennett flipped through Noah's phone and scanned through the pictures until he found a suitable one. They had gone to the tavern after the engagement party for dancing and a few more drinks.

The picture Bennett had found was Megan and Noah as they sat at a table and raised their glasses to each other with a beer.

Bennett sent the picture to his phone and posted it online with the tag, "Had a great time last night."

Twenty minutes later, he finally got the message.

> Where are they?

> I can't keep doing this anymore. I'm done.

> We shall see. You have been warned.

Lucky for both men, they had experience in waiting— long, endless hours in a cruiser when nothing happened shift after shift. Noah sat on the living room couch, and he had a perfect view out the front window.

Soon as the BMW stopped on the street, he slipped into the bedroom while Bennett hid in the bathroom.

After he brought the silenced Glock up to his head, the young man readily complied. Noah took the knife out of his hand and tapped on the door.

As Stewart stepped out of the bathroom, Noah saw the man's eyes open wide. "Long time, no see, Carmelo."

He seemed to shudder, and his shoulders slumped. "I … I didn't know you were here."

Whatever confidence he had vanished. Carmelo knew Stewart was a cop, and they had him, at least for a break and enter.

"I was just going to scare your parents, that's all."

Noah kept the weapon pointed at the back of Carmelo's head. "Frisk him."

Bennett started at the head and worked his way down, only finding the knife sheath, car keys, a thick wad of cash, and a cell phone. He placed the items in his pocket and nodded. "He's good."

Noah spun him around and escorted him out of the backyard. Carmelo started to walk toward the parked car before Noah forced him to walk into the single-car garage's side door.

"What's going on? Are you arresting me?"

Once he turned on the light, Noah guided Carmelo to the middle of the garage, where two winter tires sat, stacked on top of each other. A spool of red sixteen-gauge electrical wire sat on the ground behind it.

"Sit." Noah shoved him toward the tires.

As soon as he sat, Noah handed the pistol over to Bennett. His partner didn't flinch, and his hands remained rock-steady as he aimed. Stewart stared down at the man who was going to kill his parents.

Noah used the wire and wrapped it several times around Carmelo's wrists, behind his back, and tied his legs to the tires.

Rope tended to stretch and distort, but there was no give in the wire.

Noah tucked the Glock into his belt before making sure that the man was secure.

"What is going on? I want to see my lawyer!"

Noah cuffed him in the back of the head. "Shut up. Answer only when I ask a question. Got it?"

"What the—"

Noah hauled off and threw a right cross. He clipped his jaw and rocked him back on the tires. The wire held, and he didn't tip over.

Noah grabbed Carmelo's knife and proceeded to strip away the insulation at various points. Carmelo's eyes grew wide when he saw what was on the workbench beside him. A battery charger.

"I swear, I was just going to scare them!"

Noah hooked the two ends of the wire to the clamps, then walked over to the end of the plug.

"Bennett, I want you to step outside. You don't have to be a part of this."

Stewart just shook his head. "I'm good. I know what he was going to do."

Not arguing the point, Noah gave a slight nod before he turned to Carmelo. "I'm going to ask you questions. You will answer truthfully. The alternative is going to be much worse."

Carmelo nodded as he watched Noah's hand hold the end of the plug.

"Who's interested in Megan Brooks?"

He looked back and forth between Noah and Stewart. "I don't know a Megan Brooks."

Stewart pulled out his phone and scrolled to the picture he just posted online. "That's Megan. Who wants her dead?"

Carmelo let out a short laugh. "Her name isn't Megan, you dumb fuck."

Noah had enough.

He plugged the battery charger into the outlet. Carmelo immediately stopped as the electrical current flowed through the wire. It burned his skin and shocked him at the same time. Carmelo spasmed and jerked as he fought against the bindings. The wire held.

He pulled the plug out of the socket, and Noah leaned forward. "Let's try again. Who is she, and who wants her dead?"

Carmelo talked fast and spilled everything he knew. He failed to notice Noah's cell phone propped up on the workbench as it recorded everything. It was angled so that the two police officers were not in the picture.

Plausible deniability was everything, and they would need it for what came next.

Chapter 31

An hour later, Bennett and Noah sat back at the kitchen table and discussed their next move.

"Nothing he said could be considered as evidence. It was given under duress."

Bennett sighed. "I know, but now we have a starting point."

Carmelo knew the woman as Rachel Parisotto, and the people he worked for wanted the money back she had stolen. He didn't know anything about her being alive or dead or the explosion. Carmelo only knew his boss's boss was still interested in locating the money.

"I find it hard to believe that this Rachel person is Megan. It just doesn't make any sense. If she had any money, she wouldn't be living on a grade school teacher's pay."

"What about the money you found in the storage locker? The name is the same, and I know what you think of coincidences."

After he thought about the possibility, Noah was at a loss. "Someone thinks Megan is Rachel, and they even look the same. Also, they planted evidence in Megan's apartment that led to a storage room with Rachel's things and some money. That has to be it."

Bennett shrugged and looked as confused as Noah felt. "I'm not sure. What I want to know is, why did they kill her? Who did it?"

Noah tapped the name on the paper. "William Ryan. Carmelo works and reports to him. He'll lead us to the answers."

"What do you plan on doing with him?" Bennett jerked his thumb toward the garage. Carmelo was still gagged and blindfolded, tied up on the tires.

"I wish I could just shoot him, but I have a better idea."

~

Fifteen minutes south of Bennett's parent's home was Garfield Park. On the north side of the park was a large conservatory, and on the south were trails and outdoor gardens. The lawn and trees were well maintained, and many used it daily. Families strolled through the area, or parents sat on the benches to watch their children play. This area was also well patrolled by Chicago's finest.

Across the street were several businesses in a long strip mall, and between the stores were small alleyways barely six feet wide.

Bennett dropped him off behind one of the stores and helped Noah before he strolled out on the sidewalk. Stewart kept his hands deep into his pockets and casually looked along the length of West Adams Street before he left.

Noah took a deep breath and held the wooden board tight while waiting.

Forty seconds later, two shots were fired, and the screech of car tires echoed in the alley. It was immediately followed by screaming up and down the street as panic set in.

Bennett tore into the alleyway, dropped the gun and the baseball hat, and sprinted away behind the shops. Before he turned the corner and disappeared, Noah stood ready.

Moving the Glock on the ground into a slightly different position, Noah yelled. "Help! Help! I got him!"

Standing out on the sidewalk, he waved his hand in the air and yelled for help once again. Many tentatively emerged from their temporary hiding places and looked along the length of the street. An older man stepped out of a doorway and slowly walked toward him.

Two police officers had their pistols drawn and hid behind their car doors as they looked for the target. The young cop tried to see through a window as he yelled into the radio handset. Smoke rose in a steady plume from underneath the hood of their cruiser. The two rounds went into the grill and stopped the vehicle in the middle of the street.

"Over here! I got him!"

Quickly a crowd gathered around Noah as he pointed into the alley. Stretched out was a man that wore the same gray jacket and his red baseball cap lay just above his head. The smoking gun was on the ground, inches away from his right hand. One teenage girl sobbed at the scene while fumbling to find her phone. An older woman near the back mumbled, "What's the world coming to?"

There was a large wound across the fallen man's forehead. He was knocked out cold. Noah panted and held up the wooden board. "I just bashed him with this. It was leaning against the wall."

The two police officers rushed through the crowd and quickly kicked the gun off to the side. The taller, older cop felt for a pulse before, then nodded to his partner. "He's out cold."

The tension seemed to leave the crowd at once as they talked and asked questions. Cell phones made an appearance from the group, and hundreds of pictures were taken. Twenty people swore they saw the whole thing happen. Witnesses claimed how they saw a man as he knocked him out flat when the shooter ran into the alley. An older woman found the plank against the wall and showed it to the police officers.

As the one cop rolled the suspect over and put the bracelets on him, the younger one called it in. When they asked who knocked him out, they had over twelve different descriptions of him.

The good samaritan was nowhere to be found.

Chapter 32

Anthony wiped his mouth with the linen napkin and placed it on the table beside his empty plate. Twice a week, he went for lunch at the small café next to his office building.

Rosie's Diner was in serious need of repairs and was near bankruptcy several years ago when Luciano Property Management stepped in as a financial backer and partner.

Rebranding the diner into a café and a thousand other small changes turned the greasy restaurant into a popular high-quality place for a meal. Rosie was also his grandmother's name, and Anthony had a special place in his heart for it. Hence Rosie's Café and Bistro rose from the grease and ashes of the prior establishment.

He never paid for his meals, but Anthony always left a twenty-dollar tip for the waitress. His dealings with the owner did not extend to the staff, and he knew times were tough.

Anthony was about to return to his office when William walked through the front doors and approached his table. William Ryan was an Irishman that had worked for him for over eleven years. Will oversaw the family business's day-to-day operations and 'took care' of many problems that arose. His dark suit seemed to hang from his thin frame, making him look ill from profound weight loss. His gold-framed glasses repeatedly slid down his nose, and he absently pushed them back up while he waited patiently. His resemblance to a white-haired grandfather cleverly hid the cold interior, deceiving many who crossed his path.

Anthony nodded toward the chair opposite him. "Join me."

Will wasn't much for platitudes or small talk, and he jumped right into it. "The police called the office. An employee of ours, Carmelo Marrelli, decided to start shooting up a police cruiser. They recovered a company vehicle nearby. The police have impounded the car and have him in custody."

After living in the Chicago area for over fifty years, his Irish accent was faint but noticeable. More so when he became excited or after a few drinks.

Anthony frowned. "I don't like the attention this puts on us."

"He's recovering in the hospital, under guard. He was knocked out pretty hard. I have people trying to get more information."

After a few seconds, Anthony stood. "Find out what happened and why. Remind him about certain manners of etiquette."

"Not a problem, I will—"

Anthony cut him off and raised a hand in the air. He pointed at his ear, then the restaurant ceiling.

The walls have ears.

"I'll get back to you soon."

Will got up and, with a quick look around the room, left Rosie's. Anthony pulled out a crisp twenty-dollar bill and tucked it under the side of his empty plate.

Fires needed to be put out.

Everyone in Chicago knew what could happen if a fire got out of control.

* * * * *

Noah calmly drove the Hyundai through the streets of the Windy City while he glanced at his partner's knee. Bennett bounced it up and down non-stop like a jackhammer. He had an abundance of nervous energy and excess adrenaline.

"All good?"

Bennett looked in the passenger mirror and confirmed they were not being followed. "That was a little crazy."

Both knew how unreliable witnesses were, especially in high-stress situations. They had interviewed countless people for minor traffic accidents, and rarely were the stories ever the same from person to person as everyone has different recall capabilities. A man who wore a red hat and gray coat ran away and was captured immediately. Testimony would support the narrative, and there wasn't any reason to doubt a difference.

"You did well. You kept your head."

Noah had mixed feelings about giving up the Glock, but he knew it was worth it. Carmelo was officially out of the picture. For what crimes he had been about to commit, he would be getting off lightly.

"Do you think they will find the car and the prints?"

They had worn gloves and thoroughly wiped down the pistol before they knocked out Carmelo. They stripped the 9mm and took the rounds out of the magazine. Noah made sure Carmelo's prints were on each casing, especially the first two fired and lying on the street in front of the cruiser and throughout the weapon. There wouldn't be any dispute he fired the Glock or that it was his.

Fingerprints don't lie.

"They would have locked down and secured the area. The first thing we do is check the vehicles after looking for evidence. I'm sure they would have done the same procedure."

Stewart pointed ahead. "Turn right here."

The forty-foot sign had a picture of a hamburger tilted at a slight angle, and the Star Burgers letters shot out the side. "Best food in Chicago, hands down."

As they parked, Noah's phone rang. He showed it to Bennett before he placed it on speaker. It was Lieutenant Piekenbrock.

"LT, how are you?"

"Good. Do you have a second?" Noah could hear the noise of the station in full swing behind him.

"For sure, go ahead."

"The feds have taken over the case, but we just got some information back you should know. The search into Rachel Parisotto turned up negative. However, I now have US marshals knocking on my door. They will be arriving later today."

Fuck.

The implications ran through his head, and various scenarios ran rampant. All the possibilities pointed in the same direction. "Do they want to talk about a sealed case?"

"I'm not sure. The marshals won't talk until they are here in person."

"Understood. Do you have any other information on the victims?"

Noah could hear the LT flipping pages of paper. "All are related to the Luciano crime family. Mafia."

"Understood. Thank you."

"I have to run. Take care, Sarge."

After he disconnected the call, Noah looked at his partner. Stewart's mouth was agape, and his eyes were wide in disbelief. "Do you think Megan was—"

"I don't know what to think. However, I know enough not to jump to conclusions. Let's go inside and grab something to eat, and then we can figure out our next step with Mr. Ryan."

Noah had to be careful. His ideas called for a delicate touch, not just a board to the head. He tried not to glance at Bennett. His partner wouldn't like his next decision, but he knew it was the right call.

Chapter 33

William Ryan walked along the hospital corridor and carried a briefcase. He wore a dark suit and headed straight for the police officers. "I need you both to step to the side, and any attempt to listen in on our conversation will result in charges for you both. Is that understood?"

The young constable, the size of a refrigerator, looked the man in the suit up and down. "Stay here. I will see if the doctor approves visitors." It sounded like he wanted an argument.

Will didn't respond and just stared at the cop. After a few seconds, he had enough. "Go if you are going to go. Quit wasting my time."

The cop knocked on the door before he stepped inside the room. He emerged a few seconds later with the doctor and the nurse. The doctor talked with Will. "He has had a severe concussion, do not agitate him. Make your visit brief."

He nodded his acceptance to the conditions, and Will gave the cop a dirty look, then brushed by him and entered the hospital room.

Carmelo lay back on the bed with his eyes closed. He looked like death warmed over.

"Are you going to live?"

He opened one eye and looked at Will. "I wondered if you would show up."

His voice was a whisper of its former strength.

"What do you remember?" Will placed the briefcase at the foot of the bed, then stood next to Carmelo.

"I was taking care of business when they got the jump on me."

Will kept an eye on the door to ensure they were not disturbed. "Who got the jump on you?"

"That cop from Arrow Point and Bennett."

"They did this to you?"

Carmelo opened his mouth, but he paused. "I don't know. It's rather hazy."

"Why did you shoot at the cops? Were you drinking?"

Carmelo stared at him, and his eyes narrowed. "What are you talking about? I did no such thing."

Will filled him in on what he knew, the possible charges and evidence piled against him. Carmelo groaned in disbelief. "No way, man. I would never do that shit."

"Calm down, I believe you."

William pulled two sheets of paper and a pen from his suitcase. They were standard blank forms. "Here, sign these."

Carmelo couldn't focus enough to make out what was written on the papers before signing. They were placed inside the briefcase when he finished.

"First, you have a tough choice to make. The police are drawing up dozens of charges on you for the attempted murder of two police officers. There are witnesses and enough evidence to send you away for over fifty years."

Carmelo seemed to panic. "I didn't do anything."

Shaking his head, Will added, "There's a second option. We take care of your aunt for you and your cousin once you are gone. You are family. However, you were dealt a bad card. Right now, there is no third option."

Carmelo sunk farther into the pillow while tears trickled out the corner of his eyes and ran down into the bandages. He would be eighty years old when he got out. With a double attempted murder on two cops, there would be zero chance for parole.

Carmelo sighed. "Sorry, William. I tried my best."

With a glance at the hospital room door, Will made sure no one could see inside. He pulled out a tiny plastic bag from his briefcase. There was a small amount of white powder inside, about the size of a dozen grains of sand.

White sand.

"This will be quick and, most likely, quite enjoyable. You're a good kid. Talk to the cops when you get a chance. Confess everything. Aim for tonight when you're ready."

Lifting the blanket, Will tucked the small plastic bag into the little pocket of Carmelo's jeans.

"We'll take care of your family. See you on the other side, Carmelo."

William gave him a brief hug before he closed the briefcase and locked it. He ignored the cops as he passed them in the hallway. The lawyer's mind was already on to the next problem. There was more work to do. When it came to cleaning up other people's messes, few could match him.

*　*　*　*　*

Two police officers stood guard outside the hospital room while the emergency room doctor and nurse finished examining Carmelo. Someone checked on him every twenty minutes. His right wrist was still handcuffed to the bedrail in a private room while they reassessed his progress.

The nurse inclined the bed into a seated position and flicked a light back and forth over his eyes. A large bandage wrapped around his head, with a secondary dressing that held an iced pack in place. The dark circles under his eyes would blossom into a spectacular set of bruises. Carmelo couldn't shake the migraine, and his body ached from head to toe. So far, he refused to say anything when questioned by the police or respond appropriately to the doctor.

It wasn't time.

The pain took over his whole body. With each beat of his heart, Carmelo's eyes seemed like they would burst. The doctors said he had a fractured skull and a concussion, but he would be fine. Besides the lawyer and the hospital staff, he didn't have any visitors. His family members wanted nothing to do with him after they found out about his line of work.

Despite the fact that he still gave them money and cared for his family, Carmelo knew they wouldn't visit.

A sergeant from the Chicago Police Department came into the room to see if he would give a statement without his lawyer present. She was persistent. Carmel glanced at the clock on the wall and nodded. When he agreed, the woman couldn't believe it and brought in one of the constables from the hall as a witness.

He held his end of the bargain, and Carmelo confessed to everything. He also admitted to a few things that he was not up on charges to give them some misdirection. He wouldn't make it easy for the pigs, and even with his last statements, he would protect those he worked for—he owed them.

After forty minutes of interrogation, they left him alone.

The sun had been down for a few hours. In that time, he has said his peace with God and asked His forgiveness a dozen times.

Carmelo wasn't surprised by the lack of a response.

Not wanting to live through the pain or go through the next day, Carmelo pulled out the little bag. He had sold a great deal of the white powder over the last five years, and he knew how potent such a small amount was.

Once he licked his finger, he rolled it around inside the bag before hiding it back in his jeans. It was challenging with only one arm, but they wouldn't remove the handcuffs no matter how much he begged.

Before he could change his mind, Carmelo opened his mouth and sucked all the powder off.

He didn't have long to wait.

His heart rate doubled, then doubled again as the drugs took effect. When he began to shake violently, it was already too late. One small grain of fentanyl was enough to kill a grown man quickly, and he just took twenty times that amount.

When the nurses ran into the room and turned off the alarms, they couldn't do anything to save him. Carmelo lay dead with his eyes wide open and a small grin on his face.

Chapter 34

After they sanitized the house of any sign of their presence, Bennett drove them on a Chicago tour. He was mainly going around to avoid being in one spot for any length of time while brainstorming ideas.

Online, they found three names that matched William Ryan in the Chicago area. One man was a student, and the other a lawyer at a local firm. The third man, listed as Bill Ryan, appeared to be in the Air Force by the uniform in his profile picture. There was little doubt that the person they were looking for was the lawyer.

The initial rush from earlier was gone, leaving both men anxious about the next step. Taking on an organized crime family was never part of their training, but Noah knew one thing. "For the next phase, I need us to split up."

They were at a coffee shop downtown off the marketplace district. The weather was colder than last week, so they sat inside.

Bennett objected. "I want to help."

"I know, but we dealt with the threat against your parents. I don't think things are over in Arrow Point. You're going to be needed there more than with me."

He sat back and looked skeptically at Noah. He didn't have an appropriate reply.

"I'm also not going to mention what my next step is. That way, you can't testify. I'm going to drop you off at the airport, and you can catch the next flight back to Casper or Cheyenne."

"I wish you would reconsider."

Noah knew the risks they had taken. He didn't want to cost Bennett his job or jail time for them both. Noah pulled out the wad of cash that Carmelo had on him. It was over six hundred dollars.

He passed the money over and stood. "That will more than cover the flight. Let's go."

Despite the late hour, there still seemed to be heavy traffic, and Bennett mentioned that it never stopped in this area. All too soon, Noah pulled up to departures at O'Hare, and Bennett reached over to the backseat and grabbed his bag. "Are you sure?"

Noah held out his hand. "I'm sure. I'll keep in touch and hopefully be home soon."

After a firm shake, Bennett closed the door and headed inside the airport. Noah could tell he wasn't thrilled and didn't understand fully. He needed answers, and with what he was about to do, he didn't want Bennett involved.

When he walked out of the drug store, Noah tore open the package and pulled the white plastic tab. The burner cell phone began the boot-up sequence, and one minute later, it registered on the network.

The sun had set, and the night was cooler in Chicago than in Wyoming.

As he sat in the rental car, Noah went over his notes. *Who was Rachel? Who killed those men in Arrow Point? What did the Luciano family have to do with it?*

There could only be one reason for the US marshals to be involved with the Arrow Point Police Department. He knew they dealt with the witness relocation program. Megan was either Rachel or someone who thought she was.

He looked up the phone number and dialed.

"Steck Law firm, how can I help you?" The woman's voice said the greeting too fast and Noah could barely make out the sentence as separate words. *StecklawfirmhowcanIhelpyou?*

"I need to speak with William Ryan."

"He's gone for the day. Can I take a message?"

"This is Sergeant Hunter, Arrow Point Police. Have him give me a call." He left the new burner number.

"I'll make sure he gets this message first thing in the morning."

Noah could tell she was about to hang up. "He will want this message right away. Tell him I expect him to call me back within five minutes. Have a good night, ma'am."

After he disconnected, Noah leaned back in the seat, took a deep breath, and checked the time. Eight o'clock.

Three minutes later, the phone rang.

He just held the phone to his ear and waited. Finally, the lawyer spoke. "You're playing a dangerous game, Mr. Hunter."

Noah heard a faint accent but couldn't place it. "I'm sure you wish to talk with me."

William chuckled. "I doubt you're looking for legal advice."

"Let's get right down to it. Who is Rachel Parisotto, and what is the Luciano interest in her?" Noah couldn't help but grip the steering wheel tight as he waited for an answer. He could hear Ryan as he clicked a pen several times in the background.

"I'm afraid I do not discuss client business, especially with cops."

Noah continued, "Why did you kill my fiancée?"

At this, William laughed. "Is that what this is all about? I can assure you that neither myself nor my client had anything to do with that."

He ran a hand through his hair in frustration. Noah glanced at his notes before he decided to switch tracks. "I have the money that Racheal stashed. I want all the goons called off and to stay out of Wyoming."

The clicking of the pen in the background stopped.

"I'll call you back in an hour from a different number." William Ryan disconnected the call.

Noah smiled and started the car. As he pulled out onto the main road, he felt like whistling. He had poked the bear and gotten a response. As to what the answer would be, it was yet to be determined.

Thirty minutes later, he pulled into the Bass Pro parking lot in Bolingbrook. He only had half an hour before the store closed to pick up a few items. He should be done before the lawyer called back.

With a stack of cash from the black bag, he went inside for a quick shopping spree.

He needed to be prepared.

Chapter 35

Anthony Luciano had finished a late dinner with his wife, Kristina, when he got a phone call. After a few seconds, he hung up and went to the front door. William stood outside.

"We couldn't discuss this over the phone."

Anthony agreed and escorted him into his office. They made sure the door was closed behind them. He preferred something simple for an office, but his wife had decorated the whole house. It had floor-to-ceiling white open bookshelves with a dark hardwood floor, covered in a light gray area rug. The executive desk was from the seventeenth century and made from dark polished mahogany.

Being in the office made him on edge, but Anthony had learned to live with it. The chairs were comfortable, though.

"Sit, tell me what you know."

During the past eight years, William had only knocked on his door twice. Anthony had no illusions that this would be important.

"The Carmelo situation is resolved. The problem with the company car will be dealt with in the morning. It's all covered."

Anthony leaned forward, waiting for the critical news. He seemed surprised to note William appeared hesitant. "Spill it."

With a deep breath, he began. "The cop from Arrow Point called. He thought we killed Rachel, and he said he has the money. He wants us to back off."

Anthony didn't know if he wanted to swear or throw something expensive. In the end, he leaned back in the chair and closed his eyes.

"Rachel's dead?"

William pulled out a few pieces of paper from his suit jacket's inner pocket and unfolded them. "House explosion six days ago killed one Megan Brooks."

Anthony leaned forward and slammed his palm on the antique desk. "Who the fuck killed her? Who?"

William jumped but didn't answer. He slid a second paper across the desk for him to read. From the top desk drawer, Anthony pulled out a pair of reading glasses and scanned the document. The anger left him in a wave as disbelief took over. "Who killed our men? Jesus."

"The feds have taken over once, and our information has slowed. I'll see what we have for contacts with them."

Anthony handed the papers back. "Do you think it was this cop?"

William was hesitant. "I'm not sure. It doesn't make any sense. He was engaged to Megan."

Anthony took off the glasses and rubbed his eyes. "He has the money?"

"That's what he said. I'm supposed to call him back shortly."

"I'm not worried about a small-town cop. I'm more worried that someone else is acting on certain information and is taking out our guys."

William pushed his glasses back up his nose and tilted his head. "This information is being held tight. Less than ten people know, and four of them are now dead. I haven't heard back from Ernie yet, but things are not looking good for him."

Anthony stopped drumming his fingers on the desktop and made a choice. "Call the cop back. I have an idea."

* * * * *

Noah had just left the sporting goods store and stashed his items in the back seat when the burner phone rang.

"Go ahead."

"Sergeant Hunter, I presume?"

"Have you thought about my offer?"

Noah heard Ryan switch the phone to the speaker, and a third person spoke. "I'm afraid that your offer is not valid."

The man's voice was deep and resonated slightly. A confident, smooth voice, someone who was used to being obeyed.

"Mr. Luciano?"

"Correct. As I said, your offer is invalid. There's no one from my organization working in Arrow Point."

"I have your money. I want all of your dealings finished with my town. I will then give it back to you."

Both men chuckled on the line. A feeling of dread made his stomach flip.

"I could care less about any money you have. What I do care about is who killed my men and Rachel. Guess what your new job will be, Noah Hunter."

With a quick look at the items in the back seat, Noah knew his plans were rapidly going south. "I have a job. It's definitely not working for you."

"I have a signed confession and statement from Carmelo Marrelli. He was beaten and tortured by a police officer from Arrow Point, a Mr. Stewart Bennett, and his partner, who resembles yourself. Then he was set up for a crime he didn't commit."

The feeling in his stomach magnified, and his mouth was suddenly dry.

"We also have footage of you and your partner arriving in Chicago at the airport." After a long pause, Luciano continued. "Are you ready to hear about your new job, Mr. Hunter?"

Noah wasn't sure what to say, the tables seemed to have turned, and his bluff had been called.

William Ryan sounded excited, and Noah detected an Irish accent. "You're going back to Arrow Point, and you're going to find out who killed our men. You work for us now, or the information we have will be sent to the proper authorities."

There was a tapping on the speaker of their phone. "Is this thing still working, Noah?"

"Yeah, I'm still here."

Anthony spoke just above a whisper. Each word was exact and intense. "Find out who killed Rachel. That's your priority."

Noah didn't know where to begin. "I don't know anyone named Rachel."

"Oh, you do. You were engaged to her. You will find out who killed my niece. I expect results."

Noah stared at the phone in shock as the call was disconnected.

Chapter 36

Lieutenant Piekenbrock threw his gym bag in his locker when he heard his name being paged upstairs at the station. Straightening a blue flecked tie against his gray suit, he closed the locker and headed to the cube.

The meeting last night with the US marshals didn't go even remotely as planned. They didn't give up any information except wave a document that legally obligated the APPD to share any information. The two marshals then left abruptly, ignoring the whispered comments behind their backs.

Once upstairs, the LT looked around before spotting the special agent in charge.

The FBI had taken over the conference room and set up a small command center. Three other people were busy working in the long room with Gardiner at the end of the table. Two laptops lay open in front of him. He was on the phone, and when he noticed Zane standing outside the door, he quickly finished the call and stood to meet him.

"Morning. We have another body reported at seven o'clock last night. This one is most likely related. We're waiting on forensics to finish up."

"Where did they find it?"

"North of the hotel where we found Nick in the car. The body was in the woods. Local hunters spotted birds circling overhead and went to check it out."

Piekenbrock was surprised. He hadn't been notified of the new lead.

Information seemed to be flowing only one way. "Identification on him?"

Gardiner shook his head. "No, the wildlife has been at him for a few days before he was found. However, I am fairly sure it's Ernie Hale. We are about to step up our surveillance in Chicago on the Luciano family. The district deputy is waiting for the court orders to be approved."

"Do you need anything from me?"

Gardiner nodded. "We're going over all the statements. I need to talk with Sergeant Hunter."

"I got a text from him early this morning. He will be back at work tonight for the seven o'clock shift."

"Okay, I'll stick around and talk with him."

"Do you have any leads on the explosion that killed his fiancée?"

"That is one of the things I wanted to talk with him about. I noted on his personnel file that he had previous military experience. The chemical signature was similar to C-4 explosives."

The thought of Noah blowing up his own home and Megan made Piekenbrock shake his head. "I know where you may want to start digging. I would warn you to tread lightly here. What you may be suggesting isn't a possibility."

Gardiner shrugged. "I have to check out all possible leads. You know this as well."

Zane turned slightly so the agent couldn't see his right fist clench. The knuckles cracked from the force. Unable to answer appropriately, he just nodded before walking away into the captain's office. Soon as he walked into the empty room, he resisted the urge to slam the door. Barely.

The thought of Noah being a suspect was outrageous.

The fucking G-man made his blood boil. He had worked with Sergeant Hunter for almost eighteen years, and he knew him well enough. The FBI was barking up the wrong tree and wasting time.

Before he could change his mind, he dialed Noah's cell phone from memory, but it switched over to voicemail almost immediately.

"Hunter, I don't want you to come back to work." Zane paused as he thought about the options. "Consider yourself on extended leave. Beware the watchers."

* * * * *

An hour after sunrise, Noah safely landed in Casper. He had managed a few hours of sleep on the flight, just enough to recharge his batteries. With his return to Wyoming, the weather had changed, becoming cooler. October was only a few days away, and the slight hint of frost in the air announced that summer was officially gone. It would be an early winter.

Noah threw his bag on the passenger seat of his pickup truck and looked at the passenger window.

A crack ran from the base to the top. It looked like a lightning strike—another thing he had to take care of one day. The truck's damage brought back the moment of the explosion, and Noah gripped the steering wheel tight enough that it shook. The frustrations and emotional rollercoaster were taking their toll, and he felt like he was drowning.

Slowly he relaxed his hands and rested them on his lap. He had to get a grip, and going off the deep end wasn't an option. Too much depended on his ability to function correctly. He had never believed in meditation, but after twenty minutes of sitting in the airport parking lot with his eyes closed, Noah felt better.

The knot of tension left his shoulders, and the headache receded.

"Okay. Let's worry about today. Tomorrow can take care of itself."

There would have been a problem boarding the plane at O'Hare airport. With a bag of money, he would have been flagged and had too many questions asked. Remembering the boxes he found in the rental car, he took an idea from his abductor's playbook. He had the bag of money shipped to his apartment in a small pre-paid box. It should arrive tomorrow. The shipping label stated it was used clothing. Noah felt it was safe enough to ship a few million dollars in cash that way. He would find out shortly.

That left the issue of finding out who killed those men and being pressured and blackmailed by the head of a mafia family.

All in a day's work.

Noah chuckled to himself and felt better. Once he switched the phone on, the message from Piekenbrock almost brought back the feeling of apprehension. He wasn't exactly sure what was happening at work, but he was confident the FBI was part of the veiled warning.

"What the hell is going on?"

It felt like a curtain was drawn across his life. He was having trouble believing in reality. Arrow Point was not known for organized crime, and with Megan being involved, it seemed hard to comprehend.

What I need are answers.

Forensics results must have come in, which would shed some light on the case, but he was out of the loop. It was time to fix that.

Instead of heading back to the apartment, Noah located the lawyers, Zorch and Associates Law Office on East 1st Street. The two-story office building shared a parking lot with a bank. They had called the other day, and with the new information from Anthony Luciano, he wasn't sure what to believe anymore.

At eight o'clock in the morning, the offices were already open, which surprised Noah. The foyer was beautiful, with a high-polished stone receptionist desk and leather couches in the seating area. In the corner next to the window, a rather large fern seemed to be taking over. A folded piece of paper rested on the edge of the desk.

Ring once for service.

Following the instructions on the note, Noah pressed down on the top of the bell and waited. By the time the chime finished echoing in the air, he could hear the clack of high heels echoing across the stone floor.

A woman in a pale green dress suit moved behind the counter and smiled at Noah. Her dark hair was done up in a bun, and her frameless glasses suited her. "Good morning. How can I help you?"

"Noah Hunter, I received a call the other day, but unfortunately, I couldn't make it in. I was busy with work."

"I was the one who called you. I'm Monica Zorch, pleased to meet you."

"You as well."

"Come with me into my office." With a quick smile, she turned and walked down the hallway to the right of the reception desk. Noah passed a few offices on the right and a large conference room on the left before reaching Monica's corner office.

A glass desk was centered at the rear of the office, with bookshelves surrounding it on three sides. Two computer monitors sat to the side of the desktop. There was a small table at the far end of the office with a coffee machine with a few mugs sitting on top. Two large comfortable chairs faced the desk, and she gestured for Noah to choose while she sat down.

"Coffee?"

Noah shook his head. "No thanks."

"Did you bring a copy of the death certificate and identification?"

"Yes." Noah handed over the paperwork and pulled out his wallet, showing her his ID.

"Thank you."

Placing the papers off to the side, Monica opened a file on the shelf behind her. "You can go to the bank next door and transfer any funds, should you wish."

She slid the paper over to Noah. It showed two bank accounts, a savings and a checking account. "Here is the statement designating you as beneficiary. In case there are any legal problems with the bank or the IRS, just contact me."

"Thank you."

"Megan had left everything to you, including her possessions, vehicle, and cottage."

Noah was confused. "Cottage?"

Pulling out another piece of paper, she passed it across the desk. "I'm not sure if it is a cottage or a cabin. It's an hour's drive north of Arrow Point. Fifty acres of property and a structure."

What was Megan doing with a cabin?

Noah signed several forms and initialed where he was supposed to.

Monica stood and shook his hand. "I'm sorry for your loss."

"Thank you very much. This is new to me. Apparently, I'm now going for a drive."

A few minutes later, Noah was in his truck heading back to Arrow Point. He tried to wrap his head around all the evidence pointing toward Megan and her dual life. As far as he knew, she was a public-school teacher who liked to snuggle and watch movies on Friday nights. He had no knowledge or even the slightest idea that she was covering up anything.

Was their relationship even real?

Lost in his thoughts, Noah got back on the interstate and slowly drove home, hopefully toward some answers.

Chapter 37

Back at the apartment, Noah quickly showered and changed into his last pair of clean clothes. One of the trips today would have to be a shopping excursion for more outfits. He hadn't worn the golf shirt in a long time, and the jeans were tight. However, the weight of the Glock on his right hip was familiar and reassuring.

The second cupboard beside the fridge had several hooks on the inside. It's where Megan kept her spare keys for the apartment as well as her car. Noah had tried the third set for the apartment door, but they didn't work. Unsure of what they were for, he left them hanging. Now, he bounced them in his hand a few times.

Keys for the cottage property?

He slipped them in his pocket, put on a light blue jacket, and drove by the station. He wanted to avoid the FBI for the time being. With the parking lot being near empty, he decided to take a risk.

He didn't need to go upstairs to the offices. The storeroom was on the lower level, so he used his passkey to enter. Noah walked back out to his truck one minute later and threw the stainless-steel oversized briefcase into the back seat before heading west along Main Street.

The scene kit would be essential to continue the investigation, and he would rather have it and not need it. He had signed them out many times over the years, and they were kept stocked and ready for use.

Noah tried to ignore the last commands of Anthony Luciano. He would have been investigating the murders regardless. However, he would eventually have to deal with the mobster. For now, he would get back to work in a less than official capacity.

He wanted to go over the first murder scene again at the trapper's cabin and the national park campsite. He would also need copies of the forensic reports. Although the FBI would have them, that may prove difficult, but not impossible. Hopefully, that would fill in some of the gaps. Yet, he was missing a critical piece of information that would tie it all together.

When in doubt, start back at square one.

While camping and hiking with his brother, Noah had found many trails leading into the area, the paths crisscrossed and ended at the foothills, and some led to an area north of the old cabin. Earlier, they didn't have the time and resources to sweep miles of wilderness.

Driving his truck off-road, Noah passed where the shack used to be and parked another fifty yards along the trail. Brush and a few trees scraped along the sides of the truck on the way in, but with the cracked window and other damage from the explosion, a few more marks on the older Chevy did not worry him.

When he stepped out of the vehicle, a light breeze picked up, and he threw on his APPD windbreaker. It didn't have 'police' across the back, but it did have a white embroidered blue fabric logo. Noah wasn't sure what he was looking for—anything out of the ordinary. The actual crime scene had been examined many times. With the shack physically removed, that left the surrounding extended area.

Closing the truck's door, Noah started along the faint path through the grass. He wasn't sure if it was a game trail or not, but he had seen plenty of deer out in this area previously.

Occasionally, he would look under bushes and step off the path to examine an area, but he mainly headed north. After fifteen minutes of plodding along the trail, he slowed. With the wind across the fields, he wasn't sure if he heard something or not. He stopped and tilted his head to the side, slowly turning in a circle to listen intently.

It sounded like a rather large group of mosquitos, but he couldn't pinpoint the location.

Looking straight up, Noah found the source. A black four-bladed drone flew well over a hundred feet in the air and circled the open field. Seconds later, the drone stopped its flight path and descended. When it was within fifty feet, Noah saw a small camera mounted to the front.

Someone's watching me.

Moving his right hand to the butt of his pistol, he waited. He hadn't been to the range in over a week, and this would make a great target. However, within seconds, the drone did a one-eighty-degree turn and headed west, maintaining a steady altitude.

Noah didn't see anything else, so he turned into the long grass and followed. This area had nothing but hundreds of square miles of countryside, and it was known for people to come out here to camp and hike.

Noah lost sight of the drone, but he did see some movement near a cluster of trees fifty feet ahead. Changing his angle slightly, he slowed the pace and kept his right hand near the holstered Glock.

As he got closer, a tall woman stepped out from the trees. She faced him and waved.

Constable Angie Dickinson. She wore a pair of khaki cargo pants and a dark green windbreaker for the cooler weather. Her hair was pulled through the back of a baseball cap into a ponytail.

She lowered a backpack to the ground, a big smile on her face, making her eyes light up. Her dimples made her appear to be much younger.

"Sarge! Are you checking up on me?"

"I was just out for a walk, checking the trails. What are you doing out here?" As far as he could tell, Angie was alone.

"My ex left the drone at my place, and I thought it might be good for looking around. I needed some chill time anyway."

"Anything?"

She shook her head, making her long hair swish side to side. "Nothing. The batteries in the drone don't last too long. I've only been out here for half an hour."

"Have you heard any more on the case?"

"Since the feds took over, I was politely told I was in their way. Captain Richardson reassigned me. I'm back to traffic stops off the highway."

Noah nodded. He had been there more than a few times during his rookie years. "I'm still off work, officially. However, I needed to keep looking around. Heading out to the national park next. Not sure what I'm looking for exactly, but I have to do something."

Angie shrugged. "I'm not doing anything, and I'm on rotation for my two days off. Need some company?"

Noah thought of the task in front of him before answering. "Two eyes are better than one, right?"

"Right."

"If you're up for poking around a campground, I would be glad to have you along."

Smiling, Angie picked up her backpack and slipped her arms through the straps. "Ready."

"Did you drive out here?"

"No," Dickinson followed Noah. "I rode my bike. I left it in the bushes where the shack used to be."

"We can throw it in the back of my truck."

During the hike back, they kept their eyes peeled for anything unusual. The only thing Noah saw were a few old beer caps and a rusted crushed pop can. Angie found a small campsite off the trail, but it hadn't been used in weeks, if not months. Disappointed at the lack of progress, the officers headed back to the truck. Noah felt Megan's keys in his pocket, and he was unsure if he wanted Angie with him when he checked out the property. Noah didn't want to get her involved with the Luciano family. If the mob knew about Angie or put her at risk, Noah couldn't live with it.

However, it did feel better to have someone watching his back. He would have to be more careful.

What else could go wrong?

Chapter 38

After loading her bike in the back of the pickup truck, they headed east through Arrow Point and pulled into the national park before noon. On a Thursday morning and off-season, the campsites were empty. Noah drove around the dirt roads until he found the site. There was no barricade tape, but the firepit was devoid of ashes or dirt. It hadn't been used recently.

"Have you seen the report on the items found here?" Angie asked. She had gotten out of the truck and looked down into the cleaned-out pit.

"Nothing."

Shrugging, she added, "It was mostly the charred remains of the wallet with the fake identification. There were enough fibers in there to suggest that clothing was burned, but they couldn't make out any details."

Forensics did their best, but besides burnt fabrics and melted plastics, nothing else was identified.

"Did they find anything else in the area?"

"Nothing was mentioned."

"Okay, let's start there. By the way, far as I consider, you are back on the clock. I'll authorize your pay for working on a scheduled day off."

Getting paid for special duty or working on their rotational days off was almost equivalent to being paid double-time. Far as Noah was concerned, the department could pay up. They were doing the work.

"Awesome. Thanks. Let's get working then."

Angie started by checking all the other campsites in the immediate area while Noah headed into the woods. For decades the trees had been scoured by campers looking for fallen trees or branches to use in a fire while camping. The result was that there were many little pathways in the area, and the ground was clean. There wasn't anywhere for something to hide, and it was somewhat exposed.

After fifteen minutes of searching, Noah failed to find anything.

"How are you doing, Sarge?"

Dickinson was returning down the dirt road toward the truck. "Nothing."

"Same here. There were the remnants of a fire at one of the sites. However, it was just wood that was burned."

She brushed her blackened hands on her pants. "I'm just going to clean up."

The comfort station was thirty feet away, just south of the truck. The large building was divided into the men's and women's sides, with stalls and a long row of sinks in each. Noah hadn't been here in years, and he doubted it had changed.

"Washrooms should still be open. Women are on the far side."

"Be right back."

Noah sat on the Chevy's tailgate, pulled out his phone, and fired off a quick text to Lieutenant Piekenbrock. He wanted to keep the LT in the loop and to ensure Dickinson would be getting paid.

"Sarge! Come quick." Angie cried out from inside the women's washroom.

Noah sprinted across the grass. He didn't recall drawing his pistol, but the Glock was in his right hand while he ran. He heard Angie's muffled swearing as it echoed out of the screened windows.

His shoulder checked the bathroom door, and it flew open and banged off the wall. The pistol rose with his left hand as he swept the room.

Angie stood outside the third bathroom stall and waved him over.

"Go inside and have a look."

It took a few deep breaths to calm down. Noah nodded and holstered his weapon. Once inside the stall, he had to stand slightly sideways at the toilet bowl to close the door.

"Jesus …"

The beige stall door inside had a simple circular latch that would send a bolt out into the frame. Dried blood was smeared around the lock and near the top, where someone had closed it firmly. He could almost make out details in the blood. It was definitely a dried, smeared palm print.

"How the hell did they miss this?"

Angie winked. "Maybe they were all men and didn't want to come in here."

After opening the door from the bottom with his hiking boot, Noah stepped outside. "Okay, I have to call this in."

"I just chose this one at random. However, bad news. I still have to go."

"Did you touch anything else?"

Angie shook her head. "No, just the outside door to push in and the edge of the bathroom stall door."

"Let's keep it clean as possible."

Noah had heard horror stories of suspects walking free because of contaminated evidence. Procedures were not followed correctly, and cases got thrown out of court. With her jacket sleeve down, Angie opened the outside door. Noah realized he had left his phone on the tailgate.

He was about to pick it up when the back tire on the truck exploded, and he almost jumped out of his boots. A round was fired from across the campgrounds, and he couldn't pinpoint the location with the echo.

"Get down!"

Noah immediately faceplanted in the dirt and rolled behind the truck. He barely noticed that he had drawn his pistol once again, and it was at the ready. Dickinson joined him as they sought cover.

"Are you okay—" Angie was cut off as another round fired into the rear quarter panel, right above the tire. "Son of a bitch!"

Noah knew the rounds were fired from a long gun, but nothing near the same caliber that Bennett had fired. They didn't have enough punch to go through the full bed of the truck.

"I need my phone, take this and fire two rounds over the truck when I tell you."

Handing over his Glock, Noah crouched down behind the rear driver's tire and took a deep breath. Angie looked shaken but would be okay. He nodded. "Now."

As soon as she stood and fired the first shot over the truck's cab, Noah darted around the tailgate and grabbed his phone. He made it back by the third shot safely.

Dialing 911, Noah gestured to Angie to keep the gun while he talked. "Two police officers being fired upon at Powder River National Park. Code 30. Located at site one-one-four."

"Powder River National Park, site one-one-four. State police were notified and en route shortly. Hold in there."

The woman on the line sounded calm, and Noah appreciated it, even though it didn't quiet him down at all.

He took the Glock back from Angie. "They haven't fired in a minute. I'm going to have a quick look. Stay low."

Constable Dickinson was doing good, despite having a slight problem with her breathing. It was the first time she had been fired upon, affecting everyone to one degree or another.

Keeping low, Noah crossed over her legs and moved to stand behind the engine block. It would help provide cover in case a round tried to make its way through the vehicle. A quick look over the truck's hood didn't reveal anything, and Noah quickly ducked back down and waited a few seconds.

One of the tricks he learned in the infantry was to avoid sticking your head up at the same location twice in a row. A possible enemy would have previously targeted that spot and could have it lined up in his crosshairs. He moved two feet toward the front bumper, then crouched and scanned the ground in front of him. He could see over one hundred yards through the campground. There were trees randomly scattered all over and bushes, but he couldn't see anyone firing on him.

However, he did recognize a noise that echoed across the park. A car door slamming closed and a vehicle peeling off.

Punching his hand down on the hood, Noah swore. "Fuck!"

Angie joined him and looked around. "Was that them leaving?"

"Yeah." Noah walked around to the other side of his truck and looked at the rear tire. It wasn't just flat. It had exploded from the bullet, and large pieces of torn rubber were scattered on the ground.

"So much for pursuit." Angie kicked the tire and looked at the damage the second round caused.

"I'll get the gear out and put the spare on."

"Just a second. I have an idea."

Angie grinned and gave Noah a quick wink.

Chapter 39

At two-hundred feet in the air, the plates were impossible to read, but the vehicle was rapidly getting closer. The blue four-door Nissan turned right of the national park and headed east along the interstate. He squinted as it came straight toward them, trying to make out any details. A plume of dust rose behind the vehicle as it caught the shoulder of the road.

"Can this thing record?"

Angie pressed the button on the display screen. "Recording now, but it won't last long."

The drone flew at its maximum speed of twenty-five miles per hour. Noah estimated the vehicle was accelerating and would be doing close to sixty. They didn't have to follow the roads, and Angie flew straight over the trees to intercept.

The main highway outside the national park headed west toward Arrow Point and east toward Casper. Had the escape vehicle turned left, Noah wouldn't have been able to identify it.

Trees flew by on the display screen as the drone reached its maximum speed, although the Nissan would pass too far to make out any details.

Angie used her thumbs on the controller, and the drone dove at a sharp angle. They could almost make out the driver, but the image was too brief.

"Just a notch closer ..."

Noah stayed at her shoulder and followed the aerial chase. When a red light flashed on the screen, he had to ask. "What's that?"

"Warning light."

The drone got within a hundred yards of the speeding car when it abruptly stopped in mid-air and reversed its course.

"Safety features, it returns when the battery is low or reached the maximum range."

Seconds later, the drone approached over the tree line. It headed right back to where it was launched, a miracle of GPS. Angie folded in the props and placed it back in the zippered pouch in her pack.

"Out of batteries. However, I think I got some usable footage."

She disconnected her phone from the controller and scanned through the saved video. "Nebraska plates, hard to make them out. Driver is wearing black clothing and gloves."

The best image was blurry, and it was hard to make out any details. The range was too far and the quality of the picture too low. They could make out a blurry image of the driver—a figure dressed in black gripped the wheel. You could see the spacing between the sleeve and the gloves, showing white skin. From the angle of approach, the drone couldn't capture an image of the driver's face, but the bottom of the chin was visible.

"I can't tell if they're male or female, but Caucasian for sure."

"Good job, Angie. At least we have some information. I want to buy a drone now."

"Okay, I really have to use the restroom now. Be right back."

Noah grabbed his phone and updated 911 on the suspect's description vehicle and direction of travel. "Hopefully, the state police will be able to get them."

She headed off to the men's washroom while Noah examined his truck. It took a beating but still worked. He couldn't change the tire until the state police showed up. There was evidence to collect and pictures to be taken. Sliding his hand into the pocket of the jacket, Noah gripped the keys tightly.

He needed more answers, and hopefully, the next stop would provide some. Noah certainly could use a break right about now.

~

Twenty minutes later, the state police arrived and locked down the whole campground. Noah and Angie spent over an hour going over their statements and walked them through what happened. At one point, Noah had to talk them out of taking his truck as evidence. They settled for just pictures.

They couldn't find the bullet in the tire, but one of the troopers found a distorted piece of lead in the truck bed. The second shot had fallen to rest on the liner under Angie's bike.

The trooper wore the standard blue latex gloves and laughed as he picked up the bullet and held it out. "Thank God for ricochets. Not sure, but it could be a .308?"

Noah closed the truck bed. "Looks like it. Are you guys all done taking pics?"

Four state troopers had surrounded the truck for the hour and photographed everything. They even picked up the 9mm brass casings from Noah's Glock to document and log as evidence.

John Gaston came back with the other two troopers. "We didn't see anything from the firing position. There were some tire tracks where they peeled out. We are done making the impressions."

It was only last week when he saw him at the trapper's cabin. It seemed a lifetime ago.

"Constable Dickinson will send you the footage from the drone soon as I drop her off at the station."

"Sounds good. Let's get that tire changed, and you can get out of here. Forensics is on the way to process the bathroom. It's beyond our paygrade."

A few of the guys helped Noah, and they had the tire changed within ten minutes. The damaged tire slid into the truck bed, and Noah turned to Angie. "Ready to head out?"

"More than ready. Sarge, what do you think is going on? Why would someone follow us out here?"

As they headed west, back to Arrow Point, Noah drummed his fingers on the steering wheel while thinking of the various scenarios. Finally, he let out a big sigh. "Best I can come up with is that it was a warning."

"A warning?" Angie looked skeptical at this.

"Someone had a chance to take us out, but they hit the tire and the truck, and we couldn't follow."

She took a deep breath and let it out slowly. "It's possible."

"Grasping at straws here. Hopefully, the state police will find the vehicle."

Soon, they pulled into the station's parking lot, and Noah helped Dickinson unload her bike. "Good work today, glad you were there."

With a quick smile, her dimples made an appearance. "No problem. I'll send the footage and pictures. Call me when you are up for more exploring."

As Angie walked away, Noah opened the door and was about to get in the truck when he heard something he hoped to avoid.

"Ah, Sergeant Hunter. Glad I ran into you. Let's go have a quick talk."

Noah had forgotten about the feds. When he turned, an agent stood three feet away with a big shit-eating grin on his face.

Chapter 40

Special Agent Brandon Gardiner closed the door to the conference room and gestured for Noah to sit in the middle. The FBI agent already had his laptop and paperwork spread out at the head of the table. The subconscious position of power, Noah noted.

"I just need to go over your statement and reports and clarify a few things."

The conference room was still set up as a command center for the FBI to conduct their investigation in Arrow Point. Noah noted the agent had made himself at home.

"Not a problem. How can I help you?"

Noah removed his jacket and hung it off the back of the chair before he sat.

As he logged in to the laptop, Gardiner didn't waste any time. "How long have you been with Arrow Point Police Department?"

"Eighteen years now."

He scrolled down on his tablet for a few seconds. "Can you confirm your relationship with Megan Brooks?"

"Yes, I can."

Noah just sat there staring at the agent.

After an awkward silence, Gardiner looked up from the screen, frowning. "Well?"

"Well, what? I just confirmed my relationship with Megan. What else did you want?"

The agent leaned back in the chair and studied Noah. "What was your relationship with Megan Brooks?"

"That's better. She was my fiancée."

"How long have you known her?"

"Personal question, with no bearing on any relevant case. Next question."

Noah wasn't sure what he was up to, but he had been at this a long time, and he wasn't about to get into an area of his life that he didn't want to. None of his damn business.

"What was your role in the military before joining APPD?"

Noah drummed his fingers on the tabletop monetarily before answering, weighing his options. The odds were that he already knew the answer. "Infantry."

He knew where this line of questioning was headed, but he didn't think the FBI agent would go there.

He was wrong.

"Did you handle or use explosives while in the infantry?"

Noah's insides turned to ice. Cold anger made his stomach muscles tense, and he lost all expression. Once he stood, Noah leaned forward on the table. One hand reached out and slammed the agent's laptop closed. The small camera lens had pointed in his direction. He couldn't confirm it recorded the interview. He just assumed it was.

"You've crossed the line with me. Next time you step over it, you better bring company with you. You're going to need help getting back to the other side."

Gardiner's mouth opened in shock, and he couldn't get out a word.

Hunter grabbed his jacket and left the conference room. He tried to slam the door, but the soft-close hinges kicked in, and the door closed whisper quiet.

Damn door.

Noah waved to a few people on his way out, but overall, he wasn't in the mood to talk. He hoped the FBI would brief him on the forensics reports, but after hearing from the LT and this meeting with Gardiner, that wasn't likely to happen.

The pressure to find the answers and keep Luciano at bay was minimal, and he tried not to think about it. He was more worried about Bennett and any repercussions for him. The fact that Gardiner even hinted that he would have blown up his own house infuriated him.

There was one thing Noah had to take care of that didn't involve getting shot. Replacing the truck tire and the mundane task of buying more clothes would cool him down. Unless he wanted to be naked while doing laundry, it was essential. He would also need to order more uniforms for work, but he could easily wear plain clothes for a while.

Time to get some running around done and not worry about the feds.

There was enough on his plate.

* * * * *

Anthony Luciano closed the door to his office and sat down behind the desk. He adjusted the picture of his newest grandson and smiled. He was about to make a phone call when a knock sounded on the door.

"Come in."

Anthony's hand automatically drifted near the second drawer on his right. When William Ryan walked in, he relaxed. Will had forgone his usual suit and wore tan slacks with a burgundy sweater opened to show a golf shirt underneath.

"Come in, Will, sit down."

The lawyer nodded and closed the door behind him. Once seated, he seemed nervous and had trouble meeting Anthony's eyes. "I know this business is personal, but I have thought about this a great deal over the last few days. I would recommend you drop any interest in the cop."

Anthony leaned back in his chair and just stared at Ryan.

Will ran a hand through his thinning hair, seemingly more nervous about overstepping his bounds. "I'm not saying anything about Rachel or the family situation. However, the body count is excessively high, and the feds have something that we need to talk about."

Anthony raised his eyebrows. "What do they have?"

William reached into his pants pocket, pulled out his cell phone, and quickly scrolled to a picture. A long-bladed survival knife was lying on a stainless-steel countertop with a forensic, black, and white ruler next to it for scale. The plastic evidence bag beside it was labeled with an eleven-digit code along with yesterday's date.

"Is that …?"

Will nodded. "I believe so."

Anthony gripped the armrests on his chair until his knuckles turned white. "Who do we have on the inside?"

"At that level, just one guy. However, getting just this one picture was difficult. If we use him, it will cost, but it needs to be done—in my opinion."

The armrests creaked as Anthony's hands shook. "I will not drop it. I want this wrapped up by the weekend and gone away permanently. Have the cops taken care of. I don't want any further links back to us. If you can't handle this, you are of no further use to me."

Fearful of his employer, William stood and nodded before leaving the office. He quietly closed the door behind him.

Anthony closed his eyes and tried to calm down, but the image of the knife kept coming up in his mind.

"I still blame you, my brother. Why didn't you just listen to me."

When he slammed his fist on the desk, it caused the picture frame of his grandson to jump and fall off. Getting control took some effort, but he managed. Once the decision was made, the rest would be easy, if not costly. Anthony called his accountant.

The financial arrangements would be worth it.

Chapter 41

Noah juggled several bags in one hand while he dug the keys out of his pocket. As he approached the apartment, he saw the driver had left the parcel in front of the door. Written on the side of the white box, in black magic marker, was *Used Clothing*. He switched the bags to one hand and brought everything into the apartment. A few million dollars sitting around unattended wasn't a great idea, as long as no one knew. Noah was worried about porch pirates, even though the risk was reduced in the apartment building.

It hadn't taken long for several new outfits. Now Noah wouldn't have to do laundry every few days. Along with the tire replacement, the old truck got an oil change. It would hold out a little longer.

Earlier, a phone call from his insurance company confirmed they would not rebuild. They offered fair market value for the home and contents. With all the memories of his house, he didn't want to rebuild anyway. For now, the apartment would do.

After putting away the clothing and a few groceries, Noah sat at the laptop and pulled out the paperwork from the lawyer. Using Google Earth, he located the cabin address and zoomed in on the area. It was heavily forested, and he could barely make out a small clearing at the end of a long road or path. The image wasn't as detailed as he would like, but there was a hint of a roof or structure. The surrounding area appeared to be all wooded, with a swamp immediately north. If he didn't know the exact address, he doubted he would have been able to spot anything from the satellite images. Even with the specific location, he was unsure.

Closing the laptop, Noah turned to the box he had shipped to himself. With the FBI on his case, asking about his explosives training, and no doubt digging into his background, he didn't want to have to explain this amount of cash on hand.

The cabin would be an excellent place to lay low and hide the money. Noah doubted anyone else knew about it. Anywhere that he could hide the money in the apartment, someone else would be able to find it. They all pretty much had the same training.

Noah looked around, and the urge to get out overwhelmed him. He wanted to solve the murders and find who was responsible for Megan's death, but he couldn't do it from here. A new base of operations that no one knew about sounded perfect.

Before he changed his mind, Noah went into the bedroom, opened the closet, and pulled out Megan's large suitcase. He loaded his clothes and money, along with the laptop and an extra box of ammunition inside. What little space that remained, he filled it with canned goods and food from the kitchen. He wasn't sure how well the cabin was furnished or how rustic it was, but he wanted to be prepared.

The sun began to set, and a brilliant display of pink clouds decorated the horizon.

Red sky night, soldier delight.

Noah hoped the adage would prove true. With one last look around the apartment, he was ready. However, when he noticed the green plant in front of the window, he chuckled. When he had first dated Megan, he had stood on the same spot to look outside. The plant was parched, and the large leaves looked like they were drooping. Noah poured water from his glass into the dirt. He had taken care of the plant for years. While it never seemed to get better, it never died. It took Megan over two years to catch him in the act of watering the plant before she burst out laughing. He never knew it was plastic, and he had watered it at least once a week.

Smiling at the memory, he closed the curtains.

"I can't leave you here by yourself, little buddy."

Once he loaded the truck, the plant sat in the cupholder. Some memories were worth keeping.

~

Noah topped off the last of the gas cans and loaded them up into the back of the truck. His shopping spree at the big box plaza in Casper could only be described as fast and furious, and the truck bed was full as a result.

A new Honda generator, gas cans, a small barbeque, and a thirty-pound tank of propane, as well as a large chopping ax, were his latest acquisitions. He loaded a new Winchester twelve-gauge shotgun and placed it in the front seat along with an extra box of shells. A few more odds and ends he tucked into his suitcase. The protein bars and cans of ground coffee sat on the floor behind his seat. With that, his essential items were covered. Everything was paid for in cash. Noah didn't want to be traced by credit cards or debit purchases. He didn't know the capabilities of those who were watching. Better to be safe than sorry.

With his cell phone off, Noah headed north along interstate twenty-five.

The directions from the lawyer placed the property sixty-six miles north of Casper. As far as he knew, Megan had never been in the area except traveling to Yellowstone on one of their weekend trips. Noah had taken her camping one weekend, but the bugs and sleeping on the ground were not her thing. She had preferred to stay home and relax most of the time or in a hotel while he camped.

During the scenic drive, Noah went through different scenarios in his mind. There was no evidence in the apartment for the feds to discover because he was innocent. Of *that*, he was sure. Of course, their relationship wasn't perfect, but he would never kill Megan or blow up his house. Anthony Luciano believed Megan was his niece Rachel and the US marshals were involved. It led Noah to figure out she could have been a part of the witness protection program.

There were too many questions left unanswered. However, Noah did know the FBI would have some of those answers from the forensic reports. He needed to get his hands on all the accounts. Without involving others, he had to get back to work.

Although he only had two years in the infantry and one tour, he did learn one thing. Always have a fallback position prepared. The items in the back reaffirmed he was as ready as he would be in that regard.

An hour later, Noah spotted the sign on the west side of the interstate. Fire Route 34.

He hadn't passed a town in over half an hour, and there was nothing but thousands of square miles of forest. There had to be other cottages and homes out in the area, but so far, he hadn't seen any.

Shortly the side road turned to gravel. It didn't look like it had seen much use, with large potholes and divots all over. Despite the heavier load in the back of the truck, the older Chevy didn't have any difficulty in the near off-road conditions.

Following the directions, he drove three miles along the twisting road. Noah passed a few gates that were closed. They were secured with large padlocks on the side of a post or tree.

He came to a similar gate at the three-mile mark, fourteen feet long and made out of tubular metal. There were two thick poles driven into the ground on either side and a thick chain wrapped around it. An old stone fence to either side of the gate, overgrown with trees and brush, prevented anyone from circumventing the entrance.

When he stepped out of the truck, the air was cooler than Arrow Point, and it woke him up. Noah wasn't too surprised to find one of the keys on Megan's chain fit perfectly. The short length of chain fell and clattered against the gate. He drove the truck through and locked it behind him. Despite the rural area, he didn't want any unexpected company.

The dirt road twisted and turned through the woods for almost half a mile before he arrived.

An A-frame cabin sat at the far end of the clearing, lit up from the truck's headlights. The roof was covered in tin sheets, and the front of the building had two large windows on either side of the front door. There was a small front deck with a few wooden chairs.

It looked like the perfect place to lay low.

Noah pulled out a tactical flashlight and got out of the truck. When the sun had set, the clouds had disappeared with the light breeze. A million stars blanketed the sky, and Noah took a moment to appreciate the view. It wasn't a sight he would usually see in the city.

The moment of serenity was shattered when the flashlight picked up a red reflection to the right of the cabin. It was the taillights of a vehicle parked near the back.

Switching the flashlight to his left hand, he drew his Glock and took a few steps closer to confirm. Fire ran through his veins as the rage swept through him.

It was the blue four-door Nissan with Nebraska plates from the campground.

Chapter 42

Stewart Bennett threw the gym bag into his Honda's back seat and looked across the parking lot. A series of cars were parked at the Tavern. Many had stopped for a few drinks or maybe an early dinner. The parking lot was getting full, and by nine o'clock tonight, the bar would be busy.

He drummed his fingers on the red roof of his car and contemplated going in for a quick beer. He started back to work in the early morning and wanted to get back into the routine. That meant getting up a few hours earlier and going for a run. There wasn't any point in wasting a good workout at the gym by going to the bar after.

Since returning from Chicago, he had trouble sleeping, and for two nights, he tossed and turned. Getting back into a schedule helped, and burning off the nervous energy at the gym felt good. His parents checked in early that morning by phone, which reassured him. They were doing fine and had no problems. He didn't mention that he went to Chicago, but his dad hinted some things were out of place in his garage.

Noah and Stewart were positive they had placed everything back exactly as they had found it, but he knew his father. If something were an inch out of place, he would have noticed it. Stewart emphasized that everything was fine *now* before his dad got the hint and dropped it.

With a remorseful last look at the bar, Bennett pulled out of the gym parking lot and drove east on Main Street. For the ninth time in an hour, he checked his phone, but Noah hadn't checked in. He should have been back from Chicago yesterday, but there hadn't been any word. When he called, it switched over to voicemail almost straight away.

"Sarge, it's Bennett. Give me a ring when you get this message."

Frustrated, he turned on the radio and almost instantly tuned it out. Noah and Stewart did the same thing while they were on patrol. They kept the radio on low as background music, barely loud enough to make out details so they could concentrate on the road and not miss a call. Over the years, they had known officers who were disciplined for missed calls. Bennett knew they liked to crank the music to a level that drowned out everything, and they paid the price.

As he sat at a red light, Bennett couldn't help but think of Chicago and what happened with Carmelo. The gut rot started once again, and he worried over the repercussions. Carmelo did have it coming to him. Of that, he was sure.

When the light changed, a gray Ford sedan ran the red and squealed through the intersection, right in front of Bennett. The tires spun, and the back end swung out before it accelerated. In reflex, Stewart's hand reached to turn on his flashers before realizing he was in his civilian vehicle.

"Jesus Christ. What a moron."

As he looked both ways, Bennett quickly followed to keep his eyes on the Ford and the driver. They wove in and out of traffic and cut off other vehicles. A chorus of horns sounded in its wake.

"Okay, buddy. Enough of that."

Bennett stepped on it and soon caught up to the erratic driver. When he got the plate number, he would call a uniform on them.

As Bennett closed the gap, the Ford turned right off Main Street and headed south on County Road 44. The Honda slipped on the turn and almost clipped the far sidewalk, and he couldn't help but swear. There was a large difference between a Civic and a police cruiser. They raced past a few stores and a residential area before leaving the downtown area. Within a quarter-mile, he began to close the distance on the Ford.

Bennett was relieved to see one driver with no passengers. Probably a kid.

The gray car slowed on the far side of an intersection as if it were searching for something. He could read the personalized plates now from fifty feet away.

TEA4ME.

The plates gave him pause. He had seen them before around Arrow Point—most people have. They belonged on a Toyota minivan owned by an older lady. Anne had a small catering service and delivered homemade sandwiches all over town and any leftovers she would provide to the shelter. Noah had known her for most of his life.

Goddammit. Stolen plates.

Bennett picked up his cell phone to call it in, which was his mistake.

He never saw the large dump truck as it drove through the red light and collided with the driver's door.

The collision's sound echoed for a quarter-mile as the red Honda flattened and then bounced off the front of the five-ton vehicle. Shattered glass littered the intersection and interior of the twisted wreckage.

The steering column and wheel now rested in the passenger seat from the impact, and Bennett's lifeless body was crushed against the far door.

* * * * *

The older driver of the gray Ford parked and stepped outside with a screwdriver in his hand. He didn't even glance at the wreckage as he promptly switched the rear license plate. The old Colorado plate was registered to the vehicle. Once inside the car, he did a U-turn and parked it safely behind the intersection's white line.

The man lowered the window and yelled to the dump truck driver. "Ready?"

The dark-skinned man behind the wheel gave him the thumbs up before shutting off the truck.

Pulling out his cell phone, the Ford's driver paused, then took a few quick rapid breaths before dialing. "Hello, 911? I need to report an accident! Oh my God …"

Chapter 43

The barrel of his Glock led the way as he crept around the corner of the cabin. With the flashlight in his left hand and the pistol in his right, Noah scanned the grounds. The small flashlight was over twelve hundred lumens, and the area was lit in a white brilliance. The shadows leaped and twisted with every turn, and a lone night bird sang from high in a tree. One minute ago, he enjoyed the night air and the stars, and now he cursed the darkness. Despite the powerful flashlight, Noah couldn't see far into the trees. A dozen people could have him in their sights, and he would never know.

Slowly, Noah moved forward along the right side of the cabin and approached the blue car. The flashlight lit up the interior, confirming it was empty, and the keys were still in the ignition. The hood was cold to the touch. The vehicle hadn't moved in a while.

When he lifted the handle, the dome light turned on, and he quickly searched inside. The glove box and armrest storage were empty, with nothing under the seats. Noah pulled the release lever for the trunk. Inside was the factory cover for the spare tire and jack, but nothing else.

There was no such thing as coincidence. The Nissan had to be the same car from the national park.

Gently, he closed the trunk and shone the light in the backyard. There was only one additional building, six-foot-square, with cedar shingles on the roof.

An outhouse?

At the cabin's back door, he had a quick peek inside. The kitchen looked dated but functional, and with the open floor plan, Noah could see the sitting room. Two armchairs faced a couch with a coffee table next to a small wood-burning stove on the side. A steep set of stairs led to the loft. Despite it being well maintained, the decor reminded him of the late 70s or early 80s. There wasn't anywhere for someone to hide unless they were upstairs.

The far side of the cabin had three cords of wood stacked between two large trees, next to an old, rusted wheelbarrow covered in branches and leaves.

If someone were hiding in the woods, it would take a team of thirty people with night-vision equipment and K-9 to search unless he could requisition a helicopter with thermal. Noah would look around later, but he couldn't do anything about it for now.

Once he turned off the truck, he knew it couldn't be put off any further. The front door was locked, but it easily turned with the right key.

The cabin had a musty smell from lack of use. However, there wasn't any dampness or odors. That was a good thing, and it meant the roof was tight and didn't leak.

Nothing happened when he flicked the light switch inside, but he found some candles on the small kitchen and the coffee tables. Once they were lit, the place almost seemed quite comfortable. There was a slight chill in the air, and he thought it was colder in the cabin than it was outside.

Using the flashlight, he started in the kitchen and worked his way back to the living room. He searched for any clues or hints about the Nissan or anyone that had lived there previously. The cupboards held the usual kitchen items, but there was no food. Noah tried the kitchen faucet, but no water came out.

There were a few outdoor hunting and fishing magazines on the kitchen table that were dated fifteen years ago. Noah once again pulled his pistol and poked his head into the loft. The slanted walls of the cabin gave the space not much headroom, except in the middle. There were two small windows at either end and a large double bed at the far side, as well as two small single beds tight up against the walls just past the stairs. From the fifth step, he could see under the beds, and besides dust, he could tell no one had been here in a long time.

Outside the front door, Noah turned off his flashlight and let his eyes adjust to the night. The faint glow of the candles inside cast a weak light through the windows, barely letting him see any details on the front deck.

Without any threat or direction for him to focus, he holstered his pistol once again. Someone had their chance to place him in their crosshairs at the national park earlier today. If they were hiding in the woods, there wasn't anything he could do about it.

Noah unloaded the gas cans and generator from the truck bed and stacked them on the front deck, near the door. He didn't know where to hook them into, so he would figure it out in the morning. Once the large suitcase and supplies were inside, he lit the remaining candles.

"I'll have to add candles to my list."

The flickering light gave the room a warm glow, and it brought life to the old cottage. When he saw the small pile of logs and kindling beside the wood stove, Noah knelt and opened the iron door. The ashes need to be cleaned out, but he would do it later. The box of matches left on the coffee table still worked, and a few minutes later, the flames caught the birch bark and kindling. Slowly, he fed in more branches and a few split cedar logs. They had been inside the cabin drying out for years, so they caught fire quickly.

Leaving the door to the woodstove open an inch, Noah looked around, unsure of his next step.

He had enough food to last ten days if rationed, but he knew work beckoned. The easiest way to get more information was from the reports and further investigations. He would get up early and be there for his seven o'clock shift, whether he liked it or not, hopefully, before the feds arrived.

Noah quickly made up a bed on the couch. It would be quite comfortable inside the cabin with the fire, and he didn't want to sleep upstairs. He may as well go to bed early. Who knows what tomorrow would bring? His old section commander used to tell everyone to rest when you can. A lesson he learned rather well.

Not wanting to leave the shotgun in the truck, Noah stepped outside. The woodstove's added light gave the interior a warm glow, and he could see the narrow path from the front door to the truck. The night breeze felt good, and he decided to crack a window to help air out the cabin.

He was about to open the door when someone on the far side of the truck spoke.

"Hi, Noah. How're you doing?"

Chapter 44

Lieutenant Piekenbrock raced south along the county road from Arrow Point in record time.

His siren screamed and echoed throughout the city, and the vehicles cleared from his path. The city's peaceful calm was shattered as two other cop cars followed suit, and the fire truck was sixty seconds behind them.

The responding officer had radioed the station with the horrible news. Everyone stood in shock before a flurry of activity swept the officers. Zane was first out the door, and he would be the second respondent at the accident. The large dump truck remained on scene, and the older driver was distraught. The officer had him off to the side while he was being reassured and assessed.

Piekenbrock parked and slowly walked over to the wreckage. He gripped the distorted metal that used to be the driver's door and closed his eyes once he saw the former officer.

"Sorry, Bennett. Not a good way to go."

Death was an old acquaintance. They had met many times over the years.

Others had finally arrived, and he held up a hand to keep them back. The LT shook his head. "Nothing can be done."

In a daze, he walked over to his cruiser in time to watch the fire truck pull up, and they prioritized the scene. Piekenbrock sat on the hood of his vehicle and stared at his dress shoes. They were flecked with oil and transmission fluid, but he never noticed.

Constable Luttrell waited until the LT glanced up. "Sir, I've talked to the driver. He was headed eastbound on forty-seven when the Honda ran the red. Bennett appeared to be on his cell phone and not looking at the road. A witness was stopped at the red light, on forty-four in the northbound lane, said the exact same thing."

"Jesus Christ." From the vacant stare, Zane could tell that Luttrell was in shock. They had all worked with Bennett for years, and he was a good man. "Thanks, Glen."

Piekenbrock heard the firemen deploy their hydraulic claws, and the passenger door peeled back from the frame. They had already cut the front window support and opened the roof like a tin can.

Unable to watch further, he got up and went back to brief the rest of the guys standing around. Captain Richardson arrived in his truck, dressed in a golf shirt and shorts. News spread quickly in the small town.

When they lost one of their own, it was felt by all.

* * * * *

Noah didn't even think to go for his Glock when he heard the voice. He wasn't able to move his arms. His eyes filled with tears, and the heartache almost crippled him as he gasped for breath. The moment in time stretched on for an eternity. Unable to stand, he dropped to one knee beside the hood of his truck while tears trickled off his face. A lone gut-wrenching sob escaped.

Megan came around the front of the vehicle and put her hand on his shoulder. She stood there and cried along with him. "I'm so sorry."

Noah just shook silently while letting another sob echo in the night. He opened his eyes enough to see her dark hiking boots and black pants. Noah touched her leg—he needed confirmation that she was real, and this wasn't a dream.

Megan helped him to his feet. "Come inside. We need to talk."

Noah numbly followed her back inside the cabin, where they sat on the couch. He stared into the candle's flickering flame before he could look her in the eye. "I have an idea what happened, but I need to hear it from you. You owe me that at least."

Megan placed her hand on his knee and nodded. "They found me. I had no choice." Her eyes teared up once again. Her shoulder-length blond hair was gone. It was now cut above the ears and dyed a dark brown. Noah absently noted that the new style suited her.

"Why didn't you come to me?"

"My uncle knew everything about me, including you. They were going to destroy everything. He would have started with your family, friends, and then you."

Noah wanted to reach out and hold her, but then something clicked. "You were the one that tortured the man in the trapper's cabin?"

Megan pulled her hand off his leg and nodded. He saw a resolve in her eyes that was clear. "I'm not going back to my uncle. Ever. I have worked too hard to be free of him. What they were going to do to me was nothing compared to what I put him through. I needed answers to protect myself, you, and many others."

Closing his eyes, Noah pictured the scene when he first walked into the shack. The fact that the school teacher he knew, fell in love with, was capable of that rocked him to his core. "Start from the beginning."

Megan left her hand on her knee palm up, and Noah automatically reached out and held her. He turned on the couch to face her.

"My mother died when I was young, and my father raised me in Chicago. His name was Gregory Luciano, and he worked with my uncle Tony. When I was little, I had no idea what they did for a living. I just grew up around drugs, violence, and tough men, as if it were normal. I didn't know any different."

Noah wanted to ask questions and pry for more information, but he knew this wasn't an interrogation. Besides, he wasn't sure if he could handle everything at once.

"I probably would have stayed there with the family, however, almost seven years ago now, my uncle and father had a big fight over the business. My father had enough, and he wanted out. I was working in the offices for my uncle at the time, mostly accounting and moving money. I was twenty-two years old, and I knew what business they were in, and I sided with my father. If he wanted out, I would go with him."

At this point, Megan stood and moved to the front door. She stared outside, lost in her memories. "I watched my uncle kill my father, and I was next."

Noah could see her left hand twitching for the door handle, and it looked like she was ready to bolt. She turned around and leaned against the door. "So, I went into work the next day, and I transferred most of the money from several accounts into an offshore fund. I tried to disappear."

Noah already knew the answer, but he had to ask. "What about the police?"

She smiled slightly and shook her head. "They either work for him or the other families. I wouldn't have lasted three minutes."

Noah, once again, stared at the candle while he tried to process the information. The shock slowly faded away, and he wasn't sure of the feeling that replaced it. Anger? Fear? Too many emotions warred inside his head and heart—a battleground with no winners.

"My uncle kept sending people to find me. He never stopped. I went to the US marshals, and I testified for them in return for a new identity and life." At this point, Megan came over to the couch and knelt in front of him. When she held his hands, it felt good. His inner conflict rose to new heights. "The case was thrown out in court due to lack of proof. My word wasn't good enough to convict. I still wanted to start over, but they wouldn't stop. That's why Megan had to die, and if it weren't real enough, they wouldn't have bought it."

The information threatened to overwhelm him. "Why didn't you tell me? Why?"

Megan lowered her forehead until it rested in his hands. "I wanted to, and I came close dozens of times. I really wanted a fresh start and to escape my old life. If you had known, you would have been in too much danger, or worse. You would have joined me and thrown away your career."

As he took a deep breath, Megan looked up, and a warm glow filled his chest. Her green eyes sparkled with the candlelight, and he could tell the answer to his next question without asking. The love was real, but Noah wasn't sure that would be enough. There was still too much he didn't know.

Frowning slightly, Noah needed another piece of the puzzle. "Who was found in the house? How did you get out? Who was cremated and is now in my truck?"

He wiped away a few tears that rolled down her cheek.

"You know George at the County Coroner's office?"

Noah nodded. "I've met him a few times."

Taking a deep breath, Megan let it all out. "I explained everything to him and basically bought him out. Donny disappeared, and I got a Jane Doe and hid her in the basement the night before. I had to make it look real. Unless a body was found, it wouldn't have worked."

"Jesus …"

Noah wasn't sure what to say next. He was at a loss for the depth of the cover-up and her abilities. She wasn't just a grade schoolteacher.

"What do you want me to call you? Where was the name Parisotto from?"

"I like Megan." She smiled. "I'm used to it now, and it would feel strange if you were to call me anything else. Parisotto is my mother's maiden name. I wanted to distance myself from the family."

"And the warnings?"

At hearing this, fresh tears flowed down her cheeks. "I didn't want anything to happen to you. I wanted to keep you away so that you wouldn't get hurt or worse."

"Where did you learn to shoot then? I thought you hated guns?"

"I had my first rifle when I was eight."

"Okay." Noah couldn't sit any longer and got up to pace while Megan sat on the couch. At the woodstove, he threw another log on the fire. "What's next."

"I know my uncle. He won't stop until everything is wrapped up nice and neat. You are a loose end he can't afford. He will have people coming after you."

"That's already happened." Noah quickly filled her in on what happened with Anderson and his trip to Chicago.

As Noah finished, her jaw dropped in shock. "He has killed plenty of people or caused them to disappear permanently, for much less. You have no idea what's going to happen next. You and Stewart are definitely in his sights."

Noah made a decision. He didn't question it because deep down inside, it felt right. "I won't let him hurt you or my friends. What do you need me to do?"

Megan threw herself into his arms and squeezed him tight. They stayed up late into the night, talking and holding each other. Noah knew he should have turned her into the feds, but he made his choices.

The war inside his heart won out against logic and reason. There was no going back now.

Chapter 45

Noah crept down the stairs of the cabin without disturbing Megan. They had talked to the early morning hours before he went upstairs and made the double bed where they spent the night. Although Noah wasn't sure he slept much, he held Megan while he ran through everything in his mind, over and over again.

He crossed the line when he didn't call in Anderson. That was enough to face disciplinary actions at work and place his job in jeopardy. Bennett would have been justified and cleared of any charges. However, flying to Chicago opened a whole can of worms he couldn't contain. Ten to twelve years in jail, if he was lucky.

He slipped a protein bar into his jacket and picked up his hiking boots. Noah got dressed outside on the porch so Megan could sleep. Despite having gone through an emotional rollercoaster in the last week and the revelations from last night, Noah was in a good mood. He wasn't sure what direction his life was currently going, and the woman he loved was officially declared dead. A mafia family was out to get him, and he had problems with the FBI. Besides all that, things were great.

How could it get worse?

Noah couldn't help but chuckle as he drove back up the winding driveway and secured the gate behind him once again. Megan mentioned only two people, three including Noah, knew about the property. Her lawyer made all the arrangements with the seller over five years ago to keep Megan distant. The annual property taxes to the county were paid through her as well. Megan considered the cabin a fallback location—her haven.

When he turned south on the interstate toward Casper, the traffic was light. He made good time and would be in Arrow Point within an hour. As he picked up his cell phone to check for messages, Noah caught himself at the last second. He didn't want to turn it on and possibly alert anyone of his location. He wasn't sure the depth of involvement from the feds yet, or what abilities the Luciano family had available. Megan, (he couldn't think of her as Rachel) had cautioned against using cell phones.

She hinted at her uncle's resources, and it bordered on being scary. Money opened many doors that should remain locked. When questioned, Megan didn't say exactly where she had gotten the explosives from, and he wasn't sure he wanted to know. Still, anyone who could set them on a short timer and crawl out of a basement window before they went off—was determined and not to be underestimated. Noah listened to her advice.

Noah didn't confirm to the FBI special agent that he had received a fair amount of training with the infantry for explosives. He wanted to stop that line of questioning before it started. He recalled at the grenade range, a team would pack the unexploded ordinance with C-4, and once they were at a safe distance, they would detonate. Noah worked with the engineers for two months, where he learned how to shape the charges and wire them for various situations. He would never forget the demonstration. A metal drum was placed on top of a small charge, and when it detonated, it had sent the barrel over fifty feet into the air. The number of explosives needed to demolish his house would have been close to eighteen pounds, he figured, if not more.

The sun had risen when he came to the Casper city limits, and Noah figured it was safe to turn on his cell phone. He wanted to confirm with the staff sergeant that he would be on this morning's roster. There were too many directions from which threats could come at him, and being at work seemed his best option. He wasn't one to hole up in the woods and let all this blow over.

He picked up on the first ring. "Staff Sergeant Hutchings."

"Steve, it's Noah. Just letting you know that I'll be coming in. I had left a message with the LT."

"Jesus, Noah, I tried to get a hold of you last night. Did you hear about Bennett?"

A cold knot settled in his gut. "What happened?"

"He ran a red light on forty-four, and he was T-boned by a Mac truck."

Fuck!

"Oh my God. Is Stewart …?"

"Yeah. Best we can figure, it was quick."

"I'll be at the station in forty minutes."

"Talk to you then."

Noah made it into the parking lot of the APPD in thirty minutes, and he backed his truck into the rear parking lot. He sat behind the wheel while his mind whirled around several thoughts. He had almost no recollection of driving the last half-hour, lost in his memories.

"You have no idea what's going to happen next. You and Stewart are definitely in his sights." He whispered what Megan had said to him last night.

He took a deep breath, turned off the truck, and walked into work. His only remaining uniform hung in his locker, and it didn't take long to get dressed. Immediately, he felt better to be back in uniform and ready for work. As Noah passed Bennett's locker, he found that it already stood open and cleaned out. A single cross hung on a chain with Saint Michael, the (unofficial) patron saint of most police officers, over the opening. The silver Archangel stood with a sword in one hand and a set of scales in another. Whether you believed it or not, the traditions held firm.

The chief would have called and talked to Bennett's parents to inform them. Stewart didn't have any children, and he was single. There used to be a girlfriend, but they parted ways last spring.

As Noah walked upstairs to the cube, he could sense a pall over the station. When one of their own was injured or died, they all felt it and reacted accordingly. Once they saw Noah, they came over in small groups to ensure he was okay. Everyone knew that they had been working together for the last four months. Surprisingly, FBI Agent Gardiner came over once everyone else had cleared the area to shake his hand.

"I'm so sorry, Hunter. I just found out this morning. My condolences from my team and myself."

Reservations aside, Noah could see genuine sorrow in the agent's eyes. Shaking his hand firmly, he nodded. "Thank you. It's appreciated."

"If I can do anything, let me know. I just talked to Constable Bennett yesterday morning. A fine young man and officer."

Noah noticed Piekenbrock as he observed the exchange from the captain's office. The LT waited for him. "Will do. Thank you."

As the agent walked away, Noah changed his mind. "There is one thing you could do. Do you mind if I read up on the investigations?"

At this, the agent paused. He appeared to be thinking of several different things to say at once. What surprised him more was when Gardiner stepped forward and whispered near his ear. "Do you think that Bennett and these cases may be related?"

"I know you have a job to do, and I know why you ask certain questions. I have been there myself. Regardless, if I like or disagree with it." Noah took a deep breath before he continued. "There are no such things as coincidences. His death may be retaliation or related."

Agent Gardiner stood a few inches taller than Noah, and he leaned down as they locked gazes. Noah stared back and didn't blink as he grew uncomfortable. Five long seconds later, the agent blinked and nodded. "Agreed. Come with me."

At the captain's office, the LT looked surprised to see both of them there, shoulder to shoulder. "Lieutenant, we are at a critical point in the investigation. I think an officer from Arrow Point would greatly benefit us and act as a liaison between our task force and the precinct. Do you think Sergeant Hunter could be released from his duties to act as such?"

The LT looked at the two men before him and slowly nodded at the turn of events. "I can. I'll send him over to you when we're done. Thank you, Special Agent."

Gardiner walked back into the conference room as Noah closed the door to the office. Piekenbrock turned to him with a puzzled look on his face. "Are you sure about this?"

"Yeah. Some things aren't adding up."

Zane put his hand on Noah's shoulder. "You've gone through a lot this last week."

"I'm sure. I need to do this."

"Okay." The LT went to the captain's desk and picked up a large envelope and an evidence box. "These are yours. The knife has been sent for further testing by the feds."

In the box was the M1911 Colt, held down with the white plastic zip-ties, and the envelope contained the cash he found in the storage locker. Noah handed the envelope back. "Can you make sure this gets to Bennett's parents? Add it to the collection."

When an officer or member of the force had passed away or had a bad accident, the station rallied. A collection fund to help with medical bills or funeral costs was raised. Anything was appreciated.

"I'll make sure they get it."

Before he left, Noah thought of another mundane item. "Can you see about authorizing supply for a few uniforms for me? Despite working with them, I'm not ready to wear a suit. No offense."

Noah grinned at Piekenbrock. The LT wore a new gray suit and a light pink tie.

The officer waved him out of the office. "You may be closer than you think to wearing a suit to work. Go, I have a lot to do."

With a wry smile, Noah tucked the box under his arm to stash in his locker and headed downstairs. The smile quickly dropped from his face.

It was game time now.

Through the conference room windows, Noah could see all the suits as they worked on the case. He knew he didn't have much room for error with all the eyes watching him.

He had to be careful, or he would join Bennett all too soon.

Chapter 46

William Ryan slid into the back of the Cadillac as the driver gently closed the door. With the phone to one ear and one hand rifling through a briefcase, he barely gave him any attention, let alone thank him.

The Friday morning flight from O'Hare to Ronald Regan Airport in Washington D.C. was direct and lasted two hours. Landing at eight o'clock in the morning showed it was one of the busiest times for the airport, with everyone flying out of Washington for the weekend.

Ryan was on the phone or his laptop for almost the entire flight as he made specific arrangements. The driver got behind the wheel, quickly navigating out of the busy airport, and merged on the I-95 south.

Once in a while, the lawyer would hang up on a call and stare out the driver's side window at the rising sun. Forty minutes later, they pulled off the interstate, and William stored his phone and laptop away in his briefcase.

"Take the road on the next left."

The driver nodded and followed the direction. They took the split off the interstate and merged onto Fuller Heights Road.

Many stores lined the north and south sides of the street. A few were opened for business at the early hour. When they drove past Mary's Flower Shop, William leaned forward and pointed to the store on his right.

"Pull in here for a second. I'm just running in."

As the Cadillac turned into the 7-Eleven parking lot next to a delivery truck, Will reached into his briefcase and removed a dark blue baseball hat. He pulled it low with the brim down.

Once parked, the driver moved to get out and open the door for him, but Ryan just told him to stay in the car. Three minutes later, he got into the back with a small bag of items. "Okay, do you know where we're going next?"

"Yes, sir."

"Let's go."

William placed the ball cap back into his briefcase and used his hand to brush his thinning hair back into position. The paper bag rested at his feet.

Ten minutes later, they pulled into the busy parking lot of the Medal of Honor golf course. Dozens of golfers warmed up on the practice tee, driving golf balls out into a field. Many waited on the putting green for their turn to be called to the first tee-off position. Despite the cooler September weather, the golf course was still quite busy.

"Over there." William leaned forward and pointed to the far parking spot. "Back in. Pop the trunk. I won't be long."

The driver remained silent and followed the instructions. Once he stood outside, William brushed his suit straight and leaned against the rear bumper to wait with arms crossed.

An older couple drove by, and the woman told her husband to slow while adding the scorecard. Neither of the golfers paid him any attention. Ryan stood for almost two minutes as his right foot tapped with impatience. When an older man with creased tan pants and a white golf shirt pulled up in an electric cart, his foot stopped. The man's face resembled old leather from the sun and age, but his blue eyes still saw everything. Without a word, William was handed a small green duffel bag. After a quick nod to each other, the golfer pulled away and circled back to the clubhouse.

Without checking the contents, William threw the case in the trunk and closed the lid. Once in the back seat, he glanced at his Rolex and smiled. "Okay. Ready."

The parking lot for the crime laboratory at Quantico was easily the size of three football fields next to the Marine Corps base. The lab was considered one of the best in the United States and handled forensic analyst support for the bureau and other law enforcement agencies across the country.

The driver navigated his way through the packed parking lot to the far east side. The last row faced east and had a view of the Potomac River. Several boats headed north, and one lone man stood on a paddleboard across the far shore. His bright yellow jacket stood out against the brown haze and blue water as he slowly followed the tree line.

The driver pulled into the farthest spot and shut off the engine. William once again looked at his watch, then settled in to wait. Fifteen minutes later, at nine o'clock sharp, a light brown GMC SUV pulled into the parking space beside them. The driver was in his mid-thirties and wore a black T-shirt and jeans, his face was deeply tanned, and his short dark hair was combed to the side with gel. It gave him a slicked look that was five decades out of date. Several ID badges hung around his neck on a red lanyard. A lit cigarette dangled from his lips.

William stepped out of the vehicle and retrieved the bag from the trunk. The driver already had his window down. Ryan noted that his man had a visible tremor in his hand. The lawyer exchanged the brown paper bag for the green duffel bag with a grin. The technician's nerves were not his problem.

"That's it for me. I'm done." He had a thick southern accent, and his eyes nervously darted around.

William winked. "I don't think so, Mark. We have an arrangement."

The man's eyes opened wide, and a length of ash fell on his chest. "That arrangement is now done. There's too much risk."

"Is it?" William pointed to the front of the Cadillac. His driver had a cell phone pressed against the glass. The transaction was recorded from five feet away. "I don't think so. Pleasure doing business with you. I'll be in touch if needed."

William ignored the look of disbelief on his face and got into the vehicle's backseat. Such meetings proved the value of his worth. It also amused him to no end how stupid most people were.

"Somewhere out of the way."

The driver nodded, drove out of the Quantico parking lot, and headed west along Fuller Road. After they passed the same golf course, the Cadillac turned into a quiet subdivision and pulled over next to a small playground. It was empty at this time of day, and there wasn't anyone playing or out for a walk.

William stepped out of the rear passenger door and opened the plastic bag from the convenience store. He knelt beside the vehicle and pulled out the white bottle and a pair of blue gardening gloves. He upended the paper bag, and a survival knife fell onto the grass. A white tag, held on with a thin wire, flapped in the morning breeze.

With a sharp motion, the tag was torn off and tucked into a pocket. It would end up in a garbage can at the airport. Once the knife was placed into the plastic bag, Will opened the bleach bottle and liberally poured it inside. He let it soak for a minute before walking over to a sewer grate. The liquid and knife were tossed down the drain. He shook out the bag and threw the gloves inside before getting into the vehicle.

"Back to the airport, sir?"

"Yes."

William pulled out his cell phone and sent off a quick text message before settling into the seat. He was good at cleaning up other people's messes.

He thought about the next items on his agenda and wasn't worried. What he had planned would be much easier than getting rid of evidence.

Chapter 47

Noah compared his hand-written notes to the FBI reports, and he couldn't help but be amazed at the level of detail. There wasn't one test or search they had missed on the bodies, but nothing had produced a lead. Apparently, Megan had listened to him throughout the years or learned a lot from watching television. There was no evidence found at the crime scenes. No hairs, fibers, blood, or prints—and it left the profilers in the dark. They had fallen back on the usual standard, white male between thirty-five to fifty years old, with possible military training, for a suspect.

Now that he had the inside information, there was one aspect of the case Noah could not tie in. The relationship from the Luciano family to the homeless man in the northern part of town.

Did Pete see something he shouldn't have?

Did they murder him as a warning?

A knock on the door jarred him from his thoughts as Special Agent Gardiner came into the room. "All caught up?"

Noah tapped his notes. "I've read through the files, but I have some questions. A few things don't add up."

"We will brainstorm later, but first, did you want to come out with me and meet the team? They are at the hotel, and then we'll be going to the location just north of there, where the other body was found."

"Sounds good." Noah grabbed his ball cap and joined him as they went down to the rear parking lot. Gardiner opened a Chevy Tahoe and got in behind the wheel while Noah sat in the passenger seat.

As they headed to I-26 and east to Casper, the agent asked Noah, "What questions do you have? I might be able to answer them."

Noah pulled out his notepad and found where he left off. "What organized crime family opposes the Luciano's?"

Gardiner tapped the wheel with his thumb while he drove. "There isn't anyone specific. In the end, they all oppose each other. There are agents in Chicago right now trying to find that out. So far, there's no luck."

"Do you know what drew them to Arrow Point?"

He paused and gave Noah a side look, but he gave a slight nod. "We have an idea."

Noah stared down at his notes. What he was going to say wasn't written down, but he had to ask. "I'm guessing it has to do with the US marshals and Rachel Parisotto?"

The nervous tapping on the steering wheel stopped, and it looked like Gardiner deflated. His shoulders slumped, and he rested his head back on the backrest. "That's our number one theory."

Noah stared out the window, unable to look at the agent. Silence was always a good option.

An awkwardness built between them, and he decided to throw a red herring into the mix. "If it's any consolation, finding out everything you knew about someone was false, and a cover story … changes things. I'm sorry she died, but I have a job to do."

He wasn't sure whether the agent bought it or not, but he wanted to plant the seeds.

They drove in silence, and eventually, they came to the Motel 8, just north of Casper. There was only one vehicle in the parking lot, another black Chevy Tahoe, and Gardiner pulled in beside it.

Crime tape fluttered in a light breeze around the doorframe on room four. The seal above the lock was broken, and the door wide open. A large man walked out of the room in the FBI standard suit and tie. He appeared to be in his mid-forties and physically fit.

"Bert, this is Sergeant Noah Hunter. He will be working with us on the case. Noah, this is Special Agent Bert Campbell."

The men shook hands, then Campbell turned to Gardiner. "I dropped the others off at the site just north of here. They're going through the scene once again."

Noah walked up to the room and looked inside. Two beds faced a dresser with a flat-screen television, and each bed had a nightstand and lamp. A small round table and two chairs were near the window and air conditioner unit. The mirrored closet door was removed and placed against the wall. The black powder used for lifting prints covered almost every surface, even the standard art pieces that decorated the walls. Noah thought back to the motel and an old case. He had been here before, and not much had changed in the past eighteen years.

Only one bed looked slept in. Otherwise, the room looked like housekeeping had just left.

Bert stood near his shoulder and pointed around the room. "We've gone over every square inch of the room. Absolutely nothing. We did find some hair follicles in the second bed that matched the body we found just north of here, but nothing else."

Noah stepped outside and looked around the empty parking lot. "Did you check the other rooms?"

"The manager only had this room occupied for the night in question. There wasn't any need to check the others—no sign of forced entry."

Noah turned to Gardiner. "Where was the body found?"

The agent pointed. "Three miles almost due north, one hundred yards into the woods."

"And his car was here with the body in the back?"

Campbell walked out to the first parking spot in front of room four. "Right here. All four tires were slashed. We are not sure if it was related or not. We assume so, not many kids out in this neck of the woods."

Noah nodded. "I'm guessing he was dumped in the trees then. If not, he walked and was killed there."

The two agents glanced at one another before Gardiner spoke. "We're not sure. There's no evidence for either."

Noah looked around, then shrugged. "I guess I'll walk the route and join you at the other site. It's only three miles. Hopefully, I'll see something."

He could tell the agents didn't relish the idea of a hike through the woods in their suits and dress shoes. "Okay, we'll meet up with you there in an hour. That should give you enough time."

Gardiner pulled out a business card and wrote down a few cell phone numbers on the back before handing it over. "Any problems, give us a call."

Noah pocketed the card with a quick look at the time and made his way past the office and vending machines. The neon signs on the street said they were open, but a piece of paper taped on the door said they were temporarily closed.

Having two guests turn up dead must be bad for business.

Once he passed the ice machine, Noah stepped off the covered porchway, crossed the grass, and entered the woods. A small path led from the motel's front, but it quickly disappeared thirty feet into the trees. The woods were mainly cedar with the occasional birch and cluster of pine. Noah felt comfortable walking through the area, and at the most, he would spook a deer or an elk. They were a common occurrence in this part of the county. The dark blue uniform blended into the shadows, despite the yellow stripe down the pant legs.

Layers of dead leaves and soil had turned the forest floor into a soft mulch, and his footsteps were silent. However, the dry branches that broke off on his vest sounded like gunshots. A bull in a China shop was quieter than a police sergeant in the woods. There wasn't a path as much as a faint rabbit trail, but unless he was four feet tall, it wasn't going to work. One forearm guarded his face as Noah smashed his way through to a small clearing and pulled a broken-off cedar branch from his vest. This area was almost impossible to navigate without causing damage.

If someone had already come through here, there would be a trail.

They would have been in a hurry, and there would be signs. The FBI should have searched between the motel and the body many times by now. However, there was no sign of anyone else being in the area that he could see.

To find another trail, he turned perpendicular to the edge of the wood line and made his way east through the woods. Thirty feet deeper into the woods, he found it.

"Gotcha."

Noah couldn't help but grin at the series of broken branches and heel scuff marks on the soft ground. He quickly followed the signs despite not being an accomplished tracker as it led around large bushes and trees. He lost the path at one point, but he chuckled after he spotted a silver and gold chocolate bar wrapper. Noah thought he saw that same chocolate bar for sale in the vending machine by the motel office. The FBI should have processed the trail. He marked the position with several sticks so the feds could spot it—it should be dusted for prints.

After forty minutes of walking generally north, Noah found a large beech tree knocked over by the wind. It was still attached to the stump three feet off the ground, and it formed a natural shelter. A beam of sunlight came through the canopy and sparkled off an object underneath.

Two more chocolate bar wrappers and an empty water bottle lay on the ground. When he knelt and turned the wrappers over with a stick, Noah nodded. They were the same as the one he saw earlier.

Ernie Hale had left the hotel and traveled through here. There was no sign of blood, but he did see a sizably disturbed area in the dirt. Hale had slept here for at least one night.

Noah was about to stand when a dry branch snapped twenty yards ahead. It was followed by the unmistakable sound of a stick as it scrapped across nylon.

A deer would have known Noah was here and avoided the area.

It wasn't wildlife.

A beast that walked on two legs approached.

Thoughts of Bennett ran through his mind as he gripped his Glock. White knuckled on the polymer, he glanced through the woods. It only confirmed there was nowhere to hide except the knock-down tree.

He would prove a more challenging target to take down.

Silently, Noah drew his pistol, crouched, and waited.

Chapter 48

Noah's face pressed into the bark of the fallen tree, and he gently tugged on the Glock's slide with his left hand. He confirmed a round was chambered while he waited. While his heart raced, he kept breathing slow and steady. Whoever moved through the woods did it in stages. They would walk for a minute, then pause for thirty seconds before moving again. He couldn't see through the tree trunk and get a glimpse, but that worked both ways.

They couldn't see him either.

If someone legitimate looked for him, they would have called to let him know they were heading this way. Everyone had his phone number. Even a quick shout would have worked.

Finally, over his left shoulder, a flash of dark blue was revealed as the person crossed twenty-five feet out and disappeared behind a large spruce. More branches scraped across their nylon jacket, and slowly the figure receded.

Noah waited a full five minutes before he crept out from the hiding spot. He couldn't make out any details, but he thought it was a woman. Noah slid the pistol back into the holster and went in the opposite direction as the noise got farther away. It was easy to get turned around in the woods, and he pulled out his cell phone to check his position on the map. Once orientated to the ground, he headed north. Being careful of where he walked slowed him down, but more importantly, he moved without making any noise so he could hear if anyone tried to approach.

Fifteen minutes later, Noah heard the hushed tones as men talked ahead. When he eventually made it into a clearing, Gardiner stood shoulder to shoulder with Campbell and another man as they looked at a cell phone. They all wore a dark blue windbreaker with the FBI written across the back in white lettering.

The third man looked like a professional athlete, tall, and his broad shoulders gave him a tapered look. He had a short dark goatee and a military crew cut. A similar look that Noah wore.

As Noah approached across the clearing, the third man waved him over.

Gardiner turned and saw him. "See anything?"

Noah nodded. "Followed the trail from the motel and a place where he may have rested or spent the night. Not too sure of the timeline."

Agent Campbell turned to the other man beside him. "This is Special Agent George Clay. Sergeant Noah Hunter."

Noah had his hand crushed as they shook.

Agent Gardiner asked, "Did you see Special Agent Wu on your way back?"

Noah shook his head. "No, although I heard someone walking at one point, I couldn't be sure. It gets pretty thick in there at certain spots."

"Okay, I'll give her a call. Make sure she didn't get lost."

As Gardiner walked away, phone to his ear, Noah turned to Campbell. "Could you show me where the other body was found?"

"No problem. Over here."

The three men led him to an area that was almost the same. Tall grass covered the small field with a few smaller bushes randomly growing. "Right here. He had a bag with him as well, but there wasn't anything exciting in it."

Noah pointed roughly west. "The interstate is that way?"

They were far enough in the trees that he couldn't hear any traffic noise, just birds. A light breeze made the top of the trees sway back and forth.

"Yes, not too far. A four-minute walk."

"The only things I found were a few chocolate bar wrappers and an empty water bottle."

Special Agent Clay opened his phone and scrolled through a few reports. "The contents of the bag contained two chocolate bars."

The three men looked around, and Campbell spoke up. "The question is, who did he meet up with here?"

Noah looked over to see Gardiner walking over to them. "Agent Wu said she must have missed you. She is going on to the motel. We will pick her up there, then head back to Arrow Point."

They turned and headed west toward the interstate, where two Chevy Tahoes were parked beside the sign. Noah rode with Campbell, and Gardiner got in the other vehicle with Clay.

Once the traffic was clear, they waited until the other vehicle pulled a U-turn, and they quickly followed.

George Clay looked over at Noah. "How long have you been with the police department?"

"Eighteen years now. Yourself? How long with the bureau?"

George rubbed his goatee. "Twenty-two years this November. The time is flying by, that's for sure."

They followed Gardiner's vehicle into the Motel 8 parking lot. A slim woman in an FBI windbreaker climbed into the first Tahoe behind the driver. She had a serious look about her, and a permanent frown was etched on her face. Her long dark hair was tied back into a ponytail, giving her an even more stern look.

"Everything okay?"

George nodded. "Most likely. If not, we would have heard about it by now."

Soon they were headed back to Arrow Point. They drove in silence as Noah looked out the passenger window. He couldn't help but go over the options in his mind.

An hour later, Noah sat at the conference table and looked over his notes from today. The other agents went across the street to pick up some coffee while Special Agent Gardiner opened his laptop and sat next to Noah.

"Can you show me the trail you followed from the motel?" The satellite photo of the area was on the screen. It showed the motel and the surrounding forest in great detail, although the trail wasn't on the map.

"No problem."

Noah pulled out his pen and traced the approximate path he had followed. "It was about here where he spent the night or possibly went to ground. It was under a leaning tree."

He circled the area on the screen, and a thin red line appeared around the site. It included the path from the motel.

Gardiner drew an X on the screen where the body was found. "So, from his hiding spot to where the body was found, he had to have come this way."

Noah agreed. "That seems correct."

Gardiner saved the image and sent it off in an email. "Do you have any idea who he would have met up with?"

Noah pulled out his notes. "I doubt he would have had a pre-arranged meeting. So, he called someone for help and gave them his location." He found the page from the other day. "You had mentioned that Jim Anderson was a fixer. Would he have called him for help since he was in the area?"

Gardiner muffled a yawn. "That makes as much sense as anything else. I'm going to grab a coffee. Would you like one?"

"I'm good, thanks. Will hold the fort."

Agent Gardiner gave him the thumbs up before he stood and stretched. "Sorry, I had a late night. Okay, back in ten."

Noah was left alone in the conference room, and he leaned back in the chair and enjoyed the solitude.

What's my next move?

He wanted to spend more time with Megan, but that would be a problem. She would not be able to go out in public anywhere in Arrow Point or even Casper. Too many people knew her and knew that she had died.

His thoughts were interrupted by an incoming email on Gardiner's laptop. The volume was too loud, and the chime startled him. Noah noticed Gardiner had forgotten to shut the computer down.

What drew his attention sent a cold shiver of fear down his back. A burning rage quickly replaced it.

The new email message was from an A/SAG Harris, and Noah could see a fragment of the subject line: Arrest Authorized for Hunter, Noa …

With a look over his shoulder, Noah confirmed he was alone. With a click, Noah quickly opened the email.

The arrest warrant for Noah Hunter is authorized for the murder of Megan Brooks. I have attached an EW for the apartment in question.

A/SAG Harris.

The attachment showed an electronic warrant for Megan's apartment. Noah took a few deep breaths and slowly unclenched his fists.

Gardiner had been playing him. The gloves were off.

Chapter 49

Noah knew about balance, and he had seen it in action, one form or another, all his life. On his deployment to Iraq, then Afghanistan, balance was evident in every aspect. Soldiers walled off emotions and thoughts of home so they could get through a patrol—only to cry for hours when they got a letter from a loved one. Bonds were formed in days, and someone you had just met would be a best friend for life. Then next week, you helped carry a coffin because an IED took out your section commander.

As a police officer, Noah let the scales of justice guide his thoughts and actions. It wasn't his choice to implement the law or set the rules. That was for a DA or judge. Many didn't wake up with bad intentions that day. It happened by circumstance, negligence, or it built slowly by degree over time. However, those instances dictated actions, and it was his choice what the next move should be.

By all accounts, he should go to the captain or lieutenant and divulge all the information. It would save his hide legally, but the balance had shifted too much.

Some things required action outside the legal system. He was pushed to this, and instead of pushing back, he embraced it.

Noah held his finger ready and, without too much thought, pushed down on the delete key. Right-clicking on the other folder, he emptied the recycle bin for the email client. After he hit the snooze button, the laptop went into hibernate mode. The FBI agent would have to log in once again, and he wouldn't know of the intrusion. Noah's heart beat loud enough that he was surprised others couldn't hear it.

Seeing that the captain's office door was open, he left the conference room and crossed the cube. Captain Richardson sat behind his desk reading budget reports. He looked tired with dark circles under his eyes.

"Sir, may I have a quick moment of your time?"

When he saw Noah in the doorway, he smiled. "Not a problem, Sarge. How can I help you?"

"I wanted to get back to work early to take my mind off things, but I don't think I'm ready."

Richardson placed the paperwork down and nodded. "I understand. Do you have some vacation time saved up as well?"

Noah thought for a second. "A few weeks left, Captain."

"Take them, get yourself together. I will call HR and authorize the leave. I can't imagine this is easy."

Noah felt like laughing at that last statement. "You're correct, thank you. It's appreciated."

After saying their goodbyes, Noah headed downstairs to his locker and packed up his civilian clothes and any items that remained in his backpack. Without bothering to change, Noah left out the backdoor of the station. His truck was parked along the back row beside the two government Tahoes.

It was time to get out of there before Gardiner and the others came looking for him.

He turned on Main Street and headed east, then slammed a fist against the steering wheel in frustration. He thought he knew who was behind this, and he would have to be dealt with soon.

Before getting on the interstate, Noah took out his cell phone, pulled the battery, and threw everything into the glove box. Now that Gardiner had the green light to come after him, he did not doubt that he would attempt to track him by any means possible.

Even though most people knew him in Arrow Point, Noah didn't like to travel to and from work in uniform. However, he didn't want to stick around the station. Right now, time was of the essence.

The hour-long drive back to the cabin had one effect. It gave Noah time to calm down and think things through properly. He couldn't help but wonder how Anderson found him and if the feds had conducted an investigation …

Once he got on a particular train of thought, he couldn't shake it. He slammed on his brakes, put his hazard lights on, and pulled over onto the gravel shoulder.

He opened the truck's hood, grabbed his flashlight, and poked around. His knowledge of engines was basic, but he knew the old truck well enough. Anything out of place, he would spot it. Not seeing anything, he got down on the ground, searched from the front bumper, and methodically worked his way to the back. Once he was near the gas tank, he found it. A small black box with a flashing green LED light attached to the side of the tank. It was being held on with a light gray putty, and it took a bit of effort, but he removed it. Once he finished checking the truck's underside, Noah moved to the interior and started with the glove box. He checked every square inch. The rear seats in the cab tilted forward, and they had some storage room underneath. He kept a set of jumper cables and gloves inside. However, he also found a similar black box with the same blinking green light. This unit was smaller and resembled a deck of cards, with a long thin wire as an antenna.

He slipped both tracking devices into the cargo pockets of his pants.

Was there a warrant for my arrest? Did the feds plan this so I would run? Was it even the FBI tracking me, or is it someone else?

Questions ran through his mind, but he didn't have any answers. For now, he continued toward Casper. When he saw the rest area, Noah had an idea and pulled behind the gas station and fast-food restaurant. He parked between two transport trucks and waited. The first rig had a load of lumber tied down on a flatbed, and the second hauled a fifty-three-foot trailer. Both drivers were inside getting lunch, and he wasn't visible to the rest of the parking lot. The first black box Noah placed underneath the flatbed trailer, and the second box tucked up inside the fifth-wheel coupling on the second transport.

Hopefully, they would stay hidden long enough to throw any tracking efforts off and confuse them. If the vehicles traveled in different directions, all the better.

* * * * *

William Ryan hung up the phone while taking another sip of his coffee. His home office could have made any interior design magazine's front cover. A seventh-century mahogany desk sat to one end of a large room with a hand-woven red Moroccan area rug underneath. Floor-to-ceiling bookcases covered two walls, and a ladder was used to reach the upper levels. Two leather chairs were positioned in front of the fireplace with a silver bar cart between them. Many issues were resolved in this room, and if the walls could talk, incarceration would be the lightest repercussion.

He had just hung up after receiving a report from a credible source. For the amount of money being thrown at him, he better be credible. The information from last night was confirmed, leading to further actions. Ryan didn't lose any sleep because he knew how to cover his bases.

Standing up behind his desk, the lawyer brought his mug with him as he looked out the large window.

"Mr. Ryan? Mr. Quinn is here to see you."

Turning around, he saw his housekeeper standing in the doorway. "Bring him in."

Brushing back his thinning hair with one hand, Ryan turned around in time to see Mark Quinn being escorted into the office.

Mark stood just over six-foot-four, and the short haircut and dark suit gave him the bearing of a military man in his prime. At thirty-eight years old, the retired army major had managed Starr Securities for the last six years and provided everything from personal protection to corporate security systems. Quinn primarily hires former military personnel, and he had recently contracted out to the government or top executives for armed security and protection officers for Kuwait and Costa Rica. With next year's projections, he planned to expand and offer services in several more hot-spot countries worldwide. With a salary potential upwards of seven-hundred dollars a day doing much the same thing as they did while in the military, there was no lack of applicants.

"Welcome, Mark. Nice to finally meet you in person. Thank you for coming on such short notice."

They shook hands. "I was in the area, not a problem."

"Come on in, sit down."

William led them over to the leather chairs by the fireplace. "Would you like a coffee or anything?"

"No thanks, just a second."

From an inner pocket, Quinn pulled out a small black box. It had a stainless-steel band around the outside edge and easily fit in the palm of his hand. Once he pressed the indented button on top, an internal click sounded throughout the office. He rested the small box on the arm of the chair and leaned back. "I'm not much for being recorded. This ensures my privacy."

William glanced at the device and nodded. "Understood. I'm the same way."

"How can I help you this time?"

The pleasantry left William's face, and he leaned forward, serious. "We have an unknown threat toward Mr. Luciano and possibly myself. I'm looking for around-the-clock protection for the next few weeks for two people."

Quinn stared at him for a moment and made a decision. "One-hundred thousand per week, full protection for two people at different locations."

William cringed and tried not to let it show. His boss would spend the money, but they were in too deep. The potential for everything to blow up was real, and there wasn't a chance they would give it up. He did know that the people who already worked for them were not even close to the caliber that Quinn could provide. Ryan had used Starr Securities a few years ago when a cartel tried to make good on threats, and the danger was imminent.

"Prices have gone up."

At this, Quinn nodded. "True, but we deliver."

Reaching over, William shook his hand. "Done. When can you start?"

Chapter 50

With the gate locked behind him, Noah continued along the twisting dirt road to the cabin. He had no idea where the tracking devices were destined, but he needed time. If one of the rigs ended up in Canada, all the better. If the trackers were legally placed or not, it pissed him off.

The blue Nissan remained on the north side of the cabin out of sight, and a trickle of wood smoke rose from the stovepipe into the late afternoon sky. As he parked, Megan waited for him, dressed in jeans and a T-shirt. Noah didn't have to ask. He knew she was worried.

With his backpack over one shoulder, Noah gave her a quick kiss. "I'm now on vacation for three weeks."

"Is everything okay?"

"Yes and no."

When he entered the cabin, he noticed the difference right away. It smelled clean, and everything was dusted. The woodstove had a small fire that took the dampness out of the air and filled the room with warmth. He smiled when he saw the plastic plant on the table. Megan had written a note that leaned against the plastic pot.

Do not water.

"I started at the hotel and did a sweep of the woods with the FBI …" Noah quickly filled her in on everything that happened this morning, including the trackers he found in his truck. He hung his uniform on the coat hooks inside the front door and changed.

Worried, Megan got up and gave him a brief hug before she paced the small cabin. "It has to be my uncle. I know he has owned politicians and certainly police officers in Chicago, which was several years ago. I'm sure his reach has extended."

"Do you think he has connections within the FBI?"

She shrugged. "It's possible, or someone in the government high enough to influence them."

Once dressed in jeans and a green golf shirt, Noah slid the holster for his pistol back onto his right hip. He dug around inside the suitcase and pulled out the burner cell. "This is the phone William Ryan called me on. They have this number."

Megan sat on the couch and gestured for Noah to join her. She held his hand and rested the other on his chest. "I had to die for them to leave me out of their life. Are you willing to do the same?"

Noah paused, his mouth open. "I—"

Life on the run while he hid his identity. Not able to see his mother or brother again? Decisions made earlier were now in doubt. Noah shook his head. "I don't think I can. I'm not much for running away or hiding from a problem."

Megan's eyes began to water, and she nodded. "I know. I do have quite a bit of money. We could disappear forever."

Noah smiled. "I have a bag of money as well. However, that doesn't solve the problem. It just postpones it."

Megan wrapped her arms around him and held tight. "I know. Okay, come with me. I have something to show you."

Noah slipped on his hiking boots while Megan went into the kitchen. There was a floating shelf above the window that overlooked the rear of the cabin. On top were three decorative pottery vases, and Megan removed a key from the middle one.

Once out of the back door, they followed the pathway past the outhouse—the compacted trail led into the woods. Long grass and branches hung down, making their walk that much slower. The trail looked wide enough for an ATV originally, but now they were forced to walk single file.

"This is where I was hiding when you first showed up. I wasn't sure who it was until I saw your truck."

A clearing opened fifty yards into the woods, and a small building sat right in the middle. It was a ten by twelve barn shed with green corrugated sheets on the roof. A large blue duffel bag sat on the ground with a rifle across the top in front of the double doors.

"I found this place when I first got here. I changed the lock and added a few things. I haven't been inside in over five years."

Noah followed her to the door and examined the rifle. The Winchester 30-06 was a single bolt-action and a new Vortex scope. It was the same one she had used to scare him off at the national park. Megan unlocked the door and swung them wide. The hinges squealed in protest.

There was enough light to see several wooden crates stacked along the one wall across from a stainless-steel shelf unit. Stacked on two shelves were various metal containers of ammunition—everything from .22 to 50 caliber. Noah couldn't help but let out a whistle of appreciation. The shed rivaled the armory at the police station. Everything was covered in a layer of dust, and there were small tracks over the crates. A squirrel or mouse had tried to make this place home over the winters.

Megan lifted the hinged lid on the first crate and showed Noah the shotguns stowed inside. They were lined up six across on a wooden rack and coated in a preservative oil. "Shotguns here. Next crate has pistols."

The middle crate held AR-15s with empty magazines. "I wanted to be prepared for anything."

Looking at the green metal ammunition boxes, Noah felt it was enough to equip an infantry section and prep for war. "It looks like you are prepared, all right."

From the middle crate, Noah grabbed a Browning Hi-Power at random and engaged the slide. The shed and crates had kept the moisture out, leaving them rust-free. The excess oil would have to be removed before use, but the action was smooth.

"Impressive." Noah wasn't sure if he meant the collection or Megan. Quite possibly both. Once he placed the pistol back with the others, he made his decision. "I'm going to Chicago. I need to see this through. If your uncle thinks you are dead, I want to keep it that way."

"I wanted to keep you safe and disappear." Megan stared at their feet. A lone tear trickled down her cheek before it fell off her chin. "I'm going with you."

Noah held his breath. He knew that would be her answer. "I don't want to be all manly and tell you it's safer here because we know it isn't. You don't have to mention that you can take care of yourself. That's obvious. I would feel better if you stayed here, though."

Megan wiped her face and looked him in the eye. Noah knew that expression.

He had seen it many times. The look of a stubborn mule, and she was about to dig in her heels.

"If you are going, I am as well. End of story."

Noah knew it was coming, and he was right. Megan crossed her arms and tilted her chin slightly while she waited for his reply.

He decided in two seconds. "Let's do this together."

Megan's mood changed in the blink of an eye. Once again, her arms encircled him in a tight embrace. Over her shoulder, Noah looked at the weapons cache. With what he had in mind, he hoped that none of this would be used. However, one phrase he learned in the military leaped to mind.

Prepare for the worst, and you won't be disappointed.

Chapter 51

Noah and Megan spent the night by the woodstove as they drank a bottle of her favorite Merlot. Plans were made, discussed, then discarded as being too risky. Long hours passed as they decided on a course of action by candlelight. However, many times throughout the evening, they took breaks. Noah was glad there were no immediate neighbors to complain about the noise.

Early the next morning, Noah made several trips to load the truck with essentials. After Megan climbed in the front seat, he took a moment to grin at the cabin. No matter what happened, the place now held great memories for him.

They drove east, with the rising sun in their eyes, and only stopped to fill the tank. Now that Noah had a plan, he didn't want to waste time. Just after noon and five-hundred miles later, they pulled into Lincoln, Nebraska. It didn't take long for Noah to find a specific business that bordered on a residential and an industrial area.

The small garage sat on a busy street corner, with a large banner stretched over the bays advertising oil changes. The business sign on the post had faded so much that it was unreadable. Outside, twenty vehicles were for sale and parked at an angle to face the intersection. Next to the garage was a twenty-foot camper trailer with multi-colored flags stretched across the front and helium balloons on the railing. A blue neon sign was lit in the window and announced they were open.

"This should do it." Noah pulled over, and they both got out of the truck and stretched. He knew of similar used car lots in Wyoming. Noah was about to put his theory to the test as he strolled with Megan and viewed the selection of vehicles. It didn't take long for a man to walk out of the trailer and head over. He was tall and slim, with a worn jean jacket that matched his jeans. The large white cowboy hat suited him somehow.

"Hi there, y'all. Let me know what you're looking for, and I can help you. Name's Hank."

Noah wanted to roll his eyes, but he just smiled and pointed to the four-door Jeep Wrangler halfway down the line of cars. "We're interested in that."

"Good choice. Just came in, low miles, and it was hardly driven."

Megan turned away to study the car, and Noah could hear her mutter.

The Jeep was easily fifteen years old, and Noah was reasonably sure the green paint hid repaired body damage of some kind. The tires looked somewhat new, and the black soft-top didn't have any holes or rips.

Noah's truck was too well known, and that left few options. He didn't want to draw any further attention to himself, which led them to Hank.

"Does it run fine?" Noah walked over and looked at the spare tire mounted to the rear swing gate—it looked original.

"Our mechanics have gone over it. We guarantee there is nothing wrong with it."

Megan looked to make sure there weren't any apparent problems.

Noah turned to Hank. "If it runs good, we'll take it."

He grinned at the easy sale. "Come on into my office, and we can make arrangements to have it ready first thing Monday morning."

Noah noticed Hank's faint Texan accent had disappeared with the excitement. "I'm in a hurry and hope to finish this transaction right now. My Chevy as a trade-in as well."

The salesman looked at Noah's truck and winced. A few holes in the rear quarter panel could be repaired, and the passenger window would need to be replaced. Noah was sure that with a wash and coat of wax, the truck would be an easy sale for Hank.

"I'm not so sure …"

Noah gave up. "How about I give you the truck and cash for the difference. Just sign the ownership. I'll register it myself. Deal?"

Noah stuck his hand out and waited. Hank thought it over, then grinned as they shook. "Y'all have a deal."

~

Noah drove into a rural subdivision and pulled over to the side of the road, where he turned off the Jeep. Megan was fast asleep in the backseat, and after initially driving for eight hours, she found herself nodding off. Restless and glad to take over, Noah moved their bags and suitcase into the far back, and she found a place to curl up and was out in seconds.

It was four o'clock in the morning, and most lights were off in people's homes. At this hour on a Saturday morning, most folks were still in bed sleeping. Except for a brief stop for fuel, they had driven straight through to Chicago from Wyoming. If they didn't stop for the Jeep, Noah figured he could have done the drive in fifteen hours. A heavy foot and a badge as backup helped at times. Megan had insisted they pay cash, and Noah wore an old hooded sweatshirt pulled up to help disguise his features every time they stopped. Since he left Wyoming, he had removed his Glock and tucked it under the driver's seat. Being a police officer in Wyoming with open carry was one thing, but he didn't need to draw attention or cause a panic elsewhere. Illinois residents were required to have a permit if they concealed carried or in a vehicle.

Noah adjusted his watch an hour ahead to match the time zone difference before he gently shook Megan. "We're here."

Some people are groggy and sleepy when they woke up. Megan, however, was always able to sit up and be fully functional in the blink of an eye. She was instantly wide awake. A habit Noah hated and wished he had at the same time.

"How far away are we?" Megan brushed her short dark hair back and slipped on a dark blue baseball cap.

"West 95th Street, near the Dan Ryan Expressway."

Giving her head a little twist to crack her neck, Megan was surprised. "Sorry, I must have been tired."

"I filled up in Davenport, and you didn't even move. I was fine, so I let you sleep."

During the drive, Megan mentioned that the plan was simple. Find and kill Anthony Luciano, and the pressure would be off. There wouldn't be any retaliation from the family or organization. Her uncle didn't trust anyone else enough to run the day-to-day operations. No lieutenants would seek to rise to the kingpin position. Another organization would likely move in, but that was the way of things.

"You have no problems taking care of your uncle?"

Megan had shaken her head. "I watched him kill my father, his brother, in cold blood. He wanted to kill me as well. Whatever we had once is long gone. No regrets."

As he drove on through the night, those words echoed in his mind. The schoolteacher he fell in love with was still there, but there was a darker side to Megan he never knew about or believed possible. He knew that possibility was within himself, but he chose to ignore it and concentrate on doing the right thing. He tried to do the right thing. Noah saw the consequences, at times daily, and he knew it all came down to choices.

When this was over, decisions had to be made, but for now, he had a job to do.

Climbing up the middle, Megan sat down in the front seat. "Get on the expressway and head north."

At this hour, the traffic was light, and they made good time. Noah made one quick stop while Megan wrote down some information. After crossing the downtown core, Noah pulled over in front of a small office building and a restaurant.

Megan looked at him. Cold steel had settled in her eyes, and it disturbed him. "Are you sure?"

After a deep breath, Noah nodded. "I'm sure. Ready."

With a glance at Rosie's Café and Bistro's sign, Noah got out of the Jeep and grabbed the small backpack before they went for a walk.

Chapter 52

As usual, Anthony woke early and made his way down to the kitchen for a morning coffee, dressed in a robe over his pajamas with matching dark blue slippers. He pressed the button on the coffeemaker and got a mug ready. By habit, Anthony moved to the kitchen blinds.

"Sir, please do not open the windows."

For the last twenty-four hours, he did his best to ignore the presence of the bodyguards, but they never let up. Carl sat at the glass kitchen table with a large finger to mark his place in a paperback novel. Carl wore an open-collared blue dress shirt and navy pants. His jacket lay over the back of his chair. He also had a loaded Sig Sauer P226 on the table, ready to use. A Glock 19 as a backup rested in a shoulder harness.

Carl stood six-foot-three inches, and at forty years old, he appeared to be in prime physical shape. His bald head gleaned from the overhead light, and his eyes tracked Anthony with a feral intensity. An earpiece wire ran down the back of his shirt and plugged into a comms unit on his belt.

"Do you ever sleep?" Anthony poured a coffee before sitting at the table and opened his laptop. Carl ignored the question and reported. "The perimeter patrol has had no problems. Team two is stating all green."

Anthony had asked to be kept up to date with Ryan's security as well. For the amount of money this was costing, he wanted to be informed of all details.

After a sip of coffee, Anthony started his morning routine. Emails, news reports, and stock updates were essential before business. When the home phone rang, both men were startled.

Before it could ring a second time, Anthony picked up. "Calling at this hour, it better be good." After a moment's pause, he closed his eyes once he heard the news. "I'll be right there."

"Everything okay, Mr. Luciano?" Carl bent the page of his book and placed it off to the side.

A fury overcame the older man, and when he abruptly stood, the chair almost tipped. "I'll be leaving in five minutes, have the car ready."

Carl updated his partner over the radio and slipped on his jacket. Anthony barely retained a grip on his anger. The coffee mug was seconds away from turning into a projectile and smashing against the tiled floor, but he held back.

Someone was going to pay for this.

* * * * *

Noah and Megan sat outside a Starbucks and had a morning coffee and a few pastries on a green bistro set. Another fire truck drove east on Monroe Street and turned north on South LaSalle, sixteen feet from where they sat. That was the second truck within minutes. A few others from the coffee shop watched the drama as well, but an equal number also ignored it.

As Noah blew on his coffee, he watched the Chicago Police as they blocked off traffic and allowed the second ladder truck to join the first. Billows of smoke rose into the morning air as firefighters fought to contain the restaurant's fire before it spread. Only a narrow alley separated the nearby office tower, and the crews worked fast. A news truck had parked on a side street, and a reporter and cameraman sprinted to get as close as they could to the scene.

Megan nudged him with her elbow. "Over there."

A silver S-Class Mercedes sedan stopped on the road short of the blockade. A man got out of the back seat and just stood and watched. A large bald man scrambled out to join him and scanned the streets instead of the fire. The driver remained behind the wheel.

He has protection.

Anthony Luciano wore a dark suit with no tie, and he appeared to be aging as Noah watched. He leaned on the car for support while the other hand held his head in disbelief.

He could see the bulge in the jacket of the bald man as he regularly scanned the crowds and rooftops. Noah could see him talking to Anthony at the same time.

"That's him."

Noah nodded absently. He recognized the military bearing of the guard right away. The level of awareness was easy to spot. "He has some high-level security with him."

Megan pulled her baseball cap lower. "He's new. I'm sure that isn't his old driver."

"This may change a few things."

Megan turned to him. "Do you think they're with him all the time?"

"The bald man is armed, and he seems to be apprehensive because the person he is protecting is out in public. Too many directions for a threat to come at him."

She just nodded and shifted her attention to her uncle. The guard eventually coaxed him back into the vehicle, and the driver immediately did a U-turn and drove right past them. Luciano appeared dazed and stared straight ahead.

Megan reached out and held his hand. "Did you want me to do it? I'll be fine."

Noah pulled over her napkin and wrote on it with a black pen. "I'll be good. You're way too memorable. Every time I close my eyes, I keep seeing you."

Megan stuck out her tongue at him as he grinned.

Noah picked up the napkin, tucked it into his hoodie pocket, and walked down the street to the barricade—straight toward the nearest police officer.

Chapter 53

William Ryan sat in his home office, fielding calls non-stop since breakfast. The first was from Anthony. He could tell that the world was going to end for someone. He was cold and emotionless and spoke in clipped sentences before hanging up abruptly.

"Rosie's is on fire. Find out the details. I want it dealt with immediately."

Ryan's contacts in the fire department had nothing. They were unable to get inside the building yet for the fire marshal to conduct his investigation. Another phone call had a senior detective scramble out of bed and at the scene within ten minutes, and he waited on that report but wasn't hopeful. It was too early for an update. Investigations take time, something he didn't want nor cared to explain to Mr. Luciano.

After twenty minutes of not raising anyone on the phone, William knew he had to go over to Rosie's and try to get some answers directly.

A knock on his office door made him jump. His housekeeper stuck her head inside. "Mr. Ryan, there are two police officers at the front door."

"I'll be right there."

William slid into his suit jacket and headed to the foyer.

"Allow me to get the door, please."

Allen could have easily played on any basketball team if he could shoot. He had to duck under the door frame at six-foot-nine inches when he walked in from the kitchen. Allen already had his Sig Sauer P226 out, and a long finger stretched along the barrel. He wore a custom suit and shoes, his long stride crossed the foyer in two steps, and he turned to William.

"Stand back in the doorway and do not come out until I say so. Anything happens, run to the back door, and my partner will begin extraction procedures. Understood?"

William nodded and stepped back into the doorway to the office. Allen activated his comms set for his partner. "Bravo two, opening the front door."

Allen held his pistol along his right leg and opened the door an inch until the two Chicago police officers were visible. "Identification and badges, please."

At first, the officers could not see who opened the door until they looked up. Allen's dark skin and eyes almost made him invisible as he peered at them from above the door.

Both officers were stunned, but they opened their wallets, showing their credentials. "We would like to speak to William Ryan."

"One moment, please." Allen closed the door and turned to his employer. "Would you like to talk with them?"

Hopefully, this had to do with the phone calls this morning. However, William's contacts never reported back in person. It was a security breach he would have to address. "I will. I think they have information for me."

Allen nodded and moved to the door. Sliding his pistol into a holster, he covered it up with his suit jacket and opened the door.

"Mr. Ryan will talk with you. Please remain outside."

The younger officer looked up at the giant in front of him and took a slight step back. The older cop merely nodded.

William stepped forward and asked. "How can I help Chicago's finest this morning?"

The first officer pulled out his notebook. "William Ryan?"

"Yes."

"Are you the owner of a silver BMW, license plate NTGUILTY?"

Soon as he spelled the letters on his plate, Ryan knew these cops were not here to give him any information. "Yes. That vehicle is mine."

"Can you tell me your whereabouts this morning at six o'clock?"

A sinking sensation started in his stomach and then spread. William needed to end this encounter before it got out of control. "I was here at home. Anything else?"

"We do have a few questions for you."

William pulled out his business card from his wallet. "Any further questions, please contact my law office, and I may or may not answer them. Have a good day."

His Irish accent was fairly pronounced as he handed over the card to the startled officer. William closed the front door with a slam and twisted the deadbolt.

The lawyer looked up at Allen and shrugged. Without a word, he quickly stepped back to his office.

Ryan needed answers, now more than ever, before the world started to crumble.

* * * * *

Noah grinned as he watched the police cruiser pull out of the crescent-shaped driveway. "He's going to be pissed."

Megan chuckled. "To be honest, I really don't care."

Noah used the nearest driveway to turn about before they headed back to downtown Chicago. He couldn't help but compare it to his old military briefings. It was time for the next phase of the operation.

Earlier in the morning, they needed a critical piece of information for the plan to work. Noah had followed this same route before heading to the restaurant and parking near the restaurant.

Noah told the officer that he had seen a vehicle fleeing the scene before the fire had started. He had easily remembered the BMW's license plate and wrote it on a napkin. Gladly, Noah handed it over. When pressed for a name and identification, Noah had said he wanted to remain anonymous and didn't want to be involved. He had received countless statements from witnesses and the public in general with those same words. An officer usually created a name to go along with the recorded information, UNSUB (unknown subject).

Noah pulled his backpack forward and handed it to Megan. "Help yourself. I can go with you if you like?"

"I'm good." Megan chose a stack of bills at random and tucked them in her jeans. Once they pulled into the mall parking lot, she kissed his cheek and jumped out at the main entrance. "I'll be right back. I'll meet you at the last row, and then I need to go to another store and pick out some more clothes."

"I'll be here."

Noah watched her walk away, and his heart twisted in a knot. He leaned forward, rested his head against the steering wheel, and closed his eyes. Despite Megan saying she would be okay with the confrontation with her uncle, he had his doubts.

Noah knew what he had planned would test that theory.

Chapter 54

Anthony hurled his dinner plate against the wall. Shards exploded throughout the kitchen with a sharp retort, and Carl rushed into the room with his gun drawn. His head swiveled on a pivot, scanning for targets. "Are you okay? What's wrong?"

Anthony leaned forward on the kitchen table. Both fists clenched and shook with rage. "Have William Ryan brought here. Immediately."

Carl walked out of the kitchen to the front door and made a call. Anthony leaned forward and closed his eyes while the flush receded. The last email from a police captain remained open on the laptop. He didn't need to read it for the third time. Twice was more than enough.

It took several moments and deep breaths before he could stand upright.

"You made your bed. Time to lay in it." His words sounded hollow, even to his ears.

With hasty steps, Anthony went to the bookshelf in his office and reverently pulled down a box. The walnut had been lacquered to a high-gloss finish, with an intricate design hand-carved on the front.

Ante nihil nisi familia.

Before my family comes nothing.

The box belonged to Anthony's father, who used it for a more morbid purpose. It used to hold the smallest finger of his enemies before Anthony repurposed it. A loaded M1911 Colt rested inside, cushioned on red velvet. It was a copy of the pistol his father gave him for his eighteenth birthday. It didn't have the same carved wooden grips as the original, but it would do. The weapon was old but still fully functional, much like himself. With one quick phone call, resources were activated as his army was mobilized. Anthony had spent decades building his empire, and it was time to use them.

Once he was done, he tucked the pistol into his waistband and sat behind his desk. Angry fingers drummed a beat on the desk while he waited.

*　*　*　*　*

Ten minutes later, Noah opened the packaging, and pulled the little plastic tab to activate the burner phone while Megan did the same. The first thing they did was program each other's numbers.

"Here you go." She had bought a car charger for each of them.

Megan needed a few outfits for their next part. "Thanks. I'll be back here in an hour. If you need me sooner, just call."

Megan got out of the Jeep with a quick kiss and headed into the shops at North Bridge, a massive shopping mall in downtown Chicago. There's something about the gigantic complex with over fifty stores that made him uncomfortable. For him, shopping should be over and done within five to ten minutes. Noah gladly dropped her off, pleased that he didn't have to go in. He needed the time to himself.

Noah picked up the burner phone and logged in to the mall's free Wi-Fi as the countdown ticked away in his mind. The next two stops were only a few minutes away.

From the motorcycle shop down the street, Noah bought a pair of gloves. While good for the job, the tactical gloves he used on the police force lacked a key feature of the biker gloves. Plastic reinforced knuckles and extra padding on the palm. They were designed with an accident in mind to prevent injury, and with the plastic ridge across the back, it was the equivalent of wearing brass knuckles. As far as he knew, they were banned by police forces within several states for official use. They also masked his fingerprints quite nicely.

The next destination was three minutes away on Dearborn Street. He found parking on a side street, threw some coins in the meter, and darted inside the tall building. Noah scanned the menu board in the lobby. The offices were located on the first floor, and within moments he walked through the glass doors. Several people gave him a strange look when he glanced at his watch and slammed his wallet on the counter.

"I have fifteen minutes. Your time starts now."

* * * * *

Megan and Noah sat in the front seat of the Jeep and ate their sandwiches. The sun had begun to set at seven o'clock, and despite the twilight hour, they had a full visual. The nights were cooler in October, and soon winter would have its icy grip on the Windy City. There was only an occasional jogger or a couple out for an after-dinner stroll along the sidewalks.

"It's starting." Noah put down his water bottle and pulled out a set of binoculars Megan had bought. From two-hundred yards, the magnification brought the image into clear focus. A black Chevy Suburban pulled around from the back of William Ryan's home and parked out front on the crescent driveway. It looked like the entranceway of a hotel or resort with recessed lighting and stone columns to either side of the door.

From the driver's seat, a man in a dark suit and tie got out and scanned the area. Noah couldn't see a phone or microphone. He had to be using an earpiece.

A few seconds later, Noah whistled. "Can you see that guy?"

He passed the binoculars to Megan. "He makes Ryan look like a child."

The bodyguard stood almost two feet taller than the lawyer, and the contrast was almost comical.

The two men escorted Ryan into the back seat before they all took off. Noah and Megan ducked under the dashboard, out of sight, as the vehicle drove past.

Noah grabbed his backpack. "Ready?"

“Let’s do it.”

“Let’s do it.”

Chapter 55

Anthony laid the Colt pistol on top of his desk and pointed the barrel toward the nervous lawyer. William had seen the half dozen enforcers in the hallway and kitchen before being escorted into the office. They could have started their own football team with their size and amount of muscle.

Ryan's eyes flickered from the weapon to Anthony's expressionless face. His Irish accent was so strong, and it was challenging to understand him. "I have no idea. My BMW has *not* moved from my driveway in over a day."

Anthony glanced at Allen and Carl as his finger twitched on the trigger guard.

They stood inside the door of his office. The two men stared at one another before Allen looked at Anthony and confirmed William's story.

Anthony slid the pistol to the side, opened his laptop, and spun it around so William could see. "Explain this."

The witness statement given to the Chicago PD described his vehicle and plate number, leaving Rosie's before the fire started. Ryan read it twice in quick order and shook his head. "Obviously, I'm being set up. Who would benefit most from your organization going down?"

Anthony dismissed the two security officers. "You can wait outside."

Both men quickly left the office. They didn't want to be involved.

William took a deep breath and tried again. "I have worked with you a long time. You can say I am heavily invested in success for both of us."

Anthony tapped his fingers on his desk while staring at his lawyer. "Do you think another organization is moving in? Feds?"

William shook his head. "I haven't heard anything from any of our contacts. It might be time to reach up higher. I don't know of any other family that would try to muscle in. You are too well established in this area."

Anthony leaned forward. "Call Frank. I need to know if any law enforcement is stirring up the pot."

Frank Donavan was the current Lieutenant Governor for Illinois and had been a long-time associate of the Luciano family. The reason he had received enough funding to run his election campaign was in part due to the fact that his granddaughter and Anthony's oldest granddaughter were long-time friends.

"He may need another contribution."

Anthony nodded slowly. Money seemed to be hemorrhaging lately. "I'll give Joe a call, and I'll need more disposable cash."

William was visibly more relieved with the attention shifted. "What do you want to do about Arrow Point?"

"Call the cop. I want an update."

William pulled a cell phone out of his pocket and dialed the last number. He had three different phones on him at all times for various purposes. There were also a few extra sim cards that he would switch out when required.

After a minute, he hung up. "No answer. Not even voicemail."

Anthony's fingers hit the desk fast and faster, and then he pushed himself back. The nervous energy made him restless, and he paced the small office. "Do you think the cop would be here in Chicago?"

William's eyes widened. "I can find him fairly quickly, I believe."

"Do so. On your way out, dismiss the goons."

William quietly closed the door behind him. Alone, Anthony stared out the window as he sorted the facts out in his head.

Could the cop be responsible? How would he know about Rosie's?

Everything came back to Rachel, the money, her death—even Noah Hunter. Soon as he applied pressure on the cop, he was attacked. While the fire could be a coincidence and a genuine accident, he had some doubts.

It was too well-timed to be random.

There was only one way to flush out the prey and throw them off balance. Strike where they were most vulnerable.

* * * * *

Noah and Megan walked along the sidewalk and moved up the side of the lawyer's home toward the backyard. Security cameras were mounted above the front door, but he could only see motion-sensor lights along the side. They crab-walked under the windows until they got to the corner. Despite this area of Chicago having homes large enough to be mansions, the properties were not that large. The backyard only extended another forty feet past the rear of the house. Half was interlocking brick with a small bistro set just off the rear door. The back half of the yard was a raised, tiered garden with several small immaculately shaped bushes that resembled spheres.

Above the rear French doors, a security camera was mounted next to security lights.

Noah asked, "Do you think the camera is being monitored?"

Megan pulled her ball cap down low to hide her features. "For the amount of money he has, I would say, yes. What's the response time, though?"

Noah closed his eyes for a moment. "In Arrow Point, if an alarm goes off, it usually takes two minutes for a security company to give us a call. Depending on location, we are anywhere between two to ten minutes response time."

"So, if we are in and out in three minutes, we should be good?"

Noah reached into his backpack and pulled out a twenty-one-inch collapsible baton. With a flick of his wrist, it fully extended down beside his leg. He pulled the hood of his sweater over his hat.

"Three minutes. In three, two …"

Chapter 56

Special Agent Gardiner placed the items back in the freezer before turning to Agent Campbell.

"Anything?"

They had served the warrant for Noah's apartment, and a surprised but willing superintendent had unlocked the door. When Noah slipped away, he had immediately reported to Harris. There was confusion about an arrest warrant and why Hunter wasn't detained already, and the lack of electronic correspondence. By the time they had sorted out the problem, it was mid-afternoon, and Noah Hunter was nowhere to be found.

Agent Wu showed him the trackers on the police sergeant's truck. The first GPS signal showed the vehicle was currently in Nebraska, and the second was en route to the west coast. The Nebraska field office was called to hunt down the first signal, and they found it in a grass ditch on the interstate. No sign of the Chevy truck. The second transmitter was in Oregon, and the vehicle was located on Interstate 84 West. Hunter had slipped it into a transport that carried a load of lumber. Gardiner was furious, and he tried to take it out on the police chief and the APPD.

Chief Birch just smiled. "This is what happens when you are not sharing information as you promised. You are no longer welcome in my station. You have ten minutes to vacate, or you will be forcibly removed."

Unable to retaliate, Gardiner had his team pack and leave. They rented an extra room at the hotel to use as an office. It wasn't the first time they had done this, and it would not be the last.

Campbell placed the dishes back in the cupboard. "Nothing."

They had done a primary sweep of the apartment, and now they started the secondary search. So far, they have had no luck.

Gardiner slammed the cupboard door. "I think we're wasting time here. Do you know if this hick town has storage units for rent?"

Both agents were just involved in a case where the suspect lived in a storage unit to stay hidden. "I'll take a look. It worked once."

Gardiner scanned the apartment yet again, and he couldn't help but feel it had been sterilized. No current receipts, electronic equipment, or an indication that someone had been here recently.

He moved to the window and looked out over the lights of Arrow Point. The FBI agent wanted nothing more than to get out of this place and back into a large city. Small towns pissed him off.

He glanced down at the long display table in front of the window, where people would display pictures or allow plants to get some sun. It was empty. However, there was a large circle where something recently sat. There was a clean spot in the dust.

"He's gone." There was nothing left of Hunter's house, and this apartment was his last known place of residence. Some old clothing that belonged to Hunter's fiancée still hung in the closet and the dresser—but nothing of his. "If the personal items are gone, he isn't coming back."

Campbell agreed. "That's usually the case."

"Unless we can force him to return." Gardiner had one more trick up his sleeve, and he had a feeling it would work.

It usually did.

* * * * *

Noah held the baton ready, and Megan stepped forward with the roll of duct tape. Beside the door handle on the French windows, she formed a large cross over the pane of glass. Noah whipped the baton in a tight arc and smashed the window as soon as she stepped back. Usually, the shards of glass would fly inside, and the noise could alert a resident. The duct tape held most of the glass together and acted as a muffler. Cheap but effective.

Once she peeled enough tape back, Megan reached through the hole and unlocked the deadbolt.

"Three minutes. Let's go. Office first, then master bedroom." People tended to hide items of the most value in one of those places. Noah slammed the tip of the baton down on the paving stone. It would only collapse under force.

Soon as the doors opened, Noah paused. He couldn't hear any alarms or beeping. Moving through the kitchen, he led the way down the long hallway as they searched for a home office.

The lawyer's home looked like he was about to enter a contest for best decorated. It was perfectly laid out, down to the indentations in the pillows on the couches. Nothing looked like it was used, and it made him feel uneasy.

"It looks like a showroom. Does Ryan even live here?" Noah couldn't help but shake his head.

"Far as I know," Megan whispered as she stood in the office doorway. "In here."

The antique desk was clear of clutter, with just two computer monitors, a keyboard, and a mouse. The drawers were unlocked, but Noah couldn't find anything relevant. Megan worked her way through the bookshelves.

While he searched the top drawer, Noah knocked the mouse, and the screens came to life. "It's asking for a password."

Megan paused her search, then shook her head. "No idea."

Noah found a set of Medeco security keys in the bottom right drawer, used for heavy doors or buildings. Noah had a similar one on his keychain for the front door of APPD.

"I have a set of keys, but nothing else. You?"

"Nothing. Bring the keys. They look familiar, and we're going to need them soon." Megan gestured to the stairs. "Bedroom next?"

Noah followed up the grand staircase as he pulled two flashlights from his pack and passed one to Megan. There was only light on in the hallway and office. The rest of the home was dark. A series of area rugs covered the polished wood floors, and a cleaning product had been recently used. The whole house was dust-free and faintly smelled like citrus.

The master bedroom was easily the largest room in the house, with the emperor bed on a raised dais. Opposite was a full living room and ornate fireplace. Just inside the door was a marble wet bar with a large selection of whisky and bourbon. The walk-in closet was the size of most people's living rooms.

"How much does a lawyer make?" Noah couldn't help but wonder. This room set the new standard for opulence. He searched the bedside tables and discovered a loaded Beretta 92 in the top drawer. He tucked it into the waistband at the small of his back. Megan moved to the large closet, and a few seconds later, she called Noah to join her.

Her flashlight showed a wall of wooden cupboards and drawers along one side. The first door she opened held trays for watches and other jewelry. The door revealed a stainless-steel safe with a digital keypad and a thumbprint reader.

"Short of using C-4, I don't know how to get in this."

Noah nodded. "We don't have time. Let's go. Our time is almost up."

Two muffled slams sounded from outside. In the bedroom doorway, Noah remained in place and held up his hand. "Car doors."

From the bedroom window, Noah had an elevated view of the crescent driveway. Parked near the road was a new black Audi Q3. Two men dressed in suits approached the house. Noah could see the comms link in their right ears and the coil worked its way down the back of their shirts. Both men were easily two-hundred and fifty pounds with short-buzzed haircuts. The taller man looked like he could bench-press a small car without effort. The larger man made his way toward the front door while the other circled to the rear.

"We have to go. Now." Noah caught a slight panic rising in her voice.

He pulled the Beretta out of his waistband and handed it to Megan. "Too late. They'll be inside as soon as he gets to the backyard. Stay close."

Moving back out into the hallway, Noah stood near the corner wall. Downstairs, footsteps pounded through the kitchen.

They were trapped.

Chapter 57

Noah heard footsteps run through the kitchen and hallway, then the front door opened. The guards talked to each other in hushed whispers, and he couldn't make out any words. He didn't need to. Noah knew they would be going through the home to ensure it was cleared.

"Fall back to the bedroom." Noah didn't know the home's layout enough to make a defensive stand or a place to hide. Megan's breathing sounded harsh, and Noah could tell the adrenaline rushed through her system. He felt the effects as well. They quietly made their way back down the long hall as muted sounds echoed throughout the residence. The guards had begun their search.

Once in the bedroom, Noah turned on his flashlight with his fingers over the lens. A look in the en suite revealed a white marble room with a steam shower and a soaker tub that could easily fit five people. A death trap if they were cornered.

"Closet?" Megan whispered in his ear.

It was narrow with one entry point. "Only option. Go."

Once inside, he slid a four-foot section of suits to the end of the rod, knelt, and drew his Glock. Noah aimed at the doorway and waited.

Megan shuffled to the opposite corner and whispered to Noah. "Check this out."

She had opened a rear door in the closet to reveal a small room. Noah then noted the camera against the back wall below an inactive strobe light. "Panic room."

When she opened the second door, the feeble light showed a ten-by-ten-foot room. A monitoring station was on the left wall. Four screens cycled through the various camera feeds, from inside and outside the home, and a keyboard and landline phone filled the small desk. A shelf on the rear wall had food and bottled water, with a chemical toilet in the corner. The couch against the right wall must double as a bed.

Inside the door was a bright red button.

Recessed into the wall were thick steel doors that would close when the room was activated.

Noah took a deep breath. "We're running out of options."

* * * * *

Johnny held the Sig Sauer P226 down by his waist with his right hand, and his left had two fingers up in the air. Then one finger. He paused and darted inside the office with his partner close behind. Johnny swept the far-left corner while Adam cleared the right side. They had worked together as a team for over eight years, first in the British 22nd SAS hostage rescue team, then for Starr Securities. Life in the delta squadron was nothing but training, deployment, reports, and more training in a vast rotation of working at home or overseas. Executive Protection was the easiest job they ever had, and the money they had made in the last three years was the equivalent of fifteen years' pay back home. Someone had to do the dirty work at times, and long as it paid well, neither man minded.

Johnny moved forward and checked behind the wooden desk before whispering, "Clear."

Their old delta section would have been cleared within a minute on a primary search. However, they had to work with a two-man team and methodically worked their way, room by room.

Adam held his Glock 17 in the Weaver stance and covered the lower staircase. Opposite the office across the foyer was a formal living room. They had a full visual, and there was nowhere to hide. Johnny pointed at the staircase, then upward. A tactical flashlight was pulled from his pocket, and he crossed his wrist. The beam was aimed in the same direction as the muzzle.

Adam used his flashlight and nodded. They were ready.

They moved right at the top of the stairs, and two bathrooms and four bedrooms were checked. The balance was between speed and being thorough. Johnny was ready to start in the master bedroom when they heard a loud metallic door clang shut. The noise reverberated throughout the large home. It was immediately followed by a loud electronic chirp that sounded once per second. They stood outside the double doors, and Johnny confirmed the noise came from inside. A bright white strobe flashed from the closet and turned the large bedroom into a dance club or disco.

Both men entered the room and swept the corners before they cleared the bathroom.

"Clear."

Johnny stood to one side of the closet door with Adam right behind him. He did a quick turkey peek around the corner and stood back.

"Panic room."

The closet was empty, and the back was a six-foot metal wall with a seam through the middle. The high-pitched noise came from the small speaker underneath the strobe light. A camera was mounted on the wall above the metal doors. There was a speaker mounted on the right side of the wall with a press-to-talk button.

Adam slid his pistol back into his shoulder holster under his jacket and walked up to the metal door. "These can only be opened from the inside?"

Johnny nodded. "Far as I know."

He holstered his pistol as well before trying to slide the door open.

Adam joined him, but it would not budge. "Who's in there? Burglar?"

"Only one way to find out." Johnny pressed the button next to the speaker. "You're trapped in there, and we're not leaving. Who's this?"

No response.

"Listen, mate. I got all fucking night to—"

The first round hit him in the back of his shoulder and slammed him forward against the wall. As Johnny began to turn, he was hit by one bullet through his left biceps and then two more into his torso. His partner blocked the second volley. Neither man wore a ballistic vest for this lightweight protection detail.

Both men collapsed to the floor. Johnny tried not to scream in pain as he bit through his lip. He slowly moved his right hand across his chest to grasp the pistol and waited. They would come out soon.

Taking a slow deep breath, he waited for almost a full minute before he heard two people as they scrambled behind him.

Fuckers were hiding under the fucking bed.

Adam twitched as his nervous system shut down.

"Are you okay?" A woman spoke.

"Yes, you?" Her partner sounded gruff.

"Good. Let's get out of here."

With the amount of blood from the shoulder wound, Johnny knew he didn't have long. He needed to get help before falling unconscious. One bullet had gone through his chest cavity, and one lung was filling up with blood. That was the deciding factor for him as he pulled the pistol from the shoulder harness while he spun to use his fallen partner as his shield.

For Johnny, life was simple. Kill or be killed.

The warrior's life was one he embraced.

A scream of pain ripped out of his mouth as he fired into the bedroom. The first three shots were erratic and not aimed.

The fourth shot proved successful.

He clipped the man who fell to the side. The woman simply turned sideways and brought up her pistol. Johnny didn't hear the round that went straight through his left eye and blew out the back of his head over the panic room door.

Chapter 58

Noah kept his hood up and his pace steady as they walked out the front door. He didn't want to draw any more attention to the home than they already had. The burning in his upper arm had faded to a dull ache, but it could have been much worse. When they reached the Jeep, Megan opened the passenger door for him and got behind the wheel.

Noah's right hand kept the pressure on the wound. "I'll be good. Get us clear of the area first."

Despite her quick reactions and steady appearance, Megan's hands shook when she tried to get the key in the ignition. After a few minutes of random turns, Noah was sure they were not being followed. On a side street, he nodded toward the back. "Small brown case behind the seat."

"Is it bad?" Megan opened the case and saw everything from bandages to a suture kit.

"I'll live." Noah took off the sweatshirt and examined his arm. The bullet had scored through the flesh. It looked like a long gash with jagged edges but only quarter-inch deep. When he flexed, the blood started to flow once again.

"You were lucky."

Megan moistened a gauze pad with antiseptic and patted the area. Noah held his breath and tried not to wince. Once it was cleaned, the second package of sterile gauze was placed on top and held in place with a tensor bandage. Being careful, Noah slid his hoodie back on and downed two Tylenol. "If we had time to do a full stakeout, we would have known when the security changed their shifts."

Passing him a bottle of water, Megan nodded. "What's next? They know we're here."

Noah pulled out the keys from the desk and passed them to Megan. "I think it's time to change our original plan, and you're wrong about one thing."

Megan frowned. "What are you talking about?"

Noah smiled and put his right hand on her knee. "They may know that I'm here, but your uncle has no idea about you. I want to keep it that way."

Megan didn't know what to say, and Noah knew she was undecided. He understood. Part of him wanted to run and not look back, and the other half wanted to stay and help Megan.

"I have a plan, but I need your help."

After talking for several minutes, Megan wiped a few tears and leaned forward to hug him. "Okay. I'm all in."

*****

Special Agent Gardiner sat in the back of the rental van with Agent Wu as they watched the monitors. For the last twelve hours, he had sat outside a nursing home in Casper while Agent Clay sat in a secondary vehicle with a view of the far parking lot. The long window van had a narrow table in the back with two folding chairs. Two laptops had a split-screen and showed the live feed from four different locations around the property.

"Checking for updates, then it's all yours."

Agent Wu arrived early for her shift, and Agent Campbell would relieve Clay. They didn't have the personnel for a large rotation, but they made it work. Agent Wu had entered the nursing home and asked to use their phone. She had left a message on Hunter's cell and informed him that his mother was not doing too well. It would be best if he came to visit. This trap had worked more than a few times and could almost have been considered standard.

The only thing worthy of note was a minivan with three large men parked next to the surveillance van. When Wu had stepped outside for some fresh air, they stared at each other for a moment. Without a word, the men got back in their vehicle and drove away. She wasn't sure what they were up to, but it probably wasn't good.

When Gardiner's laptop dinged with an incoming email, he couldn't believe what he saw and showed Wu the pictures. "This is Rosie's, next to Luciano's office building."

The Chicago field office had stepped up surveillance on Anthony Luciano, and the restaurant was one of the known places he frequented. No one would be visiting there any longer. The photos showed the whole building on fire, with scores of firefighters battling the blaze.

"Too bad the offices didn't go up as well."

"No kidding."

Scrolling through the pictures, Brandon saw a person talking to a Chicago cop. It was common practice to include crowd pictures, but the email had only included a few. Most had stayed well back.

The man wore a baseball hat with the hood from a sweatshirt drawn up over their head. Gardiner could still make out half the face and the hint of a jaw profile. The shoulder of the cop blocked too much of the shot for a full facial image. He zoomed in on the picture as much as possible but still wasn't positive. The cameraman was fairly far away.

"What do you think of this?"

Agent Wu's eyes opened wide, and she leaned forward to manipulate the image. "That's very close. It could be Sergeant Hunter."

Gardiner smiled at her conclusion. It was the same as his own, and his gut instinct kicked in.

"We're packing up and leaving this place. Straight to the airport. Call everyone in."

Special Agent Gardiner tapped the screen and grinned.

Gotcha.

Chapter 59

An hour later, Megan parked around the corner of the Starbucks. Low clouds had rolled in, and the quarter moon was hidden, but they had enough light from the street to work without flashlights. Their last purchase from Walmart helped to reassure Noah. The ballistic vests were similar to those issued by the APPD but not of the same quality. It would be better than nothing, and after the close call, it was an easy decision. Once fitted over his T-shirt and under the sweater, it was hard to tell he wore a vest. Megan, however, found it uncomfortable but knew better than to complain.

Noah lifted the rear hatch and emptied the large duffel bag from the cabin. He loaded two AR-15s and several spare magazines. The Glock was back on his hip, and the extra magazines fit into his pockets. The last item was the 12-gauge Remington. Knowing the reload time on the shotgun, he left the extra box of ammunition in the Jeep.

Megan reloaded the Beretta and tucked it into her jeans.

Noah flexed his arm to keep it moving. "It's starting to stiffen, but not bad."

Noah pulled out the selection of cell phones that used to belong to Anderson from the small backpack. He removed the battery and slid the sim card out from the new Samsung. The burner phone they had bought was an android model, and the card was compatible. He copied the contact list into the new phone and scrolled through the entries from the menu option.

Seconds later, he showed the screen to Megan.

Asshole Lawyer.

"I think that's him." Smiling, Noah sent a text.

>>I'm at your office. Get your ass here and pay what you owe me. Now!

After he sent the message, Noah picked up the duffel on his right shoulder and winced. "After you."

Megan walked ahead of him with her blue ball cap pulled low and a light blue jacket and jeans. As he followed, Noah smiled and appreciated the view.

When Noah had gone through the FBI reports of the bodies, the feds had assumed that the body was that of Jim Anderson. However, until it was proven, it did not make the report. Prints and, if possible, DNA were required. If Luciano had access to the FBI files, they couldn't know if Anderson was dead or hiding out.

As he crossed the street, the cell phone buzzed with an incoming message:

>>Where have you been?

Laying low in AP. Feds are everywhere.

>>Did you ...?

He's in hiding. Do you know where? Get your ass here and pay me, or I'll come looking for you. Would you like that, Willy?

>>I'll be there in 15.

Noah smiled. "We're good. He's on the way."

The restaurant had temporary fencing erected surrounding the lot. The walls had collapsed from the fire and formed a pile of charred rubble and beams. The odor carried for blocks when the wind shifted.

Megan pulled out the keys that Noah found in the desk and tried them in the office building's front door. "My uncle uses the whole sixth floor, and Ryan's offices are on the fourth. That's where I used to work."

When the security key turned in the lock, a wave of relief washed through him. Breaking in was noisy and drew unwanted attention, especially downtown. With hoods up and the ballcaps pulled low, Noah stepped inside. No point in making it easy for the security cameras.

With such a late hour and it being a Saturday night, the building was empty. The elevator opened immediately.

"When I worked here, I managed the investments and online banking. Basically, I was hiding funds and laundering money for my uncle."

Megan hit the button for the fourth floor, and the Beretta appeared in her hands. The law firm's reception area was relatively large, with a few couches and leather chairs for clients to wait. Opposite the reception desks were two bathrooms, and a long hallway led behind the desk, farther into the building.

"They have redecorated since I was here last."

She led him down the hall and stopped in front of a large office. The nameplate *Joe Penny – Accounting* was engraved on a brass plate to the right of the door.

"He used to work for me, and this was my office." They continued down the hall before Megan stopped at a secondary waiting area. Turning back to Noah, she grinned. "If we have five minutes, I have an idea."

Looking at his watch, Noah agreed. He had seen that look before, and he was curious as to what trouble she was about to stir up.

Her old office door wasn't locked, and Megan sat behind the desk.

"Joe always had a problem. I think it was the drinking and the drugs when he was a kid. However, his memory had always sucked." Megan waited while the computer started. "When I was training him, he kept taking notes. Which wasn't good."

Taking the keyboard, she flipped it over, and underneath, paper strips were held in place with tape.

When the system prompted a password login, Megan used the code written down. Seconds later, the home screen popped up. "I'll be a few minutes. Did you want to go get set up?"

Noah grabbed the duffel bag and continued down the hall to a set of double doors with William C. Ryan on the nameplate. The door was locked, but through the gap, he could see the latch. The blade of a pocketknife fit between, and it opened without effort. The quality of the offices seemed to be lacking. Just inside the door, Noah hit the light switches.

On the left was a small oval table with four armchairs. At the far end, a large executive desk was against the wall, surrounded by bookshelves. A few generic landscape pictures decorated the walls, along with a motivational poster—something about golf.

Two leather chairs were opposite the desk, and one of the arms looked broken. After seeing Ryan's home, Noah expected his office to be finely decorated as well, but the whole room looked as if they had a tight budget. He knew where the lawyer spent his money, and it wasn't the office.

Behind the desk, he unloaded the duffel bag. Noah spread out the weapons, including his Glock, and confirmed everything was ready to go. Hopefully, none of this was going to be used, but he may as well be prepared. Ideally, not a single shot will be fired, but he knew the odds were slim.

Shortly after, Megan came into the office. "All done." She took a single white piece of paper, folded it into a small square, and then handed it to Noah. "When this is all over, you can open it."

"Why can't I open it now?" Noah placed it in his wallet, and she just gave him a look. He knew better than to argue. "Okay, about the vests."

Noah lifted his sweater to show her the medium ballistics vest. "This is a soft Kevlar, good mainly against small arms fire. You will still bruise and possibly break a rib if you are hit, but it's better than nothing. Best of all, it's lightweight and doesn't slow you down too much."

Megan twisted and quickly touched her toes. "I'm getting used to it."

The graze wound on his left arm had stopped bleeding, and it didn't cause him too much difficulty. Noah used the Velcro straps to tighten his vest before pulling out the last items.

The two latex, full head clown masks still had the price tags on them.

Baseball hats were stored in the duffel bag as they put on the disguises. Noah's mask was white, with a bald head, light blue markings under the eyes, and a red nose. Megan's was much the same, but with short, spiked, blue hair.

Picking up an AR-15 and spare magazine along with a survival knife, she moved to the copy room across the hall and left the lights off. Placing the Glock back in the holster, Noah slung the semi-automatic rifle and picked up the shotgun.

Ten seconds after he turned out the lights, the ding of the elevator arriving on the floor carried down the hall.

Showtime.

Chapter 60

Anthony hung up the phone, sat back in his kitchen chair, and looked out the window over his backyard. He stared at the finely trimmed lawn and bushes, but he didn't see them. His thoughts were in the past and of his family. He was never much to second guess his decisions. He learned from the past and didn't dwell on it.

Jerry stepped forward. "You should really be away from the windows, sir."

The next shift for the personal security had taken over, but they seemed to be fighting a losing battle with keeping him away from the kitchen window.

"I'm good. I need some time to think."

The former marine moved to the front sitting room to keep an eye on the entrance. Jerry wasn't as intimidating to look at as the other guards were, but he seemed more aware of his surroundings and intense. The wiry man barely stood five-foot-eight, but he seemed capable.

Anthony had dispersed a small army to keep a watch on his family. Especially those with small children. He would allow nothing to happen to his grandchildren—that he could guarantee. His wife was with his first son in the Vermont area, having left early that morning. The house seemed empty without her.

The report from Arrow Point wasn't good. A crew had gone to the retirement home in Casper to get Hunter's mother, but the place was under surveillance. Someone else had thought of a way to get at the cop. Anthony didn't have time to coordinate information from his contacts. The watchers could have been working for him.

He was startled from his thoughts when his cell phone rang. Joey flashed on the display screen.

"Go ahead."

"Sir, you're going to want to make sure you're sitting down."

Joe sounded hysterical, bordering on full panic.

"Slow down. What's going on?"

"All of the accounts are empty, Mr. Luciano. Did you, by chance, move things around?"

Anthony slammed his fist against the window. It came close to fracturing, but it held up to the blow. "No. Explain."

Joe pounded away on a keyboard while he talked. The clicks never stopped. "The accounts are drained, and the money has been transferred. I can't locate it, but I'm working on it."

"You will find the money and report back *very* soon. Do I make myself clear?"

"Yes, sir," Joe whispered as the severity sunk into his skull.

After he disconnected, Anthony tried to gain control of his breathing and slow down his heart. With an almost visible restraint, he placed the cell phone gently on the table.

Having over one hundred million dollars missing will set him back more than he could afford. The last time he lost a large amount of money, he was …

The last piece of the puzzle clicked.

Anthony smoothed his suit jacket and walked into his office. He removed the Colt 1911 from the wooden case on his bookshelf. Pulling back the slide, he performed a quick press check and confirmed a round chambered.

"Jerry, get the car. I suddenly have an appointment."

* * * * *

Noah stood behind the small table in the dark office and waited. He listened to the hushed tone of men as they talked and the heels of dress shoes as they approached down the tiled hallway. Keeping the twelve-gauge down along his right leg, he took a deep breath. There was a slight moisture build-up in the latex mask, and things were heating up. If everything went well, he wouldn't be using it much longer.

Noah tried not to bring up the shotgun in reflex when the long arm reached around the doorframe and flicked on the lights. The man had to duck to see under the top of the door frame. Most men that tall were quite slim and fragile looking. This dark-skinned man was the opposite. He carried three hundred pounds of muscle, and if it came to a hand-to-hand fight, Noah knew he would be outclassed.

Soon as he spotted Noah, a pistol suddenly appeared in his hands, rock-steady and aimed at his head.

"Do not move." Despite his size, the man's voice was soft and smooth.

Behind the mask, Noah nodded and kept the shotgun down.

The large man kept his pistol trained on him and moved back. William Ryan stepped into the door frame, and his eyes widened at the masked man in front of him.

"Jim?"

Noah nodded and just stood there, eyes on the bodyguard. He kept a clear line of sight above the lawyer.

William took a step forward into his office and frowned while tilting his head to the side slightly.

"Mr. Ryan, I don't think …"

Noah pointed to the lawyer, then at his desk.

"Remove your mask so that I can confirm it's you."

Noah started counting down in his head.

On time, the three-round burst struck the second guard in the hallway, and he fell. The shots echoed, but the source was obscured. The tall man swept William inside the office with one arm against the wall while searching for the shooter behind him.

As he spun back around, Noah held the shotgun out and pointed at the guard. "Get down on the ground. Now!"

Megan had fired through the cheap wall of the copy room straight into the other guard. A quick thrust of the survival knife had given her a viewing port through the drywall. The .556 rounds acted like they were fired through a sheet of paper with the proximity.

The tall man didn't have a target, and if he moved, William would most likely be dead from the shotgun blast. He ducked under the door, and he put his hands up in the air with his fingers extended. The pistol rocked as it spun upside down on his index finger.

"Drop the gun and kick it over to me."

As he complied, Noah noticed that William had wet himself. The lawyer's mouth opened and closed like a fish out of water. The Sig Sauer slid across the floor and hit the table leg with a clunk.

"On your knees, hands on top of your head. If you move wrong, you will be shot. If you understand, nod."

The guard dropped down onto his knees and nodded. His eyes never left Noah's.

Noah absently noted they were now the same height. Megan walked out of the copy room with the semi-automatic rifle pointed at the back of his head. Once he felt the muzzle push into the base of his skull, Noah saw his shoulders slump in resignation.

Nodding at Megan, Noah stepped around the table and once again pointed for Ryan to sit at the desk while he stepped forward and covered the guard.

Megan slung her rifle and then clicked one handcuff around his wrist. She guided his other wrist down beside the cuffs and secured him tightly, just as Noah had taught her. It was smoothly done.

With someone that size, Megan wasn't taking any chances. Pulling out a long bandana from her jacket pocket, she gagged him and placed a hood over the guard's head. Plastic zip-ties were used around his ankles.

"You may lay down if you wish." Noah shifted his attention to the lawyer and pointed to the chair behind the desk again.

William slowly made his way around to sit, and his eyes continuously flicked from one clown face to the other. Once inside the office, Megan didn't say a word but kept her weapon pointed at the back of the guard's head.

"William Ryan. It's time we talked. I'm going to be Frank, and you're going to be Ernest. Do you understand what I'm saying?"

The lawyer had turned white as a sheet, and he seemed to be having trouble breathing, but he nodded. Sweat poured off his forehead while his eyes twitched.

"Let's start then. Your off-the-book records. Where are they?"

Behind the mask, Noah grinned as the lawyer groaned.

Chapter 61

Jerry pulled the black Chevy Tahoe to the front of the house while his partner stayed with Anthony. He had never learned his name, and at this point, he could care less. He was a carbon copy of one of the first guards, tall, big muscles—your typical military grunt.

The guard held up an arm while Jerry looked around the area before giving the all-clear signal. Buttoning up his brown suit jacket, Anthony readjusted the pistol in his waistband for an easy draw and then walked down his front steps into the vehicle's back seat.

The second guard sat in the back with him as Jerry drove. "Sixteen-hundred, South LaSalle Street."

Anthony kept his right hand near his jacket as if he expected trouble any moment.

A cell phone rang from the guard that sat in the back with him. After a brief conversation, he could see him harden up. "Sir, it appears the second team to protect Mr. Ryan has been found at his residence. Both men were shot. Someone may be holed up in Mr. Ryan's panic room. We can't ascertain that yet."

"What about Ryan?" Anthony felt like his stomach had crested a rollercoaster.

The guard finished listening to his briefing over the phone before turning back to his employer. "No word on the location of Mr. Ryan. His team isn't responding. Once they failed to check in with HQ, they sent someone out to their position. You are being advised to return to your home, Mr. Luciano. Added protection will be arriving shortly."

He shook his head. "Not this time."

The guard gave his command the location of travel before he hung up. He met Jerry's eyes in the mirror and shrugged. Both men were prepared.

Anthony pulled out his cell phone to make preparations.

* * * * *

"I don't have any records of that kind." William's face reddened, and his eyes darted about the room.

Noah pulled out his Glock and fired a round into the bookcase just above his head in one continuous movement. Ryan flinched hard enough that he nearly slammed his head on the desk. His glasses fell and landed on the floor. He didn't pick them up.

"Last chance. If you're no good to me, this will end quickly."

His mouth opened, but he seemed to have a hard time talking. Noah moved closer and placed the muzzle of his Glock against the man's forehead. "Five seconds. You decide what happens next. Five. Four. Three …"

Noah was getting hot in the mask, and sweat trickled down his forehead. By the count of three, Ryan nodded.

"I know where they are, but I don't have access."

"Let's go. Any sudden movement, you die. Clear?"

Noah grabbed something off the shelf and tucked it under his vest before guiding Ryan. They stepped around the guard and out of the office. Holstering his Glock, he prodded the guard with the shotgun, letting the rifle hang on the sling. "Behave, and we are gone soon. Don't fuck this up."

Megan stood back and let him follow the lawyer out of the office and down the hall, back to the elevators. "Mr. Luciano's office is on the sixth floor."

The sixth-floor lobby was different from that of the lawyers. Several display cases held small miniature buildings inside that were cleverly lit with concealed lighting. Framed pictures filled the walls of architectural drawings that the property management had sold.

Noah prodded William out of the elevator with his shotgun. They moved down the hall, passing many offices and a small kitchen with coffeemakers and a small stainless-steel refrigerator.

Ryan halted in front of a simple, unmarked, wooden door. "In here."

Noah wasn't surprised to find it locked, and the time for subtly had long since passed. He put his back to the door and brought up his right leg. With a powerful back kick, the door flew open. The interior jam splintered, and pieces scattered across the floor.

When he turned on the light, Noah saw a small office with a desk. Three bookshelves stood behind the chair, and the walls were covered in framed family pictures. He gestured for Ryan to sit as he searched and fiddled with a few items on the bookshelves.

There wasn't anywhere in this small office to hide anything except inside the desk. "Where?"

William shrugged. "Any time he brought out the books, the door was closed." He kept looking around, and every time he turned to look at Megan, she brought up the rifle and pointed it at his head. He quickly learned to keep his eyes front.

Noah went through the desk drawers and found nothing except the occasional paperwork dealing with the company and office stationery. The shelves behind the desk were filled with various books, from architectural design to a whole section that dealt with Chicago's history.

The wooden floors were solid, with no signs of a hiding spot. That only left the bookshelves. The first shelf wasn't attached to the wall, and Noah could have easily tilted it over. The central unit didn't move an inch.

He took down the stacks of books and piled them on the desk.

"There you are."

On the third shelf, Noah found a large flat area the size of a paperback novel on the back wall. When he pressed it, the shelf unit swung open on hidden hinges. Built into the wall was a steel door with a biometric palm-print scanner and keypad. The door was three feet wide and four feet tall.

Noah turned back to the lawyer and was about to ask a question when a shot sounded down the hall. Megan let out a grunt of pain and fell face-first on the office floor as all hell broke loose.

Chapter 62

Knowing he didn't have time to deal with the attackers and the lawyer simultaneously, Noah brought up the shotgun and slammed the butt into the side of Ryan's head. William didn't have time to react and collapsed into a heap on the floor, unconscious. Noah darted over and grabbed Megan by the shoulder. He pulled her farther into the office and out of the doorway. The bullet hole was in the jacket, the middle of her torso. The vest did its job, but she was stunned and probably in a lot of pain.

Noah turned off the lights in the office and crouched low. He could hear someone walking slowly down the hallway toward the office. His heart was hammering in his chest, and his breathing was unusually loud within the mask.

A second round exploded through the wall just above his head and showered him with drywall dust. Had he been standing, it would have hit him dead center.

Jesus Christ!

Noah stayed low and brought the shotgun up. He fired around the corner and down the hall with a quick darting movement and ducked back into the office. Once the ringing in his ears faded, Noah tried to listen for any activity. Nothing.

He took a deep breath and cycled another round. When he stepped over Megan and down the hall, he was tempted to take his mask off to listen but kept it on. Noah stayed close to the left-hand wall to give himself a better angle as he approached the reception area. He tried to move like he was taught long ago. Heel, toe, and glide while rolling off the heel and along the outside edge of the foot.

He was startled when a figure stood up on the other side of the reception desk.

They both fired at the same time.

Noah felt like a truck hit him on the right side of his chest. His feet left the ground as he was flung backward and down. Despite the wind being knocked out of him, Noah couldn't afford to lay there and recover. He pumped another shell into the chamber. The empty cartridge leaped out and spun on the tiled floor.

There was no other noise besides the ringing in his ears.

Pain radiated from his chest, and he had to force air back into his lungs. Even that simple movement hurt.

It was a struggle, but he stood and peered around the desk. A slim man lay on the ground, dressed in a black suit and tie. A Glock 19 lay on the floor beside his right hand.

The guard had received the full blast of the shotgun from fifteen feet in the upper torso and face, and he would not be getting up again.

The man was dressed much the same as the guards at the lawyer's residence. He tilted the head to the side with his foot to reveal the comms unit into his right ear.

Knowing they worked in pairs, Noah brought the shotgun up once again and scanned the foyer. Earlier, he didn't hear the elevator door, so that left the stairs. On the far side of the reception area was the entrance to the staircase. As he watched, the handle turned slowly.

Noah darted forward with the shotgun held firmly across his body and waited. Sweat poured down his face, and he blinked to clear his eyes. When a pistol appeared, he kicked the door with his heel as hard as he could. The man on the other side screamed as the bones in his wrist and lower arm shattered. The gun fell to the ground. Noah opened the door and saw a wiry man dressed in a suit reach behind him for a second weapon when he squeezed the trigger on the shotgun.

From three feet, the blast destroyed his stomach and shredded the skin. The guard took two steps back and fell down the stairs. He landed in a heap on the lower landing.

His ears were ringing, so Noah didn't hear the man as he approached and placed a gun to the back of his head.

"You are the most trouble I've ever had from a cop."

Noah detected the rage in Luciano's voice, and the end of the barrel shook against the back of his head with every word. There wasn't a way to move fast enough to dodge a bullet from this close, but there was no way he wasn't going down without trying.

Noah was about to spin around with the shotgun leading when a single shot rang out. He automatically ducked, and that reflex saved his life. The Colt 1911 fired above the back of his head and through a display case. In the clown mask, Megan leaned across the reception desk with the AR-15 now pointed toward the ceiling when he turned. Anthony screamed in pain and tried to hold his right calf with both hands. Noah kicked the Colt pistol to the far side of the lobby, and it rested against the elevator doors.

He grabbed Anthony by the shoulder and lifted him. "Let's go. We aren't done yet."

Noah knew he was shouting, but the adrenaline and the deafness in his ears didn't help.

He could barely hold the shotgun in his left hand, so he left it on the floor while he had to practically carry the older man down the hall back to his office. Megan followed close behind.

Soon as they walked into the office, Anthony swore at William as he lay unconscious on the floor. Shoving him into a chair, Noah stood beside the desk. He took a moment to inhale and shake his head. The ringing in his ears had lessened, but it still sounded like feedback from a rock concert.

"Open the safe."

Luciano laughed through the pain. "Not a chance. You're done."

Without a word, Noah picked up the lawyer's feet and dragged him out into the hallway. Anthony jumped when two shots rang out.

Noah walked back into the office. "You're next unless you open the safe."

He held his Glock at his waist, ready to fire.

"Is this about money? Because I have none. Not now."

Narrowing his eyes, Noah pointed toward the pictures. "Your family is next—your son, then your grandson. I have nothing left, and to put it simply—I don't care. Your choice."

Those words sunk in rather quickly. Anthony nodded, then added, "You'll leave them alone?"

Noah smiled through the mask. "I promise. Now open it."

As Anthony stood, Megan stepped forward in rage.

The semi-automatic rifle came up into a firing position as she took aim.

Chapter 63

Special Agent Brandon Gardiner had swung by the Chicago field office and raided the armory for his team. He also picked up a few junior field agents to help. The five-hour flight was direct and at the government's expense. They had driven straight to the waiting Gulfstream, and they were in the air within moments. The intel he acquired would only be good for the rest of the evening, and no expenses were spared.

Noah Hunter would be in custody before midnight.

They were one block away from 1600 South LaSalle Street, clustered around the hood of the government-issued Crown Vic, looking at his tablet. "Clay and Campbell, I want you both to come around from the north and watch the building from here."

Tapping the screen caused the area to zoom in, showing a side street with a few low-rise condo buildings.

"Wu and I will start here at Starbucks." He also pointed to the western side of the large road, past the building on screen.

"You two stay at that location and be ready to block the road or move in. Any questions?"

Gardiner scanned their faces. Everyone has been fully briefed, and they knew the target in question. "Okay, we will do a radio check and then move to your locations. Don't move until I give the word. The other agents are deployed in a net to prevent any chance at the suspect fleeing."

Everyone headed to their vehicles while Gardiner closed the tablet and adjusted his tactical vest.

Hunter would be going down tonight. Smiling at the thought of him being armed and resisting arrest, he got into the passenger seat while Agent Wu drove.

No one questioned him as to why they were at this location or the intel. Perfect.

This will be over soon.

* * * * *

Noah immediately stepped in front of Megan, brought his hand up under the rifle's barrel, and gently shook his head.

Trust me.

It must have been something Megan saw in his eyes because she nodded and relaxed.

Anthony laid his right palm flat on the sensor, and with his left, he punched in a long numerical sequence on the keyboard. With a click, the door swung open an inch.

"Done. Now get what you want and leave my family and me alone."

Noah chucked. "I know how you treat your family. When they disagree with you, you kill them. Just ask your brother."

Anthony puffed up in rage and his face flushed. "He betrayed me!"

"I heard he just wanted out. That's why you killed him. Is that why you came after Rachel as well? Pride?"

Anthony took a step forward, appearing to grind his teeth while he pointed a finger. "You do *not* abandon family. There is no getting out of our business. He knew that."

"So, once he wanted out, you had to take care of him?"

"There is only one way to leave. I had to kill him to send a message to the rest of the family and everyone involved. I didn't want to, but it had to be done."

Noah was glad of the mask. He couldn't stand the dirtbag, and there was no chance he could have controlled his emotions. "What about Rachel? Why did you send those men after her?"

"Do you have any idea how many millions she stole from me? From her own family? She had it coming to her." As Anthony's gaze shifted to Megan, Noah swung the AR-15 around and slammed the barrel under his chin crosswise. Anthony's head snapped back, and he fell against the desk unconscious.

Noah knew he hit him rather hard, but a quick check showed he was still alive. "Are you okay?"

Megan nodded, took a deep breath, and relaxed her white-knuckled grip on the weapon. "What now?"

Turning back to the safe, Noah looked inside at several stacks of cash, several inches tall, wrapped with brown paper bands from the bank. All brand new, crisp bills.

Ignoring the money, Noah opened a large blue book stacked against the sidewall. Lines filled each page, and it was set up as an accounting ledger. All fifty pages were filled with handwritten details—names, amounts paid, and dates.

There were five large blue books in total.

"Now we get the hell out of here."

Noah pulled out his handcuffs, secured Anthony, and grabbed the books. He pulled down a small silver case from the far-right bookshelf and tucked it into his front pocket.

"What's that?" Megan couldn't see what he was doing with his back to her.

"I'll explain later. Let's go."

Sliding the rifle back on his shoulder, Noah made his way back to the reception area.

Megan turned to the elevators and was about to push the button when Noah stopped her. "We should probably take the stairs if you can handle it."

Megan nodded. "It hurts pretty bad. I'm going to have a massive bruise."

Noah pulled the clown masks off and leaned forward to kiss her. The air felt good on his face, and he could tell she was just as sweaty and hot as he was inside the latex. Megan threw her arms around him and held him tight for a moment before they took to the stairs. Gingerly, Noah stepped around the fallen guard and made their way to the first floor.

Each step down jarred him, and the pain grew uncomfortable.

She held the door open for him as they stepped outside into the cool night air.

"Thank you, ma'am. I think we both need a shower and—"

Noah's words were cut off as a bullet passed through his right arm, and it was immediately followed by a second hitting his left leg. As the first shot registered, a third-round hit him in the stomach, and he fell, screaming in pain.

A hail of bullets peppered the area as they both tried to lay as flat as possible. Noah threw the books to the side and rolled in front of Megan. Another round hit him in the back. As he struggled to breathe, he couldn't tell if the ballistic vest had worked or not.

Noah looked at the door as it swung closed, and bullets pockmarked the steel. The outside of the door was flush, with no exterior handle.

As he lay there bleeding out, Noah realized there was nowhere to go.

Another round ricocheted off the ground before it exploded into his back. An inch away from the first impact. The integrity of the vest was all but gone, and he could feel it penetrate his shoulder. As to how deep it went, he couldn't tell, but it wasn't good. It was too late, and Noah could not move even if he wanted to. He focused on protecting Megan and staying conscious.

He could hear more small arms fire in the distance as someone shouted. "FBI, drop your weapons!"

A few more pops from a distant pistol when the cry continued to come for them to drop their weapons. It sounded as if fifty agents screamed, and soon enough, a car was driven closer. Noah could see the shadows dance on the side of the building in front of him through slitted eyes.

A car door opened, and footsteps drew close, accompanied by laughter. "Sergeant Hunter, if you're still alive, you're under arrest."

A foot stepped on his shoulder and rolled him over. Agent Gardiner stood above him, wearing a vest with FBI in bright white letters across the front.

"Fuck you, G-man."

Noah barely spoke above a whisper, but he could tell by the look on the agent's face that he heard him. Gardiner winked, drew his pistol, and aimed at his head.

Noah started to pray when he heard something that lifted his spirits. He couldn't help but grin.

"U.S. marshals, stand down. Stand down!"

As Noah smiled at Gardiner, his vision faded. Out of the night, a large figure tackled the FBI agent, and his pistol went flying.

Before he lost consciousness, Noah slowly pulled out the silver digital audio and video recorder and laid it on the ground beside his head. Before Hunter succumbed to the darkness, the Crown Vic's headlights made the engraving on the bottom of the recorder easy to read. *Property of the U.S. Marshals. Do not tamper.*

Chapter 64

Noah pressed the button on the gray controller, and the top of the bed elevated to place him in a semi-seated position. After three days and two surgeries, he seemed to be doing quite well. However, it would take him a while to recover fully.

Bob Murphy held out the cup, and Noah sipped cool ice water through the straw.

"Thanks."

The assistant deputy chief placed the drink back on the hospital table and wheeled it closer in case he wanted more later. Bob was close to retirement after a long career with the marshals. The deep lines on his face and thinning short white hair were earned. He wore tan slacks with a white golf shirt and a light blue sweater. He was dressed in much the same casual outfit when Noah burst into their Dearborn Street offices. The older man happened to walk by the front desk when Noah arrived. It didn't take sixty seconds of listening before Murphy went with his instinct and quickly made a deal.

Succeed, or we will disavow any involvement.

After a rapid series of instructions, Bob handed over the digital recorder.

"Good luck, Sergeant Hunter. It sounds like you will need it. Try not to break too many eggs when making the omelet."

With a quick shake of his hand, Noah made the deal that sealed his fate. He was a police officer at heart, and he didn't want to have the Luciano family get away with murder and extortion to outright bribery.

Bob looked at his wristwatch to check the time. "In eight minutes, it will all go down. I'm glad it worked out."

After looking through Anthony's records, over two hundred and twelve arrests would be simultaneously ordered across the country. The AG had signed it off, and the task force was ready to execute. The only other agency that the US Marshals could count on was Homeland Security. No one from their organization was named in the files.

"No problem, the first thing I need you to do is sign these forms. Please do not look at the dates already filled out."

Bob rolled the table over and handed Noah a pen. The three pages authorized Sergeant Noah Hunter from APPD Wyoming to work with and act as an officer for the US marshals for the duration of the investigation. Noah smiled at the backdated forms as he signed.

A knock at the door interrupted them, and a surgeon wearing full scrubs entered. "Mr. Hunter, I'm sorry to say that I have bad news." When Noah nodded for him to continue, the doctor cleared his throat before resuming. "The woman that came in with you has succumbed to her injuries. My deepest condolences."

The pen fell to the floor as Noah leaned back on his pillow and closed his eyes.

Bob gave his hand a gentle squeeze. "I'm so sorry."

Noah numbly nodded.

Losing her once was bad enough, but going through it twice?

Lost in his memories, Noah didn't notice as Murphy slipped out of the room.

Chapter 65

Noah kicked the tires a few times and got in behind the wheel of his new Ram truck. It had taken almost three weeks in the Chicago hospital to recover enough that they would let him leave. He was sore in places he didn't know existed, but the sutures from the bullet wounds were healing.

His clothing was cut off and destroyed, but Bob had brought him a clean set of clothes and a few items he found in his Jeep. Nothing was said about any of the weapons, and they all disappeared except for Noah's Glock and holster.

Repercussions from the arrests were felt worldwide as the paper trail was followed and arrests were made. Anthony Luciano and William Ryan would stand trial on several dozen offenses, and a few judges on their payroll would join them. Noah had fired into the kitchen floor, and Luciano had bought it. Without that pressure, they may never have gotten into the safe.

Bob had passed over his business card and wrote his cell phone number on the back. "If you ever decide to leave the police department, I'll ensure you have a new home with the marshals. We could use good men like you."

Patting his chest pocket, Noah felt the card inside and was reassured, but he knew that Arrow Point was home … for now.

Not wanting to drive the Jeep, Noah had ordered a new Dodge Ram from a local dealer. It was sleek and had every option. It wasn't broken in, like his old Chevy, but he liked it. The Jeep was fine, but nothing beat a truck.

It took him over three days to drive back from Chicago, and it was the time he needed. He wasn't in a hurry, and it gave him time to reflect on how the events unfolded. Noah was just north of Casper when he decided to spend an extra day before heading back to Megan's apartment.

His apartment.

Turning west off the interstate and dirt road, he eventually came to the driveway with a large gate. Taking the keys from the console, Noah got out and unlocked the gate, then secured it behind him.

A night at the cabin would do him wonders.

The trees had lost most of their leaves over the last few weeks, and the hint of frost was in the air. There would be an early winter.

Noah grabbed his backpack and unlocked the cabin. The floral smell hit him as he stepped inside.

He threw his bag on the couch and walked over to the kitchen table.

A fresh bouquet sat in a vase, and the folded piece of paper Megan had handed him in Chicago lay on the table upside down. He didn't even know it was missing from his wallet. A large heart was drawn on the back, and in the middle of the drawing was his grandmother's engagement ring. She had left him a note underneath.

I will miss you. Xoxo

Sliding the ring into his pocket, he smiled and turned the paper over. He had wondered what Megan … Rachel had handed him for a while now.

On the other side was a list of bank transactions and deposits into two separate accounts—one in the Cayman Islands and another in Switzerland. There were details and login and passwords for each, naming Noah as the sole account holder.

Oh my God!

The total for both accounts was ninety-two million dollars. Plus, the cash was in a duffel bag upstairs in the loft. Noah realized he could go anywhere in the world or do anything he wished.

"Now what?"

He let out a big sigh as he spotted his uniform still hanging behind the front door. He knew right away what he wanted to do.

Folding the note, he tucked it into his shirt pocket.

For the first time in weeks, Noah looked forward to going back to work.

Grave Choices

The Noah Hunter Series:

Book Two, preview.

Chapter 1

The headlights blinded, and the airhorn caused him to panic as they came straight for him. Steve Misevski stumbled back to avoid the transport and was nearly knocked down by the wind gust. After the curve of the road, the truck drove too close to the shoulder on the interstate. The plume of dust that trailed behind stung his eyes. He had to squint and keep his mouth closed. The red lights of the trailer disappeared into the night as the driver continued west on the interstate.

"Son of a bitch."

Steve had gone into the city to see a concert with friends to celebrate his eighteenth birthday, and he had missed the last bus home from Cheyenne. He turned down an offer to sleep on a couch, and he had stuck his thumb out to hitch instead.

The first ride in the back of an old pickup truck brought him right into Casper, and he was now on the shoulder of I-26 west at two o'clock in the morning as he tried to get home to Arrow Point. There were a few street lights on the other side of the road, but they were not too effective.

The spring weather was nice for the end of April, and Steve had to open his jean jacket to keep cool. The walk along the road had warmed him up.

Soon, another car passed him, and the driver pretended not to see his thumb as he looked for a ride. When his hand dropped to his side, Steve felt the cell phone in his pocket. He was tempted to call his father to pick him up. His mother died of cancer five years ago, and since then, his dad hasn't talked much. To even start a conversation with him was painful. Often, a whole week would go by without speaking a word.

Steve shrugged at the situation and continued west along the interstate. He had hitched home a few times over the past year, and he knew sooner or later someone would stop. It was just a matter of time.

Once the last vehicle disappeared, the night birds resumed their chorus.

An hour previous, the cloud had cleared and revealed a thin sliver of moonlight and a million stars. He kicked the gravel and tried not to scuff the new white running shoes. Soon another transport truck roared by, and it didn't stop, but he was glad to see the brake lights from the car that followed and pulled over.

Running up, Steve saw that the passenger window was down, and he could hear someone calling out from the front seat.

"Steve Misevski? Is that you?"

He leaned down to see inside, and he chuckled in relief. "Ya. I missed the last bus. Can I get a ride home with you?"

"Sure, get in."

He sat in the front seat and buckled up. The driver smiled, "I barely saw you in time. It isn't safe to be out at this hour hitchhiking."

"I wanted to get home so my dad wouldn't worry."

"No problem. Glad I saw you."

They pulled back onto the interstate, and the miles passed as the radio broadcast the news and weather report.

"Home in ten minutes. I think that was a little faster than walking."

Steve continued to stare out the passenger window. "Thank you very much, I—"

Steve didn't see the syringe as it was jabbed deep into his left leg. The plunger was fully depressed before it was removed.

"What the hell?" He started to fumble for his seatbelt, but he had trouble concentrating.

"Relax, you will be out in a few seconds."

He managed to push down on the seat belt release and turn to the car door, but as his hand reached for the handle—it lost all strength and fell back down into his lap. Steve tried to lift his head and look to his left, but it rolled around shoulder to shoulder.

His heart rate slowed, and soon, a thin line of saliva hung down from the corner of his mouth as his face went slack. Steve's attempt at a scream came out as a quiet moan as he lost the battle and slid into unconsciousness.

The last thing Steve would hear was a cheerful whistling in the car before he succumbed to the darkness.

Chapter 2

Sergeant Noah Hunter stood ramrod straight with his heels together, and his highly shone boots pointed outward at a perfect forty-five-degree angle. With his shoulders back and his chest out, he moved his fists slightly to line them up with the outside seam of his dress pants before remaining still. The white gloves stood out in stark contrast to the dark blue dress uniform.

Noah stood an inch under six feet, and at thirty-eight years old, he was in great physical shape. His dress uniform couldn't hide the broad shoulders and deep chest. He kept his brown hair short, resembled a military cut, and he had recently regrown his short dark goatee.

At the first note of the bagpipe, his right arm snapped into position, parallel to the ground, and angled his forearm toward his head. The fingers were pointed straight with his thumb tucked in tight, palm down. The index finger barely touched the corner of his right eyebrow.

He held the salute for over four minutes while constable Randy Finlay played Going Home. Those gathered around the coffin gazed at the picture of captain John Richardson displayed on top of the high-glossed casket. He looked sharp in his dress uniform with the American flag as the background, and he had a slight smile on his face that most remembered from the man.

The sorrowful and haunting notes from the bagpipe washed over the crowd gathered and continued throughout the Arrow Point cemetery. The weather was contrary to the solemn occasion. The early May breeze felt like that of the hot summer months. Last night's brief rain gave the grass and flowers a fresh look, which made the colors more vivid, and it had added a little humidity to the air.

When the last note faded, Noah's arm snapped back down to his side, into the position of attention.

Police Chief Birch had a few police officers gather around him, and he pulled a handheld radio off his belt for the Last Call.

"Headquarters to Captain Richardson, please respond."

The silence was broken as the birds sang in the trees at the edge of the cemetery.

"Headquarters to Captain John Richardson, please respond."

The Chief wiped away a few tears as they slowly made their way down his cheeks as they waited the full ten seconds.

"Headquarters, no response. Captain John Richardson, rest easy and stand down. Thank you for your many years of service—end of watch, the eighth of May, thirteen-hundred hours. Rest in peace, my brother. Headquarters out."

The casket was slowly lowered into the ground on nylon straps attached to an electric motor. The aluminum bars rotated on the frame. It descended silently as befitting the occasion and with perfect timing.

A few sobs could be heard as Noah stepped backward and performed a right turn, and waited. The eight pallbearers conducted their left and right turns respectively and slow marched off the gravesite. The last man stopped and faced Sergeant Hunter and handed over an American flag, folded sharply into a large triangle. He saluted the flag before he turned once again to join the others.

Noah held the flag firmly with two hands, and in turn, slow marched to the Chief and reverently handed it over. Sergeant Hunter saluted once again, followed by a right turn, and joined the pallbearers off to the side.

The Chief walked over to the side and handed the flag off to a woman in a long black dress. She was doing her best to hold back the tears. "I'm so sorry, Eleanor. Please accept this token as our gratitude for his thirty-two years of service. He will be remembered."

Chief Birch handed over the flag and stepped back, and gave a perfect salute before he walked off to join the others. The Arrow Point police department members filled the gravesite along with the fire services, as well as countless others. Richardson was well known throughout the community, and he had touched many lives. His recent heart attack had taken them all by surprise, and it was still hard to believe.

Wanting to give the family time alone, Noah thanked the officers. They would meet up at the Tavern to hoist a few drinks in the Captain's honor shortly. Within fifteen minutes, the parade of cars had left. Noah and Lieutenant Zane Piekenbrock hung back and waited until the area was clear.

The LT stood a few inches taller than Noah at six-foot-two, and at fifty-eight years old, he was physically fit with broad shoulders and a deep chest. His hair had turned white at an earlier age, and he kept it short. Both men were solemn as it fit the occasion. Noah would grab the picture off of the casket, bring it with them and rest it on the bar. More than a few drinks would be hoisted in the Captain's memory this afternoon.

The widow was the last to be escorted to her car by her son, and the priest left in his vehicle. The caretaker walked over to the head of the grave and brought the coffin back up on the lift. He knelt on the fake grass that lined the hole and brought it up far enough that he could reach the picture.

As his fingers brushed the top of the frame, the angled prop folded flat. The large image of Captain Richardson hit the top of the casket, slid down the side, and rested at the bottom, over six feet down.

"Crap. Sorry guys, it fell. Give me a second."

"Jesus Christ." Piekenbrock took a step forward.

Noah held his hand out, palm up to forestall him. "Accidents happen. Do you need any help?"

The caretaker shook his head. "I'm good."

Henry had worked at the cemetery for over twenty-five years, and unfortunately, this wasn't the first time he had knocked things down under a casket. At forty-five years of age, he had a lanky frame that caused his clothing to hang from his shoulders like a scarecrow. No matter how much he ate, Henry always appeared in need of a good meal.

The caretaker raised the coffin fully at the control unit, and he moved to the side and gave it a push near the head. Once it hit the aluminum bar, it easily pivoted, and it left him a four-foot gap in which to drop. The gray coveralls he wore were dirty but essential in his line of work.

Noah watched him sit on the edge of the open grave between the nylon strap and the end and smoothly dropped down from sight. Two seconds later, Noah saw the picture frame come out of the hole and rest on the artificial grass. Two hands grabbed the framed tubing, and Henry pulled himself back up. With a neat turn, he sat on the side with his feet dangling down.

Noah expected him to get up right away, but he just sat there as he stared down into the pit. With his gaze fixed below, he called out, "Hey guys? Can you come here, please?"

Noah turned to the LT and shrugged. When they stood beside the caretaker, Noah followed Henry's finger as he pointed down.

At the bottom of the grave, the toes from a white pair of sneakers pointed up through the dark soil. Farther down, they could see a small patch of denim from a pair of blue jeans where Henry's foot had disturbed the dirt.

Someone had been buried below an open grave.

Noah cleared his throat as he tried to take in the scene. "It seems Captain Richardson isn't done helping us yet."

Author's Notes

There are many people I would like to thank for their support, who have helped directly and indirectly. I want to thank my immediate family: my mother, wife, daughter, and mother-in-law, who believe and encourage me to continue writing.

I know authors and writers support each other, and it is a world in which I have been welcomed. Chris Hauty, Simon Gervais, Don Bentley, Kyle Mills, Jennifer Gardiner, Eric P. Bishop, James Downey, Jonas Saul, Bill Schweigart (to name a few) have offered advice, encouraged my endeavors. At times, even a brief word or assistance works wonders, and for that, I'm grateful. I would also like to thank Valerie Rzepka, Stan Bydal, and Glen Pitcher for picking their brain and expertise.

Arrow Point is a fictional town west of Casper, Wyoming—you will not find it on any map. I have modified a few facts and police procedures to enhance the novel. However, any errors or omissions within the story are my own.

Most importantly, thank you for reading, *The Tipping Point*, and I hope you enjoyed the story and found it entertaining.

Join me for another adventure with Noah Hunter in *Grave Choices*. It will be released at the end of November 2021.

David Darling, February 2021

About the Author

David grew up in a small town east of Toronto, Canada. He has had many interests throughout the years, including the military, martial arts, playing guitar, reading, and in his mind, he is quite an excellent fisherman. David is married and has one daughter, and still misses his chocolate lab beyond words. He plans to continue writing until they nail his coffin shut.

www.daviddarlingbooks.com for updates and new information on novels forthcoming.